A SAND FORTRESS

A SAND FORTRESS

A Novel
by
John Coriolan

Gay Sunshine Press
San Francisco

Published in paperback.
There is also a special edition of ten numbered copies, handbound in boards and signed by the author.

First revised/expanded edition 1984

Cover: Drawing by Rex
Drawing copyright © 1984 by Glenn Turner
Cover design by Timothy Lewis

A Sand Fortress was first published by Award Books, Universal Publishing Co., New York, 1968, and was reissued by Charter Communications, Inc., New York, 1978. The present Gay Sunshine Press edition is a revised/expanded version of the novel.

Library of Congress Cataloging in Publication data:

Coriolan, John.
A sand fortress.
"First published in 1968"—T.p. verso.
I. Title.
PS3553.06475S2 1984 813'.54 84-13744
ISBN 0-917342-46-1

Gay Sunshine Press
P.O. Box 40397
San Francisco, CA 94140
Complete catalog of books available for $1.

ALEX

Alex Este decided it was a Whistler type of day. The October haze over the Hudson made the Jersey shore indistinct and romantic, though the sheen on the water was sharp-focus dazzling, perhaps more Turner than Whistler.

Alex steered skillfully through the West Side Highway traffic, skimming downtown at the fastest speed he could maintain without attracting too much attention, darting from lane to lane without braking. The little car was in good shape—driving was a pleasure, an indulgence, an exhibition. Alex did not claim there were many things he did well outside his office but driving was one of them and he was enjoying the sensation of being quick and deft and absolutely in control. Cooking was more complicated—it took more planning and pains, but hungry half-drunk friends seldom noticed the finer flavors. Making people feel good in bed took a lot less thought but more innate talent and touch and concern, but there Alex was sure he was appreciated.

The leaves of the clumped trees of Riverside Park were coppery from the long dry spell while the grass was still surprisingly green. Warm air poured in through the opened section of the Peugeot's roof. The air felt wonderful but its sound discouraged conversation and Mike was evidently taking advantage of that to withdraw into his own thoughts.

Alex was not accustomed to silence from Mike. Over the period of three or four years he had known Mike, Alex had seen him mostly at parties or at the beach with people around, Mike smiling and keeping the conversation spinning along in that soft, Southern, habitually flirtatious way of his, not trying to say anything important or very witty, just keeping things balling along. Alex himself preferred to keep his mouth shut if he had nothing to say, even if some people did get the impression he was stupid or rude. They found out different soon enough. When he did say something it had pith to it and helped him get what he wanted—usually.

Alex had to grin to himself, remembering his first words to Mike. After several drinks at Tom Carlier's while everyone had been moaning over a set of polaroid shots Tom had made of a fantastically tattooed cab-driver, Alex had suddenly kidded Mike about his rather overblown Southern accent—after all, he was only from Kentucky—and his Miss Magnolia compulsion to keep conversation and commentary unbroken. "Lace-making" Alex had called Mike's polite babble. Alex had always found it a smart move to throw a complacent beauty like Mike Kincade off balance by attacking him playfully where he was sure to be most vulnerable—his bad teeth or his lack of education, his too graceful shoulder movements or his abysmal ignorance of politics or art or sports. But Alex had realized that Mike was not concerned about anything of that kind. The Southernness ploy, however, though obvious, might be unsettling for a moment and Alex had casually dropped it into a sudden silence.

Mike had smiled and said, drawling more than ever, "Well, I reckon we all have our little gambits. I think I'll just go right on with the Southern bit a while yet. But while we're on the subject, that sulk-and-insult gambit of yours is crude as shit, man, unless the insult's witty." And he had gone calmly off to pick up another drink amid the laughter. Alex had laughed too and had shrugged away the put-down.

Alex admitted to himself the Miss Magnolia angle had been pretty cheap. Mike was gay, of course, and smooth-skinned and fine-featured, but there was nothing effeminate about him. Feminine maybe, even androgynous, but never epicene. The setback had only made Alex more determined to storm Kincade's lofty citadel but it had been several weeks before Alex had managed to get near enough again to attempt any of his salve of flattery. The follow-up tactic had taken place at John Kavanaugh's *bon voyage* for one of the ballet troupes.

Mike had laughed and said, "Relax, Alex. You're the crude, direct type. Say what's on your mind and take the consequences."

Before Alex could say directly and succinctly, "I want to take you home with me," Mike had spoiled it all by babbling on, "I'm used to people like you. When I was six I had a little girl friend Charl who never wasted a word either and knew just where to grind in a bony knee. All Southern ladies aren't necessarily sweet and gentle from birth just as you Yankees aren't always so shrewd."

The "shrewd" had cut Alex to the living quick. It had been a word he had happily applied to most of his operations—by being shrewd he could outmaneuver nearly anyone and obtain what he was after. Suddenly all his shrewdness had been reduced to bad manners and a kid's bony knee. For quite a long moment Alex had not felt like stating his desire, succinctly or otherwise, although Michael Kincade had apparently waited, politely now, half smashed. Then Michael had gently kissed Alex on an eyebrow and weaved his way over to say good night to Kavanaugh. Alex had tried to catch Kincade but he was gone and, since Kavanaugh was Alex's boss, Alex had not dared dart out after Mike without saying good night.

Alex remembered that he had puzzled over that kiss quite a lot. Obviously it had been a gesture of apology for the rough verbal swat. Mike had realized that "shrewd" had hurt and he hadn't meant to be that harsh. Alex had also realized then how much his casual crack about Miss Magnolia behavior had antagonized Mike. It was only a wonder Mike had not hit him.

Over the next few months Alex had learned how thoroughly Mike detested calling men by girls' names—it was one of the sickest aspects of gay life. But in that minute at John Kavanaugh's, Alex had realized there was a lot more to Mike than most people suspected and Alex had been more intrigued than ever.

Even though he had intermittently admitted to himself he was in love with Mike Kincade and had interpreted Mike's moment of polite dreamy waiting as an invitation to ask, Alex Este for a period had remained at a distance, literally as well as psychologically. He had found that, as long as he was not the one Mike was talking to, he did not mind not being near enough to hear what Mike was saying. It had been delightful to Alex just to look at Mike and admire his special radiance—and to dream of real intimacy, of course. For radiance like

Mike's the academics and book reviewers had dug up those words "charisma" and "mana." More flamboyant terms suggested show business, which Mike never did, although Alex had found out later that Mike had been acting in a Broadway play when they had met the first time. But whatever one labeled Mike's magnetism, Alex had witnessed its effects on women, men, little children and dogs. They all wanted to touch him, kiss him, do things with him they had not dreamed of before. And Mike was blond, a genuinely radiant blond in a city where blondness was prized and imitated and joked about and everybody's dream boy was a tall blond with a neat profile, broad shoulders and a big bulge in his crotch.

Now, turning to gaze toward this special creature beside him in the car, Alex realized with a pang of real horror that it was another Mike slumped there. This Mike was not beautiful. Staring and brooding, making no attempt to charm, this Mike was anything but radiant. He was worn and hard. The sardonic twist engraved at the corner of his mouth must have been there for a long time but had gone unnoted when he was smiling and weaving his spell. At thirty-two, or whatever he was now, Mike Kincade was an ex-beauty.

The rather small but perfectly proportioned and spaced features were still striking, of course, and that long pale-blond hair the wind whipped through was still eye-catching and silky and like no one else's in the world. But while Mike's hair was not even perceptibly thinning, its luster seemed to have vanished—and Mike's whole fabulous radiance was gone, as if his wattage had been reduced from two-hundred to twenty. Could charisma be withdrawn, the mana dissipated? For an instant Alex felt forlorn and even a little sick.

How could such a change in Mike have occurred without Alex having been aware of it until now? Earlier that day Mike had been smiling when he had left his apartment and joined Alex in the car. True, Alex had not actually seen him for some time before that. They had talked on the phone but Mike was always just off to see someone, usually those people in Greenwich. Alex's weekends at the Island had not coincided with the one weekend Mike had been out there. At Ally Leverrett's birthday party Mike had arrived late from dinner with Mark Atwell, and Monique Vernon had cornered Mike when he had turned up. Alex himself had fled very soon thereafter when Pierre Gordon had marched in with a new and very flashy Puerto.

Actually it had been at Riis Park early in August that Alex had last seen Mike for more than a little while and Mike had had a hangover and had slept most of that afternoon. He had ridden back to town in Alex's back seat, sleepily fending off the unsubtle passes which that friend of Eddy's, little Donny, had kept making, passes Alex would have welcomed and received if Mike had not been along. And Alex had received those passes as soon as he had dropped off Mike and Eddy. To be second-best to Mike Kincade was not wounding to any healthy ego and little Donny had not seemed too disappointed when all had been said and done that evening.

Perhaps even then, Alex thought, Mike hadn't seemed so special to Donny who had never met either of them before. Alex was almost glad that he had never been a beauty. A pleasant squarish face with a narrow tilty nose had never been enough to qualify him for those exalted echelons. And his eyes were too ordinary, his lips too thin, his crewcut going silvery too much like that of a thousand others. His body had always been good, a little heavy, perhaps, but smooth and strong, not big enough to impress except in the embrace. But at fifty the body was as good as it had ever been, maybe better. Except for a tiny false hernia and a knee that went stiff in wet weather. Taking responses one by one—and those individual responses were what really mattered—Alex was actually more appealing now than he had ever been in his long and busy career.

The beauties of his own age, who still tried to reign imperiously, although they were rapidly falling apart, were drawn to him. His unfretting durability fascinated and reassured them. He could almost hear them whispering to themselves that if Alex could keep his façade that way with no effort at all, how much better they must appear—with all their massaging, bag-punching, discreet dyeing and expensive pilling.

Few of them realized how long and rigorously Alex Este had stuck to simple sensible diet in private, how he had trained himself to breathe correctly and balance his weight as he sat and moved. They probably thought he went to the gym every other day just to cruise, which was not true. His workout there was brief but exacting and was calculated to keep his weight steady and his muscles hard. The swimming was the most salubrious part. Salubrious. Alex liked the word. One of the deepest interests he and Mike shared was a vigilance for new usable words—usable for Alex in crossword puzzles and his private ruminations, usable for Mike perhaps in his poems and his teaching, not very often usable for either in conversation except between the two of them.

On the other hand, Mike was sloppy about a lot of things—clothes, for instance, and keeping his apartment clean. In the area of vocabulary Alex had to admit he sometimes felt a tinge of envy—Mike's approach to words was easier, more intuitive, more joyful, and he never used them to dazzle a youngster as Alex was often tempted to do. When Mike used the right word he did it so gracefully that nobody noticed the word itself. No matter how Mike might go off in physical beauty there would always be his intellectual grace and zest—he would always be young.

It was the beauties of Mike's generation—thirty, thirty-five, forty years of age—who were difficult for Alex to make out with. Difficult but attainable. He knew how to tease them along and they condescended with flattering frequency, but after tedious courtship usually. Alex had ways of finally making them feel suddenly wonderfully young and giddy again. He looked as if he could really take care of them. The really young beauties were far easier to make—except for Pierre Gordon.

The image of Pierre as Alex had first encountered him—wet, shining and merry under the shower in the men's beach house at the Riis Park—made Alex gasp as if someone had given him a nasty dig in the solar plexus. For a month or so Alex had been congratulating himself on his recovery from the craziness, yet he had to face the fact that every time he thought of Pierre as he had been in those early encounters a year and a half ago, he still experienced that catch of breath, that clutch at his heart and that sinking shamed feeling. How much longer would he have to suffer the torment of frustration and envy? An instant's vivid recall, just as he was dozing off, of Pierre wet and glistening and roguish, robbed Alex regularly of hours of sleep. And after the last time he had seen Pierre, maybe a week following the Leverrett party, Alex's heart had still throbbed in his throat. He had not been able even to raise his hand to draw Pierre's attention. Pierre had lounged there in the subway in skin-tight white Levi's and short fleece-lined rust-colored jacket and high-heeled glittering black boots. He had leaned on the seat arm by the subway door, intent on a scruffy little Puerto in tight black pants, hypnotizing the PR with the astonishing bulge at his crotch shamelessly thrust up and teasingly swayed. Pierre had not bothered to acknowledge Alex even after he had obviously seen him. Pierre had brazenly followed the kid out to the deserted Seventy-ninth Street platform and groped him even before the doors had closed. Alex winced. Was Pierre a tangible symbol of failure and frustration Alex did not like admitting he was vulnerable to? If he had never seen Pierre, would he be even more hooked on Mike?

Last night when Alex had reached the firm carefully considered conclusion that he really wanted Mike Kincade to come and share his apartment and his life, the older man had readily admitted to himself he was thinking much less of Mike's good than of his, Alex's, own pleasure—the swank of having the beautiful Mike for an apartment mate, the cachet of showing him off, the reflected glory of being seen with him, glory that reflected his own taste and charm and desirableness. And now it was apparent in the light of day that Mike was no longer the great beauty Alex had always thought of his being. Had he ever been? Yes, that was a recognized fact, not personal bedazzlement. But did Alex still want so much for Mike to come?

Alex looked closely at Mike, trying to see him in focus, as others must see him, as a stranger would see him—hunched, almost morose, pale when half the town was still ruddy with sunburn, abominably dressed. And quite beautiful. Alex found that he wanted Mike more than ever before. A great need and love for Mike surged through his chest. Perhaps he felt this way because Mike, looking so vulnerable and lonely and so much in need of someone, now would respond more warmly. Perhaps it was only because now Mike would be less competition, less enthralling to others, less justified in staying aloof. There could be less flaunting and more sharing, real pairing, Alex thought. The kind of sharing and pairing that would have been impossible with Pierre. To live with Pierre and his demands and arrogance and quirks would be hell for anyone. To live with Mike, if he were actually beautiful in the way he had been, would be wearing, especially on the ego, probably more irritating than rewarding. But this way—Mike fading a little, perplexed, off-base, bewildered—life would be easier. The problem was to persuade Mike to give up his own lonely apartment that he had grown accustomed to and come up and share Alex's roomy modern one.

And what would happen then? Would they be merely roommates, coming and going without seeing much of each other? Pals like college kids? Or would they be lovers? The one time thay had been to bed together had occurred when they had both been tired and somewhat drunk. The occasion certainly had not been as spectacular as Ron and Eduardo had claimed their brief love-making with Mike had been. Certainly Mike's was one of the smoothest, most exciting bodies Alex had ever encountered and the legends about the extraordinary size and beauty of his sexual equipment were not exaggerated. But no matter how magnificent Mike was, if he were not aroused by Alex... Alex sighed.

Mike spoke without turning, chanting some lovely autumnal lines.

"Yours?" Alex asked after a second's reflection.

"No. But thanks." Mike laughed.

My God, Alex cried to himself, he is beautiful! When he laughs like that, the beauty all comes back. Perhaps I've just never seen him serious before. Living with Mike might be more complicated than I thought. But isn't my life a little oversimplified at this point?

He wondered if Mike expected he would know the author of the quotation or if the younger man had been deliberately teasing. Or had just felt like saying it aloud and didn't really care what Alex thought. Alex prided himself on his knowledge of things cultural but had admitted to Mike long ago he was weak on poetry when he had found Mike was seriously interested in it and had tried to talk with him about Rilke and Hart Crane. Alex had had a course at Columbia in the Romantic poets and another one in the seventeenth-century metaphysicals and had audited one on Pound, Yeats, Eliot and their contemporaries, but had never found himself comfortable with any of them. All he knew about Hart Crane was that he was a notorious sailor chaser and wrote poems about the Brooklyn Bridge and committed suicide like a fool. Actually, except for Shakespeare and Chaucer, Alex preferred prose and could not quite fathom Mike's preoccupation with verse.

"All right," Alex said, "who wrote it?"

Mike turned and winked. "Emily Dickinson. Isn't she wonderful? I wish I could have met her or just seen her once. I'll bet there was a mad intensity that glowed through the demure fluttery persona she presented to Amherst. Saint Edna must have had it too but she didn't veil her light. I'd have loved to see her in action, drunk in red velvet with that flaming bobbed hair, screaming like Kassandra in Apollo's arms at a Village party."

He's trying hard to be gay, Alex decided. It was nice of Mike to try after that prolonged withdrawal. Obviously it was the sound of gaiety and not the sense he was working for.

The Brooklyn-Battery underpass was upon them. Alex slid shut the roof section to keep out the noxious tunnel-trapped fumes and the roar died.

"Are you writing again?" Alex asked.

"I've—halted. I'll have to start again, I suppose." Mike's tone did not encourage further question or comment but for Mike's own good Alex pretended not to notice and bumbled on.

"Don't forget I want to read the new poems when you get back a copy of them. I won't say anything because I don't know anything about poetry but I'd like to read anything you write." The lightly pressed "you" had been almost a declaration of love—Alex had intended it should sound that way.

Mike gave Alex a quick, clownlike, pseudo-puzzled stare and Alex knew he was supposed to laugh at his own maudlin slip but did not. He kept his eyes more or less on the road and stroked his free hand along Mike's thigh and up under his loose pullover.

Mike unzipped his fly and flopped his cock out. Alex quickly slid his hand down and gave the thick roll of warm flesh a lingering squeeze. Mike tucked it back into his pants. They rode on through the tunnel and out and through the toll line in silence, Alex abashed and Mike scowling and remote again.

Away from the river it was just another warm October day with South Brooklyn basking empty-streeted and silent.

Alex felt he had let the silence go on long enough. This could be the time of no return, their friendship could wither and never recover. Alex had to ignore Mike's cynical gesture that said Alex's meek protestation of love was nothing but commonplace sex entreaty. Mike was evidently in a strange mood—unhappy, unreasonable, reckless, ready for a violent turn. A friendship that never had been very close could be abandoned, shrugged off and forgotten in this cold whirling about. If Mike could be led to discuss what was bothering him . . . Alex chose to ignore the unusual in Mike's tone and behavior and selected a casual opening.

"It's a nice day. It may be the last one. I'm glad I thought of this." Then, before the reverberation of his voice could die away, Alex went on. "You sounded a little flurried when I called. What have you been up to?"

"Nothing special," Mike said. "A lot of nonsense, the usual odds and ends all snarled up. Quillquiar's School wants me to come back. I'd just gotten in from Greenwich when Proctor called and I'd hardly hung up when you rang. The new man they kept bragging about last spring when they knew I was leaving has turned out to be an impossible bore and a hand-waving faggot and the boys are making life hell for him. I know those sly little bastards—they probably claim they adore him and then they imitate him and quote him all over the building until he's the school joke."

"I'll bet you spoiled them for anyone else," Alex said.

"I flirted with them and bullied them and teased them and scolded them and they loved it and covered themselves with glory on the college advanced-placement exams. Anyway, Proctor called personally. I don't have to turn up for chapel if I don't choose to. Choose to! He knew how I loathed that rigmarole, I wasn't shy about speaking my mind. If chapel were optional for everyone, there wouldn't be six bodies in the pews or a priest at the altar and they know it. Someone called Quillquiar's the purest case of petrified fantasy on the eastern seaboard."

"Don't be modest—you said it."

"I wish I had. It was a digruntled math man they fired. He told Proctor the algebra text old Witherspoon taught from hadn't been used in a reputable school for more than twenty years."

"I can't imagine you standing that kind of guff for two years," Alex said.

"Two and a half," Mike said. "Actually in my classroom I did exactly what I wanted to and loved every minute of it, but outside the classroom I had to contend with that organized ineptitude and cynicism."

"I take it you said no when they called."

"I promised Proctor about six times I'd think it over," Mike said. "The school is arrogant as hell most of the time but not above begging to get something it can't get any other way. That's part of what I mean by being cynical. And I am broke. But not that broke. As long as old Witherspoon and the Twitcher are haunting the premises like two antediluvian evil stepsisters, it will never be safe for intellectual, artist or dedicated educator. Or any adolescent who isn't made of pure brass. The stepsisters hate anything that demands a fresh reaction and they annihilate anyone who disturbs them."

"What are those two? Frustrated sadists?"

"Who knows? They're too old to do anything but bicker. And having wasted their own lives, they're determined every kid they can get their clammy grasp on is going to waste his in the same sublime fashion."

"They sound like retirement cases. How old are they?"

"Witherspoon must be sixty and Twitchell may be only around fifty but they live in the far past. You should hear that pair on haircuts. Twitchy coaches a soccer team and you should hear him mutter when a boy loses the ball because his hair has suddenly flopped over his eyes. The captain, who's a stunner named Eddie Hopkins, kept his ginger curls pasted down at school and avoided the wrath of the old men very neatly but on the soccer fields his hair spray sometimes gave up and his mop became vastly tossed and tousled and he'd have scared the opposition to death if they could have seen him through their own flailing fringe."

"I think you're hooked on those kids. You'll go back."

"Eddie and I used to measure in the washroom. He could always produce another half inch by straightening out some more kinks. At one point he had thirteen inches to my twelve and a half."

"I've always dreamed of a cute kid with thirteen inches," Alex said.

"One of the seniors, a chap by the name of Murfree who had spent half of his life in analysis, was going to write me a term paper on the psychic significance of hair to the human male. He told Proctor about it very gravely and explained that he agreed implicitly with Proctor and the whole Establishment and hoped to prove that Buffalo Bill, Daniel Webster and U. S. Grant were all fairies. Proctor persuaded him to drop the endeavor."

"You never had any sex doings with any of them, did you?" Alex asked.

"Lord, no. And a funny thing is I never heard of any queer teacher's even groping a student, except some of the married ones."

"But do you really think some of the boys knew the score?"

"Don't be silly," Mike said. "Of course they did. I suppose the usual one out of three had had an orgasm with another boy and nearly all the older boys knew the score or at least the vocabulary. But in the girls' school in Pennsylvania where I taught a couple of years I never got a hint any of the girls were active with each other or even wise."

"You must have been pretty young. I suppose they had crushes on you. Teaching girls must be a temptation for a straight guy."

"You can't help noticing them of course. And even dreaming about a few special ones. But you just don't chase them—you're friends sometimes but once the year's over even that fades fast. I've seen only one of the girls I taught. Louise was my best student and we had kind of special rapport. Last year I ran into her at the theater. She's married to a wealthy man and they have a place in the country near Westport. They've asked me up a number of times but we seldom refer to those earlier times."

"I knew you'd been up there quite a lot lately," Alex said.

"Frankly I can't quite picture you lounging around a swanky Westport swimming pool."

"The swimming pool is a pond where the little river's been dammed up. And they live in ramshackle simplicity, very rustic, very expensive, very quiet."

"I still can't see you in the picture. Are you sure you're not leaving out something? Is her husband gay? Is there a beautiful kid brother who just happens to be spending the summer with them?"

"Nosy. It happens there is a beautiful divorcée over the hill a piece that Louise has decided I should marry."

"I see. Is she wealthy too?"

"Yes, but Phyllis lives in expensive Frank Lloyd Wright-Danish modern simplicity. With Mondrians and Franz Klines to look at when she's tired of color television or when I'm not there."

"So. What does she think about you marrying her? Is she hot for the idea?"

"She's hot for a husband," Mike said. "Or even a lover at this point."

"So you're sleeping with her to oblige her," Alex said.

"No."

"But you're thinking about it."

"I've thought of it. When I'm around her I hardly think of anything else. But I'm not going to do it."

"She'll get you drunk and roll you into the hay—a beautiful hunk like you. She'll love it. And so will you, won't you?"

"She's got all the makings for a real fine fuck," Mike said. "In fact I can't recall when I've had a better offer. And I'm not bragging when I say it's being offered."

"You'd think a rich babe would get out and circulate," Alex said, "go to Miami or Waikiki if she just wants big handsome studs to service her."

"Not Phyllis. She has pride and standards—all those shiny fixtures the exclusive women's colleges weld on so conspicuously. And she has an undersized weird little seven-year-old she wouldn't leave. And that house. You don't understand about a woman's house, Alex."

"I don't understand about women at all, Mike, though I can understand how a hot little divorcée would look you over and say 'I want that.' Does she suspect what you've got for her in your pants?"

"As a matter of fact she knows. Yesterday afternoon we were sunbathing down on the rocks by the stream and got to necking and the damned thing came right out of my bikini. She put it back. She took her time doing it but she didn't look at it. I kind of wanted her to but she didn't."

"Why didn't you give it to her?" Alex asked. "She wanted you and you evidently were in the mood. I don't understand about these things."

"It's complicated. I don't mean physically always. And sometimes there aren't any emotional complications. At least not immediate ones. But with a girl like Phyll . . ."

"You'd feel it meant more than, say, with me?"

"Maybe. Yeah."

"Probably goes back to your childhood or something, Mike. Did you sleep with a girl first, or a boy? Or were you seduced by your local parson?"

"Well, if you want the story of my life . . ."

"I'll listen any time, Mike."

"All right, the dirt. I was seduced by a clean little boy, another thirteen-year-old named Berty. I'd been jacking off for a couple of years without visible results but the first time Berty jacked me off I shot—so it was a very special occasion. We immediately did it twice more. We'd heard a lot of jokes so we tried everything. We wanted to try girls, too, but we didn't know any we thought would be interested except one older Italian girl. She had big tits and we couldn't figure what we were supposed to do with them so we only looked at her. Berty and I met in the local park until it got cold. When spring came I was eager to meet again but he was busy with a construction crew. He went over to a vacant lot every day at lunch time and had what he called dessert—a different man every day. Berty sat in the weeds on one side of a board fence and they came over to take a leak on the other side. They took regular turns but he was sure if I'd help him they'd come over two at a time. I wouldn't do it—I was too romantic, I guess. They wouldn't let him see their faces. So at fourteen I had an eight-inch cock and was spurned by my lover and wanted romantic sex."

"And Berty?"

"He kept it up for two or three weeks. Then he talked a couple of our friends into helping him but they thought it was a real nothing game and he was bored, too, so we all started chasing the babes and masturbating in private. Berty got married at eighteen and he's got three or four kids of his own and probably would raise hell if he ever caught one of them touching another fellow."

"You were hot for the babes at fourteen?" Alex asked.

"Sure," Mike said. "But when I laid a babe I was sixteen and the first one of our bunch to actually get into a girl. She was from another town a few miles away and was visiting a girl in the class ahead of me. We double-dated. She was hot and easy and very pretty and I figured the other couple was doing it outside on the blanket so we went right at it both nights she visited there. She loved it and I had a pretty good time too. The second time I was very grown-up and wore a rubber."

"So that was the beginning of that," Alex said.

"It was also the end for about four years. I was in love with another girl for over two years but she didn't put out. In college I didn't know any girls right off and had to work pretty hard to stay in school and anyway after a couple of months a junior and I had a thing going in the showers. All during my second year my roommate was swinging on it every time I had a hard-on and sometimes when I hadn't. It was my third year of college before I really got with a girl and had a love affair."

"The roommate didn't count?"

"He was in love with me, I suppose," Mike said. "He certainly was the year before when I wouldn't let him touch me. But I didn't love him. And that's the way it's been ever since—a lot of sex and damned little love."

"Carlo too?"

"I loved Carlo," Mike said.

"Loved?" Alex asked.

"You want to know too much. Haven't you ever slept with a woman, Alex?"

"No, and what's more I never wanted to, as far as I can remember. And I wasn't mama's darling or in love with my old man and I wasn't seduced by a bachelor uncle or the local photographer. I was eighteen and in college and the kid who taught me what I had been missing was a seventeen-year-old townie in my Sunday School class. Looking back, I realize he was a natural fairy—really swishy, blondlined curls and plucked eyebrows, but I thought he was the sweetest thing in the world for a whole fall and winter.

"In the spring I went out for the freshman baseball team and met Ralph who was just as butch as Lonnie was swish and we had it good all through the rest of college. And Lonnie and I went on being Sunday School sisters. He became a hairdresser and had his own place in Chicago and probably makes twice as much as I do. Ralph got married but used to come by whenever he was in New York. I haven't seen him for about ten years. Guess I scared him away the last time— he'd got as fat as a pig. I figure in thirty-eight years I've slept with at least three thousand different fellows. If I'd got married, would I have slept with my wife three thousand times? Or if I'd wolfed after women, would I have made out three thousand times?"

"Just sex? No love, Alex?"

"I've loved a few fellows over a length of time. Ralph. And you, for instance. And some a little more than that—to the point of obsession, which I hate. But the way you operate is probably best for most men—AC-DC, all sorts of experience. Have you ever hustled?"

"I've been paid, if that's what you mean, Alex. I never loitered around Forty-second Street and took anybody who would pay me a few bucks or picked up fat men in East Side bars or had a pimp send me customers. Not quite. Look, let's talk about something else. I'm sick of sex."

"Yeah," Alex said, "I guess we're beginning to sound like one of those dreary Warhol epics. But what else is there for us to talk about? You hardly ever go to the opera, I don't like talking about my work, I don't know anything about poetry. Want to hear what we're doing down at the Union to get the pornography laws changed?"

"Sex again," Mike said.

"All right, I'm sex oriented. You're probably still money-oriented. Want to talk about money? Jobs? The stock market? Furniture sales? The latest fashions? Cute advertising? Hollywood wind-up movies? Italian films? We're back to sex again.

Even the money-mad monsters know the basic thing is sex."

"So talk about sex," Mike said. "I'll think about something else."

"Bet you don't. Bet you hardly ever do. Be honest."

"I'm honest, Alex. I'm disgusted how much time I spend on sex, one way or another."

"Why be disgusted, Mike? What's more interesting? Or more rewarding in the long run?"

"Art."

"Sublimated sex," Alex said.

"Not completely. Sex is evanescent—you want it, you have it, it's gone. You may feel better for a while and you may have felt wonderful at the time, but it's over. If by chance you make a baby, you do have something afterward but that's only one time in a thousand even for those who do it the baby-making way. Sometimes there's communion, shared experience, companionship. But that doesn't last. Art does. It may not be very good but it's there if you want it to be."

"Do you class architecture as an art?" Alex asked.

"No, because architects don't make the buildings they plan. An artist has to both conceive and execute."

"Then musical composition isn't art, either," Alex said, "unless the composer plays his works."

"Even if he composes a symphony that's never played," Mike said, "he's an artist. All right, architecture is an art. You're an artist too."

"Not because of the architectural work I do. I'd be in the craft or skill category, but my boss is an artist. And I admit it isn't sublimated sex with him—he's got a wife and five kids in Larchmont and a ballet boy here in town about twice a week. And half the other ballet dancers in town on special occasions. He likes them lithe."

"I wasn't a dancer but I was lithe," Mike said.

"You bastard. I forgot that's where we met. Here I am telling you about John Kavanaugh and you've slept with him and I haven't."

"That's New York," Mike said.

"Just a bigger *Peyton Place* or *King's Row.* I hear that Mark Atwill is writing a book about it called *The Daisy Chain.* Do you know Schnitzler's *Reigen?*"

"No, but I know Mark Atwill."

"Is is true he won't touch a man that isn't married?"

"It's true he likes to think he's competing with women."

"Does Phyllis know you're AC-DC?" Alex asked.

"Yes. In fact she was first interested in Carlo. He went up to the Tomlinsons with me a couple of times last fall. Carlo had a long session with Phyllis one afternoon about her husband. They were being divorced at the time, so we never met him. Her husband had decided at thirty-five he was queer and wanted out. He confessed he had married her mainly to please his parents. Phyllis read books and quizzed people in her roundabout way and really tried to understand. She hoped, I think, they could work out something but the bastard was a spineless crybaby. He cried until Phyllis pacified him with a very substantial settlement."

"How much?" Alex asked.

"I don't know."

"So she was hot for Carlo first?"

"I didn't say that." Mike turned abruptly away and stared at the sunlight glittering in the Narrows, Staten Island an oriental dreamland floating in the distance.

Alex was aware he had been pushing, even gouging a little. It was his worst fault, a kind of insensitive digging into what was not any of his business. His was also a trick for mining out little nuggets of personal revelation no one else ever brought to light. He preferred being thought a little callous or crude to not knowing those special bits—especially about people like Mike, the beautiful people everyone was interested in. And being friends, they were expected to tell each other things. But Alex always felt he was more willing than Mike to share secrets. Or maybe, to be fair about it, Alex did not have any secrets to share with Mike or anyone else.

The Verrazano Bridge rose majestically before them, loomed above them, sweeping like a gigantic dancer's gesture off into the pallid, unreal distance.

Mike said, "It's like a dream. What do you dream about?"

Alex tried to follow the shift but was at a loss. "I don't dream. Or if I do, I don't remember. I always suspect that people who claim to remember their dreams are actually making it all up."

"Very interesting. I dream of old debts and not being able to graduate from college and being chased by wolves and climbing through other people's houses to get to a boat. I dream that one often. It's a city right on the water but all the crooked little streets end in cul-de-sacs so I have to go through the houses. There's never anyone in the houses—it's as if a plague had struck and they'd all gone off into the dark to die. And I sometimes dream that words march around in geometric patterns and split and proliferate, making sounds and echoes. But no colors . . ."

They had rounded the curve of the bay and were approaching Coney Island. In the haze the skeleton of the parachute jump was hardly more than a figment of memory.

Alex said ruefully, "In a few years it will all be gone—the rides and the baths. That quaint archaic tearoom under the tracks is gone. The wild times I've had in those ramshackle rings of hell. I must have started tans out there on the roof decks for twenty years. There were seasons when the activity was unbelievable in the steamrooms."

"I don't remember hearing anyone talk about them before," Mike said.

"And Bare-Ass Beach—all those lovely deserted dunes and acres of bulrushes with paths and lairs and open sandy patches just right for a blanket party of six or eight. No one wore any clothes up in the dunes and sometimes the straight families down by the water ran naked, too. And some of the papas wandered back into the dunes for a quickie. That was during World War Two. Now the beach is just another stretch of bungalows and cabanas."

"No, I wouldn't remember any of that. After all, I'm only thirty."

"Oh? Of course I realized you were about that. And I'm already fifty."

Alex knew Mike wouldn't say it: *I hope I look as good as you do when I'm fifty.* Alex went on. "Even at fifty new things still happen to me. Sometimes I feel like a stupid kid. And sometimes I find myself in a situation or a state I've seen others in and thought I could avoid."

"Yes, other people's experiences don't really teach us much—we have to make all our own mistakes right down the line.

And what may be a mistake and a bad state for one person can turn out to be the right choice for someone else."

"It depends on whether you're ready for some things," Alex said. "Do you get lonesome living alone in town?"

"Yes, half the time I'm so lonesome I could cut my throat. And sick of the garbage on the street and the noisy garbage trucks and the loonies screaming and all the creeps and the cops and the women with the raucous voices, screeching like macaws in expensive stores and theater lobbies. Out in the stillness of Connecticut there's Phyllis, all glowing and eager and anticipatory and soft-speaking when she speaks at all. There's something almost Chinese about her manners."

"Then you will marry her?"

"It's more complicated than that." Mike turned and stared at the tacky commonplace Brighton Beach stores and bungalows and flats.

"Mike, I want to suggest something else to think about at the same time. The whole point of this excursion today—aside from the sun and air and your sweet company—is that I want to suggest something. How about coming up and sharing my place with me if you decide against settling down in Westport? You know the layout—it's big enough for two. It wouldn't cost you any more than it costs you where you are now. Please give it a serious thought, Mike. Besides, I love you. Which may or may not be a good argument. I suppose I'm not in love with you. Not any more anyway, but I want to live with you. I'm lonesome, a new phase for me after twenty-five years. And I find I don't want anyone else but you."

A police helicopter suddenly loomed over them, passing them on its sweep up the highway. Alex went on. "It looks like a weird malformed dragonfly, doesn't it. Except I confess I've never seen a real dragonfly. Have you?"

"Oh, yes, we had them all summer in Kentucky, mostly around swamps and ponds. They're beautiful and a little sinister-looking but very shy and harmless. I reckon I haven't seen any around here. Where do you come from anyway?"

"Suburban Detroit. And directly to New York after college. Then the Navy during the war and back to New York after the war. I guess I've missed a lot of things, always living in a city or on a ship. I've never been on a horse or a sailboat. Or had a kite. I'd never dammed up a stream until last summer. I read somewhere that damming up a stream is a basic urge."

"Well," Mike said, "I even tried to dam up the brook that runs out of the pond at Westport but it runs much too fast. Yesterday at this time Phyllis and I were sunbathing on the rocks and talking about her seven-year-old Toby. What the brat needs is an affectionate father but neither of us would say it."

"Oh, is that the way it is?"

"Phyllis doesn't say much about her ex but he must have been a real crud. Probably was gay all along but didn't decide to admit it until home life became a little routine and the child a nuisance. Phyllis said he would never touch Toby. And Phyllis doesn't understand Toby. She's devoted to him but to her he's a stubborn little adult. Of course, he looks old and wise and he knows a lot for a child his age, but he's a baby."

"A woman like that must have a hell of a time," Alex said. "But I suppose all women do. I can't imagine very clearly what goes on in their minds. I can't remember when I last had a conversation with a woman. I work for a man, I work with other men, I eat with men, exercise with men, go to the theater with men, play bridge, drink, party, carry on with men. I hardly remember my mother and I never see my sisters and aunts if I can help it—they're all harpies and gossipmongers. Someone sold me on the Greek ideal of beauty early—women are knock-kneed and lumpy and passive, men are dynamic and beautifully constructed. Some men need women at home, I suppose, but I don't. I'm a better cook than any woman I ever heard of and who darns socks these days? Mrs. Atkin comes in twice a week and washes my shirts and swishes a duster around. That's all I want from the whole tribe."

"Alex, you have a problem. You know all the bad things and none of the compensating ones about women. They aren't that different from men, I assure you. Many a dumpy smooth-skinned fag is more girlish than an athletic flat-breasted girl—you'd be amazed. There's got to be only one real physical difference. And I say '*Vive la difference.*' Throwing out the marginal cases, women are fun to lay and they can be very loving and amusing and useful and appealing. But I don't think I'll get married again soon, even though Phyll's boobs in a boned-up bathing suit bounce like heavy cream in a crock."

"How long were you married?"

"To June, less than a year. To Carlo, two years and four months."

"Did you think of Carlo as your wife?"

"No, but we referred to each other so often as husband that I had to be very, very careful at Quillquiar's School, I can tell you. Those old biddies and the boys too were all ears for even the slightest hint of personal sex life. They were sometimes very vocal about some of their own adventures. One large square youth was indignant for a week because he'd made a fool of himself at a party, mistaking a boy for a girl. Actually I think he was less indignant than fascinated or he'd have kept the whole episode quieter."

"What happened?"

"It was one of those impromptu parties in somebody's apartment while her parents were away and kids called other kids until half the private-school population of the Upper East Side was beering it in the light of one lamp. The square youth engineered a certain doll in slacks into a dark corner down behind a sofa and did quite a lot of hot kissing before he discovered he was undressing a boy doll. Some of the other Quillquiar boys had watched his progress with Leslie and thought he knew what he was doing and were certain afterward that if he had kept his cool and proceeded with the *savoir-faire* and *cherchez le* fairy that becomes a Quillquiar senior, the lovely lad would have cooperated most enthusiastically and our disgruntled friend would have had a quick course in total participation and emerged with some corners knocked off as well as his rocks off. The kids asked me in my office what I thought and I said they'd been throwing a good many euphemisms around but under the circumstances discretion was probably better than valor. They took the hint and closed the door. They knew as well as I did that old Witherspoon had a habit of eavesdropping out in the hall if he saw the door of my room open."

"Dammit, Mike, one minute you're the most honest person I know and the next you're off in wonderland. Stop it."

"Poet's license, *mon cher.* Also ingrained Southern exaggeration designed to make a good story better. As a matter of fact that account is almost word for word of what was said the third time Jamie bewailed the look-alike fads and long-haired boys. From there, once the door was discreetly closed, the discussion ranged over items like what happens to your automatic Oedipus complex if you can't tell your mother from your father? Were we in favor of coeducational toilets? Bottomless bathing suits for all? Would our spiraling economy suddenly deflate if there were no more wars? Do the liquor distillers keep pot from being legalized? I wish I had taped the whole session."

"They sound like a lively bunch."

"All kids are lively if they're let be but most of the teachers I know loathe kids. Teachers just like having a captive audience, so they demand silence and get apathy."

"Don't kids go too far if you don't restrain them?"

"Sometimes I've had to quiet them down, if that's what you mean. If you mean asking questions and saying what they think, I don't think they can go too far. They wanted to get personal sometimes but I always managed to divert those attempts and still not discourage exploration."

"Did you let them discuss books like *Candy* and *Our Lady of the Flowers?*"

"If they'd all read them. I found that one of my senior classes had all read *Fanny Hill* so we discussed it as history and fantasy. One of the boys pointed out to me that Cleland was much more interested in the men than he was in the women and by writing it from a woman's point of view he could discuss the size and shape of each organ that Fanny encountered, climaxing in Goodnatured Dick's enormous machine which Fanny watched another character cope with. The same student also pointed out that the episode is preceded by Fanny's watching the homosexual couple and followed by the foursome and one can easily become confused about who's doing what to whom. His theory was that Cleland was ardently bisexual but had to disguise his interest in men to get his money for writing the book."

"Did the kids actually say 'homosexual'?"

"Well, they love to throw the slang around and show how

they know what's currently 'in', so they probably said 'queer' or 'swinging'."

"Is there anything those kids don't know?"

"Sure—they don't know what half the words mean. But they will find out for themselves, most of them, They don't accept the old handed-down, prefabricated concepts of decency and morality and pleasure so easily. I taught them to be wary and analyze intentions and observe what was carefully not being said as well as what was put out for the reader to see. At least they can read advertisements now and not be misled. And some are ready for Dante."

"Speaking of advertisements, Mike, wouldn't you think the advertising experts would feature the male physical endowments more obviously than they do? Supposedly women do most of the buying."

"Well, I don't know. A very well-dressed woman stopped me on Fifth Avenue once and said I should wear underwear. She was very crisp and polite. I crisply and politely told her I was wearing underwear. She said she meant of course the other kind, which she understood were called 'jockeys.' I asked her if she had a financial interest in the matter or if it were sexual. She disclaimed any financial interest. I asked if the sight of a man's covered sexual equipment aroused her to an embarrassing point or if she preferred to think men didn't really have anything there she didn't have. She trotted off in quite a state of something or other. Right up to the last second I was sure she was trying to proposition me. I'm still not sure that wasn't what she wanted to do. On the other hand, when I was teaching in a coed school I had to explain to the fifteen-year-old boys that some fifteen-year-old girls aren't ripe for sex even in wisecracks and to go easy in class. I quoted the words of some sage: 'There's only one thing worse than not having sex when you want it and that's having it when you don't want it.' They got the message. That woman on Fifth Avenue might have been a fifteen-year-old emotionally."

Marshlands and dumps had followed the stucco desolation of Sheepshead Bay. On the water side was a half-hearted park designated by signs as Plumb Beach and Plum Beach. Over to the right across the water were the Marine Bridge and Breezy

Point with its Dubuffet buildings that had been abandoned half constructed.

"It may be warm enough to sunbathe," Alex said. "I have my suit in my pocket. Did you bring one?"

"No," Mike said, "and it almost seems warm enough to swim today. I don't suppose there will be any cops around, now that the bathhouse and all the concessions are closed."

"Probably a patrol check every so often. The cops have to have something to do. One quiet weekday last summer there were two patrol cars and six cops on foot milling around between the bathhouse and the refreshment stand at the other end. It's a municipal scandal."

"I think the whole concept of a professional gun-totin' snooping special privileged police force is obsolete somehow. I don't know what to suggest to replace them but it seems to me the police as they are now cause more trouble and ill-will than their positive deeds justify."

"Of course," Alex said, "I've known a couple who were human enough when they had their uniforms off. And there was a beauty I used to flirt with on Madison Avenue. If you turned and looked back at him, he'd wink. He was there for years. It must be wearing to stand there in the middle of traffic for hour after hour."

"Yes, but I feel a lot sorrier for those nice elderly people who work in fancy stores. I have the impression there isn't even a place they could sit down if they weren't busy."

"Are your parents alive, Mike?"

"My mother died with I was ten. My father married again and my stepmother died while I was in college. My father went to New Mexico and then out to California. I haven't seen him since the day of May's funeral. He sent me money until I finished college. And after that, not a word. I'd like to see him again but I suppose he doesn't want to be bothered. Eight years. He's fifty-three now."

"Both my parents died while I was in the Navy. When my father was my age, he was an old man."

"Like Ernest Hemingway," Mike said. "All that vaunted virility, that one-hundred-ten percent butchness—a melancholy old lion, ungraceful at fifty. My father looked rather like Fitzgerald—the golden hair and the charm. He was rather short, too. And a flirt." Abruptly Mike turned on the radio. An announcer with cherries in his larynx was dramatically sweeping up to the finale of what was obviously a coffee commercial; then there was an instant of silence and horns dipped and blared a high, desolate call.

Alex identified it as the *Capriccio Italien.* He knew his habit of announcing the title of even the most trite piece of music on the air or on Muzak irritated many of his friends but he went on compulsively doing it. Mike did not seem to hear. "It's sadder," Alex went on to day, "than *None but the Lonely Heart,* isn't it? The only music I find sadder is the little refrain in the last movement of the Brahms G-minor Quartet."

"The Vinteuil," Mike said.

"What?"

"To me that bit of the Brahms G-minor is the Vinteuil sonata that winds through *Remembrance of Things Past.*"

"But that was a piano and violin sonata, wasn't it?" Alex asked.

"Yes."

Alex was a little chagrined that Mike had been so familiar with the Brahms and even had his private associations. And Mike's father being only three years older than Alex did not help his *amour-propre.* "I've read Proust, of course—I can't say I very much like all that rambling and winding and back-tracking. But his finding out everyone was gay did amuse me."

Mike seemed hardly to hear. They passed the air base in silence and went through the toll station without a real halt. In a moment they were on the bridge with Riis Park spread out before them. A light breeze seemed to beat at the car, almost in time to the jingling, yearning Tchaikovsky music.

"It's clearer out here," Alex commented. Mike nodded. He wasn't looking at the Park but over it and far out to where the sea and sky faded into one another without a line to mark their meeting. There was no conversation while Alex drove around and into the paved desert of the parking lot. Only two other cars were there. Alex parked near the lower exit and they waited for a minute until the final passage of the *Capriccio* came to a crashing climax and faded. Alex switched off the radio and they got out and locked the doors. They were walking the twenty feet or so to the exit when Alex saw the dragonflies—first one, then two more, gliding in great interlocking circles. They were like some sort of sign to him, there so soon after having mentioned them.

Mike saw them too and smiled. "Now you've seen a dragonfly."

They were smaller than Alex had expected them to be and less glittering. He tried to make sense of their circling and swooping but could not. One hovered over the hood of the Peugeot an instant and went on and away.

"What do they want, do you suppose?" Alex asked.

"What does anybody want?"

"Food? There's nothing here but cement and my car. The silly things."

"Maybe they just enjoy using their wings," Mike said.

"If it turns cold tonight, they'll die, won't they?" Alex asked.

"Probably."

A breeze wafted them away but they circled back without apparent effort.

"They're beautiful—Japanese beautiful," Alex said. He wanted one.

"And you want one for your collection."

"No."

"Good," Mike said.

He can almost read my mind, Alex thought. But I can't read his. Mike's a poet—these dragonflies and this moment mean much more to him than he shows. I never really see significances until someone like Mike points them out. It's a wonder I even noticed the dragonflies. Are our lives as aimless as this circling? Is that what Mike is thinking? My life is rigid, preset, I go in circles. And maybe it is aimless. Is Mike's life as aimless as mine? Is just being beautiful or talented or successful enough in itself? Mike uses his wings for the fun of it. So do I in a way. And when the cold night comes, we all die, whether we had any fun or not. I read somewhere that only those who've had a full sex life die happy.

Mike was moving toward the gate, da-da-daaing the Brahms theme to himself. At the break in the hedge he turned and looked back. The dragonflies had vanished.

They crossed the barren traffic lanes and went around the

boarded-up bathhouse. A few ragged scarlet cannas bloomed late in the oval flowerbeds among the dead stalks. Beside the gravel path were cherry trees with small, waxen yellow cherries among the golden leaves, and some tall shrubs were putting out whitish blossoms that permeated the afternoon there with an odor almost disgustingly sweet. The two men followed the walk around to the promenade, crossed it and sat on the steps to pull off their shoes and socks.

Wind had blown the sand over the late season litter and left the beach almost clean. Down to the left a woman leaned on the railing and watched them. Her poison-green capri pants and blouse bulged as if they might split any second. Her dyed red hair was elaborately teased up and sprayed but she was barefoot and not carrying slippers. Further along, two ancient men and a woman sat muffled and motionless on a bench. No doubt they were from the hospital for the aged there beyond the fence at the end of the promenade. Just after the war the hospital had been empty for years and the area, now a baseball field, had ragged little dunes where the boys could sometimes sneak a quick one together like kids smoking in a vacant lot. But those days had been gone for years.

Up in an angle of the bathhouse front a fat man and a stringy woman stretched out almost naked and seemingly asleep in metal reclining chairs; their skin was a uniform saddle-leather brown and dripped oil. When Alex stood up he could see tiny figures far up the beach.

The sea was quiet, as if voluntarily restraining itself to accord with the calm of the afternoon. Even the few wheeling gulls were silent. Alex and Mike trudged directly toward the ocean across the warm crusty sand. They were surprised by a figure kneeling in the damp sand at the edge of the water. The hump of shore sand built up by a storm and left with the ebbing of the tide had hidden him from them until they were within thirty or forty feet of him. He was youthful, perhaps only a boy, with a lithe olive-brown body clad at the loins in a very narrow faded brown suit; his hair was reddish brown and curly. He was squatting, unaware of them, finishing a sand castle.

Alex stopped and whispered, "It's the sand-castle boy from Fire Island."

Mike watched closely until the youth turned a trifle in his work. "It's Caswell Green. I taught him at Quillquiar's a year ago."

"Ssh." Alex drew Mike back and they retreated until the boy was out of sight again and the distance and soft slap of the surf would cover their voices. "You know him? Cas—that's what everyone called him, all right. He was pointed out as often last summer as the Tiffany lampshades in the Long Wave. You taught him?"

"Yes," Mike said. "He was kicked out at the end of the first trimester—he wouldn't work, they claimed. I didn't find out what was afoot until we returned from Christmas vacation and he was gone. I made a fuss but it was too late. He went off to a little school up in the country I was told."

"Well," Alex said, "he spent the whole summer in about a dozen different houses. Ed Darrille kept him most of the season. Cas supposedly spent every morning on the beach making sand castles like that one and the late afternoon in his shelter way down in the dunes. I think they said he called it his crib. He wasn't in it when I saw it, but I could imagine. It was just some old planks stuck in the side of the dune, no top on it or anything. He couldn't even stretch out in it. You went up and leaned on the plank across the top of the opening and Cas went on from there. Or he didn't and you went on and let the next guy have his chance. Cas wouldn't pay any attention if you spoke to him, played deaf. The chosen ones said he was an expert, fast and thorough. Some fellows he took every time they turned up—others he wouldn't touch. No one could figure out why some were accepted and some were rejected—and the same man he accepted one day might be rejected another time. Some days he disappeared—evidently he walked for miles up or down the beach. Fellows reported seeing him passing the other villages but if he ever stopped anywhere except at the Grove, no one knew of it. You couldn't depend on him but he was usually there. The guys who knew about it tried to keep it a secret but of course they took their friends down. I didn't hear about it until just before Labor Day and he left a few days after that. Charles and Owen discovered him in June and made regular trips down to him. Cas took care of Owen twice the whole summer and Charles every time. They both agreed it was worth waiting for and got erections just telling me about him."

"No one had him?"

"His various hosts had him, of course. But he wouldn't have more than one man in bed with him. He was passive and, after he'd been taken each night, he went right to sleep, no matter what time it was. He occasionally went to the discothèque and watched the dancing and talked to some girls he knew—not dykes, either—but he didn't dance or drink. He usually slept about ten hours a night. He was sick, of course."

Mike seemed to be only half-listening. "Yes. I suppose so. It's a messy situation. His father is in Greece, carrying on with the whole Greek army. His mother is a beautiful dipso from Atlanta who lives with someone very high up and very rich. Caswell was living with an aunt on East Eighty-fifth and going to an analyst when he turned up at Quillquiar's. When the facts came out, I was surprised they'd ever accepted him at all. After a month he left the aunt and the analyst and moved into an unfurnished apartment in the Village with a university student. The school didn't know until the analyst called to find out what had happened to him. Caswell wrote a story for me about the move so I knew quite a lot about it—how he preferred sleeping on the floor on a pile of clothes to staying with his aunt and how he and the university student were learning to cook on a secondhand hot plate. The aunt was pretty weird too, according to Caswell. She sometimes declined to speak aloud for a week at a time. I think the only assigned work he did at Quillquiar's was that story and another one or two for me. He called himself Andreji in the story and I asked him if it stood for André Gide and he said it did but wouldn't talk about himself. The librarian said he read everything he could get his hands on about chivalry and the Provençal Love cult; I was going to suggest he do a paper on the early Arthur poems."

"How old is he?"

"At least nineteen. He was older than he looked, I remember. He may even be twenty by now. I think I'll try to talk to him."

"Wonder how he got out here. Of course one of those cars may be his."

"I doubt it," Mike said. "For one thing, without his glasses he can't see twenty feet."

"He didn't wear glasses at Fire Island," Alex said.

"Evidently he didn't have to." Mike led Alex back toward the water. At the crest of the little rounded cliff, Mike stopped and said "Hi, Caswell."

The boy looked up. His face was not exactly beautiful but it was rather striking and very appealing. His eyes were gray and he stared as if he were looking up into the sun.

"Mr. Kincade. Gee." Caswell straightened up and brushed the damp sand off his hands by rubbing them on his chest. Mike slid down beside him and they shook hands. Alex appeared and Mike introduced him. Caswell politely said, "Hello, sir," stared at him a second, then down at his sand construction. "I've been making a fortress."

"Go on," Mike said. "We're just out for a walk in the sun. You're certainly looking healthy. Are you in college this fall?"

"Beaton." He did not explain why he was not at the college on this October afternoon.

"Good," Mike said. "Like it?"

"Not too much." He knelt and patted a tower. "Do you still write poetry?"

"Yes." Mike smiled. "At least I did until yesterday. And I may tomorrow."

"Oh. Don't if you don't want to. That's the main thing."

Alex spoke up. "How about 'Do if you want to'? Isn't that important, too?"

"Yes, the other side of the coin," Caswell said. "But not quite as important." He turned away from Alex. "Is it, Mr. Kincade?"

"I'll think about that," Mike said. "I was sorry when I heard you were gone, Caswell."

"I know. I heard about the fuss you kicked up. I had spies. The kids always find about those things, you know."

"Yes," Mike said. "I left too. Did you hear that?"

"No. I'm glad. But you waited until the end of the year, didn't you? It wasn't because of the fight over me I hope."

"Only partly. There were too many instances like that."

"But no one quite like me I hope," Caswell said.

"No, Caswell, I'm sure Quillquiar's will never let themselves in again for anything vaguely like you." Mike laughed but Caswell looked at him suspiciously. "That's why I left. I want to be where the boys like you go when they're dumped out."

"Dumped out. That's exactly what I was. Sometimes I manage to wriggle out first though. After your school I went up to a place in New England where there were thirty divorce-court orphans like myself. Woodworking if you wanted it. Skiing. Free reading, baby math. Art every other hour. I slept with a girl every night for a week and no one noticed but the girl she was supposed to share the bed with. The roommate went to the infirmary and slept with the nurse. Anyhow, I got a diploma so Beaton could take me. It wasn't bad. I was out at Fire Island all summer. I didn't see you there."

"It's a long busy sand bar. And I was out only two days. I was at the Grove."

"I was at the Grove. Did you dance at the discothèque?"

"No," Mike said.

"Neither did I. And I never went into the Long Wave except for lunch one time. And never to the Meat Rack."

"I saw you at a distance, Cas," Alex said. "I heard a lot about you."

"He told me," Mike said to the youth.

"I don't mind. Or I shouldn't mind. But I do. Well . . ." He stood up.

"I'm going to walk up the beach," Mike said to Alex. "See you later, Caswell."

"Sure. I have a crib over there by the wall. A sunbathing crib. I don't think the old folks from the hospital can see into it. I've been sunbathing in the nude most of the day. Come and sunbathe there if you want to."

"Thanks," Mike said. "I think I'll just hike for a while."

"I'll be down by the wall. That looks like a good place to get some sun," Alex said. "I'll take your shoes."

Caswell did not look up as they went off in different directions.

MIKE

The desire to turn and look again at Caswell was strong but Mike restrained himself. He did not want to catch Alex doing the same thing, somehow, and he knew Alex would be looking back, studying Caswell as he casually sauntered away, hoping to catch Caswell's eye before he was out of the lad's range.

Mike turned up the beach toward the Roxbury end and walked along the surf in the wet sand. Occasionally waves washed over his feet—the water felt almost warm. A little flock of sandpipers fled ahead of him, running evenly on their short legs and skimming off in brief flight. Unlike the dragonflies, the sandpipers were plainly hunting food and finding it from time to time but still they seemed to enjoy their exercise and were not much frightened by the man who had barged into their feeding ground. Mike was thinking that to see was to love—there was no need to possess. To see Caswell again was to love him again. There had been that unspoken response from the first. With some people it was that way—there was no need for more.

Alex and everyone else at the Island no doubt had called Caswell's sand constructions sand castles, Mike thought, but Caswell had called them fortresses. And he called his little sunbathing shelter out here a crib, too. Crib. Baby's crib? Whore's crib? Or did they only call them cribs in the South? Does Caswell think of himself as a baby or as a whore or as both? He's capable of seeing himself in both repulsive roles simultaneously and still not able to stop himself from acting them out. Or even want to. Obsession. Compulsion. Zwang. Swinging. Taking that many men every day. Taking from them—and giving them a certain measure of pleasure and distinction in return. Measure of pleasure. Who can measure pleasure? What sieve would one use?

Distinction in CG—to be accepted every time by Caswell-Cas. Or even every other time. Failure—to be turned away every time. Did that pattern give Caswell power he didn't hope to have any other way? Did he realize how much his attention had meant to some of those drones like Charles and Owen? To be in, to be elect of Caswell?

Perhaps that phase is over. The child can't hope to find men out here today to entice. Alex is intrigued—he wants to be let in.

Pathetic Alex, Mike thought, never in on the antics, always on the sidelines, running to catch up with the parade. He hears the bagpipes but he never sees the kilts. It would be fun to tousle Alex in kilts in a haystack. He has the calves and the thighs and the buttocks for kilts and tousling. But I won't live with him—he'd cry if I brought in a sailor. Alex would cry more if he didn't get to see the sailor. And if he did see the sailor, Alex would want his share right then. Alex wants to be a member of every wedding. F. Jasmine Alex. So he can talk about it afterwards—or at least talk to himself and tell himself he isn't left out, left over, negligible. Whoever wants to be negligible, left over, left out, forgotten, abandoned the way Carlo abandoned me, my father abandoned me, June left me?

I won't think of that. Not now or tomorrow, Miss Scarlett.

Members of the wedding. Wedding of the members is more like it.

Caswell. I had no idea his body was that beautiful—so sleek and exquisite of proportion. Trite, but in the case of Caswell, right. No thickness—everything minimal for sheer beauty; but not delicate either—functional. His strenuous summer certainly didn't ruin his health.

Bernie Stern became a skeleton when he went man-crazy. He couldn't eat or sleep properly, he wore himself out hunting, chasing, sucking. He said he had VD in his throat three times. He wore himself down to a naked urge. But he wore the urge out too, he got sick of his obsession and vomited it out and calmed down and he's all right now.

That was the year I slept with everyone who wanted me until I was almost as worn out and uncomprehending as

Bernie. I hardly knew where I was or what I was doing or who I was doing it with. But I dragged out before I was carried so far I couldn't get back. I was sick in bed for a week and when that was over I was awake again, the sun was shining and the storm was over. They always say such promiscuous carrying on makes you jaded and insensitive and it does for a while—I didn't care what any of those men and women wanted or got, as long as I wanted and got them.

No, that isn't quite how it was—most of the men and women I didn't even want. If they asked me, I went with them. But I never gave them what they really wanted and they had nothing for me. Or if they had, I was too dazed to realize it. And it wasn't just a flu bug I finally had, I had to be sick, sick unto death before I could go on, sick the way Michel was in Africa and Rodion in Siberia. Life imitates art.

When I came out of that phase, thin and washed out and interested only in keeping alive, I was ready for something absolutely other. Ready for Carlo, ready for love.

I wasn't ready for love when I met June—she wasn't ready, either. We just wanted to be in love and tried so hard to be, went through the motions—even some of the superficial emotions, too. We were the happiest, brightest, most-in-love young couple that ever hit the Village or condescended to grace weary old Riverside Drive. God, how we posed and danced and made love. As if we were being filmed for international release. We were the stars, the beautiful young, the precious envied darlings—we were acting out all the fantasies of the slickest advertising.

There was quite a lot of flaunting of perfection in that first year with Carlo, too. And it was perfect, not just visually, not just sexually, either—each of us was totally in love with the other and couldn't imagine wanting anything more, anything different. I still don't want anything more or different. Can he be happy with that stick Hayden? And June, can she honestly love that clod, be happy with him and their clodlet?

If she isn't, she'll never admit it, but Carlo is bigger than that. He'll have to admit it's a mistake. Even if we can't go back to the beginning, he must come back. Carlo, Carlo, I love you. How can I not love you? We were to be together forever, no matter what. If I did something wrong I'm sorry.

I want you to come back and live with me. If you ever loved our house, how can you stand that bitch-elegant stage set? Quit acting and come home, honey.

That's useless, no good, maudlin, Carlo isn't coming back, everyone knows that, everyone who ever knew us knows it now and I may as well face it.

And would I really want him to come back if he would? I'm finally free to do as I please, be myself. When Carlo was there, I saw everything, even myself, through his eyes. He was cool, he put people off, he put them into the middle distance and ranged them up and down in hierarchies—rigid and cruel and artificial. Snobbery. But I thought I was close to Carlo himself.

And how he loved being close to me, as much as I to him, our neutrons and protons commingling and forming unique, never-to-be-repeated, never-to-be-shattered Us. At home we wanted to be near enough to touch. At parties we couldn't keep away from each other and didn't even care when people teased or were cynical. We knew they were jealous or thought we were show-offs but we didn't care. At least not for a year or so. And it wasn't just show-off. That summer in Europe we were never out of each other's sight for a single hour. Half the time we couldn't have said right off what country we were in, but we knew we were together.

Now no more We. I've said We so long, nearly three years now, that I still say it. And it sounds so stupid and pathetic, an arrogant mechanical pronoun based on no antecedent. And the worst of it is I know there will never be a Carlo-me again.

Phyllis and I could say We but it would never mean as much as it did when it stood for Carlo-me. June and I tried. With a girl there are too many blank patches, areas a man can never fully know or understand. You have to take so much on faith. And hope and charity. The pieces may fit together psychologically and physiologically and make a kind of whole but there can't be the real identification.

The narcissism, you self-seeking, self-devouring, self-adoring, hyacinthine beauty. Ex-beauty.

Phyllis. She has never been in love, she doesn't even know what the possibilities are but she does know that she is missing something. That cruddy Sandy Utterman never loved her and if she loved him, it couldn't have been wholeheartedly. Do most people have to settle for halfhearted love? Never experience for one instant what Carlo and I had for two years at least? Or am I glamorizing what was only ordinary and flawed and only seemed wonderful because I intoxicated myself? If I did intoxicate myself I certainly didn't catch myself at it. At least I am that honest—when I catch myself glamorizing I admit it to myself even if I don't to poor Alex. He's so credulous. About Berty, for instance, who didn't have the whole construction crew—he had two of them but one of them had a huge whang and I was jealous. And I didn't have the lifeguard who watched Marc Ferrera and me necking. I tried to get the lifeguard but he was too shy.

Less than a month ago I walked into the john down there and found Marc surrounded by teenagers, all with stiff joints in their hands. They were taking turns jacking Marc's big one. He motioned me into the circle and I let them play with me too until we had too many faggots pushing to see. It was silly and dangerous and self-indulgent. When I was with Carlo I wouldn't have done such a thing. I wouldn't have had to do such a thing.

Carlo and I didn't make a façade to present to the world to prove two men could be happy together—we were happy. Blake and Gerry have lived together in domestic bliss for seventeen years and are still in love. They have everything a straight couple could have except children and since they both teach they have children too, have them more hours a day and more intimately than most of the kids' parents ever do. It would be different having children of your own but not necessarily better.

I could love Phyll's little Toby just as if he were my own, I think. But not having had one, how can I tell? I'm as silly as the straights who have never had a homosexual affair but think they have the right to say it's unsatisfying, bad, won't work, can't last, cock was made for cunt alone and all that other teleological horseshit which they wouldn't stoop to use about any other subject. But having committed themselves to one way, how could the straights admit something else might have been just as good or even better without looking like fools? And church and state that depend for their very existence on masses of babies they can control have been right in there making might right. If war were obsolete and the Holy Ghost went back where it came from and were forgotten about, who'd care what anyone did in bed? Or right out in public, for that matter?

What a half-assed world we live in now with all our bright new theories and freedoms and our medieval superstitions operating alternately, even simultaneously. Kissing's wonderful but kiss the beautiful mouth of a boy and you're perverse. Masturbation is expected, normal, advised. But wrap that adept hand around another man's aching cock—maybe a nice big one, the kind you've always dreamed of possessing yourself, so you enjoy the pleasures of a waking dream and he enjoys your excitement as well as the neural and kinesthetic delight of being manipulated—and kid, you are queer, Make him even more assured of being wanted by taking it in your mouth labiating it and you're a nasty little cocksucker. Slip it into his anus and fuck him good—you're not really queer because you're treating him like a woman. But if you enjoy being fucked in the ass, you're really hopeless. Even I kind of wonder about those fellows because I don't enjoy it and don't want it. There must be something special to it because so many want it—married men who'd never kiss another man or suck a cock often love that extra thrill their wives can't give them. Why don't I like it? Is not liking it the way I convince myself I'm really a man whatever I may kiss or swing on? And what's so important about being a man?

So how queer am I anyway and who cares? If I marry Phyllis, how upset will she be if I wander off once in a while? Is a wholehearted husband now and then better than a half-hearted one all the time? Is possession that important? She might feel degraded in others' eyes but whose business would it be but ours? And what dear friend, cosy neighbor, business acquaintance, PTA member, distant cousin—wouldn't think it was his business if he got an intimation of it? And how would I feel if one of them found it was his duty to tell me Phyllis was sneaking out with another girl or another man?

If Phyllis doesn't find a husband who will love Toby, gets another oaf like Utterman to her bed, what will little Toby grow into, batting around from psychiatrist's couch to boarding school? He might become like Caswell Green even without

Caswell's special fateful circumstances—crisscrossed and tossed awry, askew, aside, floundering and flaunting in cribs of his own making.

If I had known about Caswell last summer when I was out there, would I have gone down to his dune? He'd have taken me—I could tell a few minutes ago that he wants me. And I want him, but not that way. To hold, to caress and kiss for an hour, to tease and turn, kissing those curls and his ears and neck, giving him everything I've got and then taking him in my hand, not out of duty or courtesy but because I want to and I want to twice as much because he wants me to. That neat, surprisingly conspicuous basket like a tennis ball. Bait, a bid for attention, for excitation. How perverse of him to put himself inside, behind a fence where he couldn't be handled. Like Berty Roark behind that fence on Locust Avenue, the fence with the half-board that could be set aside.

The big one came to him the oftenest. Berty knew who he was. He had five girls in school, one in our class. Maybe his wife was weary of that huge thing. Were there no whores in town? The Patton sisters who ran the dime store gave it free to anybody under eighteen—they must have had some older, paying customers. Angus Walton was probably tired of them, too. And could he have just liked the idea he was giving pleasure to a crazy fourteen-year-old kid? What did he do after Berty got tired and wandered off to fresher mischief? And the Patton girls? I never heard either of them got married. Are they spiteful old spinsters now, gossiping about the loose morals of miniskirted rock-and-rollers and the noise of the motorcycles? Wait, Kincade. They were only about ten years older than you. They're probably riding motorcycles and love all that leather and swing with the best.

Noreen was married the week after school was out. I wonder if she heard about that double date I went on and how I laid that hot little cupcake Marcia two nights in a row? I told myself I was doing that so Noreen would hear and be jealous. Marcia's hair was the same color as mine and Ellen's mother said we looked like twins.

"Dear Miss Mothers: The first girl I ever laid could have been my twin. I'd always wanted a sister—and an older brother. Does this throw a new light on *Twelfth Night?* Discuss in five hundred well chosen words."

That Mexican movie star wasn't any hotter than Marcia although she tried to pretend to be. All that biting and clawing, Sylvia Salazar. But she knew how to keep me from coming until she had had all she wanted. Then wowee, zamzam, pow and I was out. Very adroit and slick. All that tan and makeup and technique, so sophisticated, so worldly. And the look on her mask-mug when I took her chauffeur's cock in my mouth. Something went out of her when she had to admit a man could be good with her and still be queer too, the possessive little bitch. And not just one of us: she'd already told me she'd had Luis every day she'd been in town and he was the best fuck she'd ever had in ol' New York. She sounded as if she'd had about six per diem. Well, *carpe diem* and back to the kliegs, Sylvia. If one of us had wandered in while she was in bed with the other and she'd got us both worked up and we'd had a threesome, she'd have enjoyed it, but to finish with her and go to him . . . oi.

Mexican. Half Jewish. Why are all the girls I get serious about Jewish? June, now Phyllis. But I wasn't serious about Sylvia. And I was serious about Noreen and Lainey. But Lainey always claimed she had a Jewish great-grandmother. Lainey wanted to be everything—Negro, Jewish, WASP, hillbilly, sophisticate, poetess, peasantess, Peter Pan-Wendy, the gal in the brassière ads, the imperturbable duchess, Madame Faustus doing a striptease in the Casbah. And I was, am, just as avid. How could we help loving each other? We were each other.

And what would Kid Lainey-de Beauvoir have said if she'd found out about the me-and-Lloyd Stark episodes before and overlapping her Lainey-and-Lloyd year? I never knew if Lainey would be furious and heave a two-pound ashtray at my head or laugh herself silly at a surprise. If we met now, could we begin again where we left off so raggedly? O the roses and the snowses of yesteryear, the sleighs, the lays, where are they now? O, Villon, how you sang at thirty! Why can't Michael Kincade sing as sweetly, as richly, as wisely, as hauntingly, so his clarion words echo down the corridors for a decade or a year or even a day?

What's in a day? What's in youth? There's Caswell's youth, bent by a wintry fever, like a crooked rose. And mine? Will I ever admit that my youth has been bent? There may be a dent or two in my halo at this point but am I not a saint still? Am I not sweet and loving, kind and gentle, pure in my love of the truth and the poetry that alone can say it out?

How can I love God? How can I not love God? God is myself, this sand, the sea, Caswell in his crib, the cop in his helicopter, the golden cherries among the golden leaves in October, the autumn-drugged bees in the silly season honeysuckle... O, la—love. I loved Carlo—Carlo—Carlo, come back. Daddy, where are you? Don't go off like that, I love you.

I love too damned many people. And no one loves me. If Phyllis really loved me... she doesn't even see me. I'm a promise of hot sex but only now and then, which is nicer; a blond clothes-model escort—shagetz but a real doll. At the beach club, the muscles on him. In the showers, the meat on him—the Roseman heiress picked herself a real stud though uncircumcised. Alas, my wife could use that. Music he knows and an eye for art, culture yet and such manners as well. And Toby adores you, Michael, he won't go to sleep until you've told him a story but, darling, not one of your Kafka ones—he's too advanced for seven as it is.

And the brat sits up at that point and laughs and I hit him. And he loves it. No one has ever touched him before. Kids need the feel of the hand.

My father never touched me—until that time. Maybe if he had cuffed me once or twice earlier, it wouldn't have had to be that way. And he wouldn't have deserted me. At thirty I'm a whimpering child, crying because it's getting dark and there's no one around. Except it's a sunny October afternoon and Alex wants me and Quillquiar's wants me and Phyllis and Toby plead silently and Caswell needs me and somewhere Ty O'Neill is waiting for me but doesn't realize it.

Ty, O Tyree Tyrone. How did we get thrown apart so fast? We came together like a flash of magic and it was wonderful and I wonder if I dreamed it. Midafternoon, the sun hot on the sand but the paths under the wiry crooked little trees green-gloomy and damp-cool; the hush and surprise of seeing someone standing like a ghost, the pale German boy looking deeper into the woods; a sound and with only that warning a dark man in a gold lamé bathing suit and oiled hair artfully combed over his dome, stalking silently by as if he'd seen a vision and even dared touch it.

Around a bend of intricately laced bushes and vines, there at the side of the path, a woods god, half deer, wholly male and glowing. Tall, brown, the black hair on his chest animal and exciting, the green wool suit about his loins decent but distended, the shoulders rounded back against a tree, the throat strong and biblical, the face oriental as the Irish and Spanish sometimes are—cheekbones high, nose short and thick, mouth square and full, unsmiling, the tilted eyes half closed but opening as I approach, drawing into their tilted fullness all the green gleam of the forest, the shadows and flecks of the sun, irradiating godlike animal passion and promise. I cannot look away. I cannot reconnoiter to see if we are alone, I have no volition except to approach and press my being against this pulsating kouros, my thighs against his thighs, my chest against his chest, my lips against his lips, and to look into his jewel-bright and expectant eyes. I dare not move or breathe or even pray once the five parts of me touch the five points of him, until his arms move and he presses me closer with his hands spread on my back. In the surge of unconditional acceptance, our bodies meet and become one, until we must draw back for breath. And then, when he smiles slowly and shyly, I lose my breath again. But I feel my cock stirring against his and the smile breaks into a flash of delight and we become a system of aching needing nerves and pounding blood and demanding muscles.

Hands touch us, caress us, probe and attempt to slide between us. We go quickly with our arms still as much around each other as we can keep them on the Indian path to the walk and to the house where he is staying and to someone else's bed, with the soft afternoon wind puffing in every now and then under the blind to cool our ecstatic bodies. Did you believe me, Ty, when I whispered I'd never been so fully excited in my life? And would you have believed me if I had said then that sexual excitement didn't matter so almighty much—it was your eyes and your smile that made me so happy?

After supper the waiting in the bar until he came in with his "house"—the two hosts I'd known casually for years and disliked, and the gilded, angel-faced j.d. I'd never seen before. Ralegh Bronsten, I hated you that moment. I'll hate you forever just for being between us when we should have been together. Their "house" came over to my "house" and Ty and I went out onto the cold deck—slowly, for we were beautiful together and knew it and loved it and wanted everyone to envy us a little and rejoice with us. And Ty said he'd loved every minute of it but had to stay at his hosts' house that night—Arnold and Rog had gone to great trouble to get this doll Ralegh out for his delectation. Ralegh was being kept in Philadelphia and was now supposed to be in New Rochelle visiting a sick sister. And Ty said they were all leaving in the morning on the eight o'clock boat and then he had to go to Boston and New Haven with a show. He didn't say Philadelphia too but that damned musical's in Philadelphia right now. And we kissed a long time without touching each other at all and went back in, he to his "house," me to mine, me drinking until they left, him not even looking back as the four of them went out laughing.

And several drinks and some time later I said okay to a leather-type and fucked him strapped to a lamp post with about fifteen to fifty guys jostling around us, grinning and groaning and groping each other. And I staggered over the dune to the beach and swam naked and alone and came out cold and lonesome as the moon. And went right down to the end of town and lay naked on the walk while everybody took turns sucking me and when that gilded cherub Ralegh took a turn I held his head down and tried to choke him to death with my big cock. He took it down his throat until I let him breathe and take my last load because it wasn't his fault and he was a first-class cocksucker and had just sucked off Ty at least once I was sure and maybe more and I wanted to mingle my gism with Ty's. And the cherub went crazy and begged me to call him in Philly—he'd come up to New York just for an hour if I'd let him suck me off again and I slapped him and told him I was in love with Ty and he said he didn't think Ty was so great so I slapped him again and let some creep swing on my meat while Ralegh crouched over me and cried on my face and kissed me. I pretended to come again and Ralegh pulled my hair and kissed my eyes and put his cock in my mouth and I sucked him off like a demon. He screamed so loud when he shot that we all had to leave in a hurry, in case a cop came to investigate.

In the morning it was raining. I shaved and staggered down to the dock to say goodbye to Ty. He had on a trench coat and the three of us huddled under it and kissed and the kid got my cock out for a last look and I had my hand inside Ty's pants and silk shorts and felt it throb and get hard but I never took my eyes from his beautiful, wild, shy face. It's an elusive face. Sometimes I can't make it come clear to me at all and sometimes I can see it as it was that first instant in the woods. I want to see it as it was when he began to smile but I can't make it smile.

It wasn't until my hosts and I were crossing later that morning that I found out his name was Tyree and that he was the latest genius in scene design and rich and had been the lover of a New Haven socialite whose wife had committed suicide and my chances of seeing him again were slim indeed because he was already working on sets for another show and was the darling of the richest bunch in town. When I told Hal and Barry how Ralegh carried on down by the Comber, they wouldn't believe me. They thought Ralegh was the cutest thing they'd ever seen and wouldn't believe he'd gotten that excited over me, especially when he'd just been with Ty O'Neill.

I find Caswell Green much more appealing than Ralegh. I used to catch Caswell staring at me in class but he was always staring at somebody or something and you never could be sure he really saw what was right in front of him. But one day in study hall I was remembering all too vividly the night before with Carlo mio and got a hard-on under the desk and realized Caswell was staring at it. And he was always pressing his thighs against the edge of my desk top and making his tennis-ball basket pop out most alluringly. I expect he absent-mindedly did that before some of the older men and that had something to do with his being dumped so abruptly. Those closet queans were thrilled at being tempted to touch it but hated themselves for not having the nerve, the sour old things.

If I had not been so much in love with Carlo last year . . . Do I sin in lusting after Caswell in retrospect?

Does Caswell sin when he indulges in orgies of phallic worship and did he when he carried out his ritual of taking living semen from eager victims? A million ignoramuses who never imagined such things could happen would adamantly bellow yes, he sins! and take joy in locking him away from decent people, lest he contaminate their sons, who would be just as eager as any if they were initiated into those ancient rites.

Sin . . .

Age . . .

. . . I've gone through thirty years of days; some rain down more brightly than others; some I have not let come to my ken for many a day or night or dreamtime, but those refused may be the very ones that hold the answers to the riddle of my oedipal sphinx, of my sphinxial oedipal demands. And the irony just as well may be that there is no answer even in those clouded-off days. I have not sinned so there can be no absolution—memory's shower can provide no cleansing ablution. If there is desire to expiate, there is still no need. I do not believe in sin, except perhaps that wanton negation of human beings, treating persons as animals, as numbers, as ghosts, as negligible. When I slapped Ralegh Bronsten he knew why and it was not because he was negligible, oh far from it. But has ignoring his notes and telephone calls been wrong of me? I don't want to see him again. Don't I have the right to say, *It would be no good; I don't want you however much you fancy you want me now?*

A perfectly pleasant man haunts me sometimes, the one who came up to me at Sixth Avenue and Forty-fifth and said, "You are the most beautiful human being I have ever seen." And then, when I said nothing, he added, "I have been in love with you for two years and you don't know I exist." I tried to look at him, to see if he were someone I had casually teased some time, at a party or at the baths or in the locker room at the beach, but I didn't want to look at him. I just mumbled something like, "I'm sorry," and went on. What should I have said? He meant nothing to me. He had nothing for me. For me? I don't know. Did that odd little episode have anything to do with my giving myself later that year to anyone who wanted me, perhaps to him? Perhaps only to him, because he had asked in that dignified way and I had refused him as if he were a dog barking. I could at least have been polite—he was honoring me.

Well, he wouldn't say that about being beautiful if he met me there now, that's one thing for sure, honey chile. No one turns and stares these days. Not at your face, anyway.

The way I turned and stared in Salzburg until Carlo caught me. He saw only the lad's hand floating up in that outrageously graceful gesture and thought I was laughing at the exhibition. But I wasn't and the girls with him weren't, either. For an instant I joined them in adoration of exquisite mobile beauty—face, body, movement, expression—all extraordinary, all blooming together. And that afternoon Carlo apparently didn't recognize him in the aerial act of the Circus Krone or the girls in the act as the ones guarding him on the street. I never told Carlo that was why I wouldn't leave with him at the intermission even though otherwise it was such a dreary little circus. In the second half I enjoyed his brief appearance without inhibition and ached to catch him and hold him. He was undoubtedly the most beautiful human being I ever saw. And caused Carlo and me to be separated that summer for one hour. Was that my first infidelity? I had never felt that way about anybody until I met Carlo. And, until that moment there in the Domplatz, Carlo had been the most beautiful person in my world and after that he was again—with that one unspoken exception—for a year or more. And still is, in his classic Italian way, although others say he is beginning to show his age a little. Ty's face haunts me but Carlo's is still the more beautiful. And I wonder if I could see that acrobat again if I'd think he was so beautiful. In the circus he had on heavy makeup and his movements were simply those required by the act. He may even have had on makeup on the street! And the movement I thought so spontaneous—some rehearsed affectation. And the adoration of his harem an act to attract wealthy Americans.

Did Carlo realize, suspect, guess—that in that instant I was taking my first step away from him and quietly begin drawing away from me so he wouldn't be the one deserted? Did Carlo ever shed one tear because we were parting? I tried to hide my tears so he wouldn't feel guilty about doing what he was going to do anyway. Perhaps he too cried in secret. No, he didn't. He was all too happy to set up housekeeping with Hayden. Carlo didn't love Hayden and doesn't now. Carlo couldn't. But he was eager to join Hayden in out-eleganting all the other East Side pairs—joining, merging, shuffling together like so many rare old cards, their collections of small but oh very tasteful paintings on one carefully calculated wall. Remington, Romney, Bonington, Dehn, Tchelitchew and Kuniyoshi mere items in a trite decoration gambit. A stupid, ostentatious, callous conglomerating that makes the collector all and the artist nothing, a dull-witted Victorian makeshift. Even that old actor's half-bedroom in Twenty-second Street with all those framed and signed photographs of dead stage stars was not so pathetic as that picture wall of theirs is to me. And Grover said everyone was calling Carlo Charles this summer out at East-hampton—no more Carl. He never really liked my calling him Carlo. Charles Castella when it could be Carlo Castella. Or maybe he's protecting Carlo from them, reserving it just for me and the halcyon blue, honeymoon gold, salad green days when he was still only a transplanted New Jerseyite and a not totally willing refugee from Mama's management and all that Montclair Jewish-renaissance opulence. He made me an English cottage setting suitable for a Southern poet gone astray and when it was finished he left. Just as June left me when she put all the proper scenery in place for us to play Bright Young Marrieds in front of. Does Alex only want me to share his place because he sees me in it? He loathes poetry but he doesn't mind my posing as a poet and lending a literary aura to his cut-and-dried and planed-down domicile.

Is that what I do—pose as a poet? Writing just enough to keep my license, my franchise, keep my conscience quiet so that calling myself a poet isn't pure pretension and a bald lie that even I, the perpetrator, would have to choke on?

And if I am not a poet, what am I?

If I could be Tyree O'Neill's lover, would that be enough for me? A sycophant, a hanger-on, an errand runner, keeper of the hearth and replenisher of the liquor supply about whom would be said, "Ty and Mike are in Europe." Or, more likely, "That faded blond who lives with Tyree O'Neill—he belongs to Ty but it's pretty clear Ty doesn't belong to him. But they say, in his day he was a figure around town." Or would they say, "He was rather notorious around town," and giggle about what Tyree would say if he heard of the way I used to carry on at parties or saw that film I made in the Meat Rack. Of course it wasn't made in the Meat Rack, it was made in the Sunken Forest, and it was in the Meat Rack I met Tyree and he had already seen the film even then, but they wouldn't know that. Ty confessed after we were worn out and resting that he had recognized me the minute I appeared on the path and had wanted me ever since he saw that film a couple of years ago and was afraid I'd stalk right by him. He didn't have to confess all that—he was being modest and honest. And he did enjoy the afternoon or I wouldn't have enjoyed it so much.

Do I yearn for him only because our affair was broken off so abruptly? Is it only frustrated sex again? Could I be weary of him in a week and find all that smoldering brilliance turning ordinary and dull? Could his shyness and modesty that were the best of him have been merely that preppy pose I've seen Quillquiar's boys assume so glibly? No, dammit, he is decent and honest and shy and too good for me. Even if he has slept with an army, he is still innocent and shy and honest. I've slept with two armies, and I'm still honest. Not shy, but innocent? How does one know? What is the alternative—guilty? I'm not guilty. I'm just a little bedraggled. Bed-raggled. That's me—Mike Kincade, bed-raggled. And Ty isn't. He's fresh and hopeful but he needs someone honest and experienced like me. He's ready for me and I'm ready for him. If we could meet and start again, what would happen? I can't even imagine and that's wonderful— a mystery, a promise. O Ty, you are my remote Bermudas and thy praise I will exalt until it "redounding may echo beyond the Mexique Bay."

How calm it is this afternoon. And beyond the Rockaway Bay the Rockaway towers aren't there any more, shrouded away, enchanted away. Enchanted calm, quieted by my reverie. Do I only think the sea is unusually calm because I want it to be calm to reinforce my hushed suspended mood? What arrogance. Blather. The sea is quiet and not because I want it to be. I am not the center, the wellspring of anything. Sometimes it seems to me that, far from being a positive force, I am only a vacuum even in my own life, a still center with a whirlwind of people and poems and things fluttering around me, still center and cyclonic envelope drifting nebulously together nowhere, meaninglessly. Chance swept these *miscellanea* about this vague nothingness that is me and they aren't ever mine because every item flutters around a dozen, a thousand other dead centers as well. Even my poems drift off and don't come back.

But even though I am nothing, not much, so little at most, I still feel, reverberate, resound—feel and turn feeling into words, make poems of sensations and observations and chronicles of my quests and conquests and quixotic contests, my hushed, damned defeats. That hath a dying sound, a dying strain. I must have said that Orsino speech a hundred times, learning it, rehearsing it, playing it. "My desires like fell and cruel hounds" pursued me. I was thinking of Lainey every time I went over those lines.

She played Olivia better than anything else. It was the only role she was really good at, if the truth must finally be told. She was better at writing and dancing than acting. Or fucking, if the truth must finally be told there too. I wonder if Loel knew I was in love with Lainey even in those early *Twelfth Night* days? I used to watch her all the time and nearly miss my own cues. He was furious with me once or twice in rehearsals—he must have known what my trouble was. But he always smoothed it over afterward. Was he somewhat in love with me even then? It was a whole year later...

It was autumn a year later. Not early autumn like this but later autumn—there had been frost and the leaves had fallen in the woods. In the woods. Not quite the way I found Ty in the woods last summer and the woodlands were a thousand miles apart and ten years but still there's an auspicious echo.

Loel, lanky and pink-skinned, stretched naked on his clothes among the bright leaves, pinky-beige on pink and beige and amber and dun and purple-green and all the gingery-cinnamon colors, his hair gingery in the sparkling light, his corduroy jacket and pants cinnamon around the edges of his naked, extended pinkness in his sultry lair by the big rock away from the wind.

Wind windier than March—he couldn't hear me clambering over the rocks, clambering aimlessly, wondering where he'd wandered off to after I'd seen him strike into the woods far ahead of me.

And then the shocking glimpse of male nakedness through the whipping bushes, and leaning over the ledge to stare. He was less than ten feet away, his eyes closed, his legs flung off into the delicate roughness of the leaves, his long cock idly dangling down on his balls and the shadow of dark corduroy. And then that sudden silent hiatus with the sun beating down fit to broil us, me breathless, not daring to sigh much less shift my weight . . . Loel massaging his chest, all of him more sinewy than I'd have expected, massaging his belly, scratching in the gingergold hair, caressing his cock and lifting it and laying it athwart his muscular belly, rubbing it roughly and pulling back the thick skin off the head, flopping it until it began to harden, letting it thrust and stiffen untouched until it was longer than mine or Lloyd's. Then the onslaught, two-handed and eager. I could have crawled back then—with the blood pounding in his ears he wouldn't have heard me—but I didn't and, if I had, I'd have missed the quick bracing of rigid legs, the upward curl of long upper body and downward plunge of head, the thorough kowtows and frozen holding and taking at the flaming crest of climax; then the loosening, falling apart and back and out and under, under the little death of receding excitement, me lying doggo, not daring to stir, much less stand and whip my semen in long raining arcs over him as I longed to do, but finally dodging softly away when he seemed to sleep. And all week I could hardly hear what he said in rehearsal for stripping him and stroking him lustfully. But not actually. It was *The Rainmaker* we were rehearsing. Destiny had been given a nudge or two and was determined to outnudge us.

Those Dionysos interpretations of Loel's—the magic stick Starbuck carried was Dionysos' thyrsos and when I cut a thick one like a big rampant phallos and brought it into dress rehearsal, he said, "Yes, that's what we want."

Edie What's-her-name, the lezzie Lizzy, said, "Well, that's not what I want. That's too much." We all knew she didn't want anything like that at all and anything male would be too much, but we weren't sure she knew that yet and didn't mean it was too much to expect the audience to take without a howl of protest—or pleasure. Anyway, a giggle. "Mr. Hastings, that's just plain indecent," she said and Loel agreed and explained again about the fertility aspects of the play and she was talked down that time.

But when I came swinging out on my first entrance, singing "It Happened in Old Monterey" with that thyrsos in my hand and the real thing in my tight tan chinos, she stopped the dress rehearsal and yelled, "Well, certainly that's too much! He's got to wear a jockstrap. You can't ask any actress to compete with that."

And Loel explained she wasn't supposed to compete, she was supposed to be overcome by it and challenged and that right there was what the play was about and she should start quivering and burning and that eventual roll in the hay should be exactly what she and the whole audience wanted to happen—the rainmaking was a verbal metaphor to accompany our physical one.

I suppose I might have been embarrassed but I wasn't. I was lost in the art of it all and delighted to show off what I had to the paying customers as much as any burlesque queen or club bunny or well-stacked secretary delights in showing off her beauteous boobs. Or well-endowed sailor delights. And the way any auto-fellator delights in showing off his trick.

I've run across three or four who could go down on themselves and didn't have to be very drunk or coaxed much to get it up and swing on it. They all claimed it didn't mean anything, just a fortuitous combination of long ramrod and long flexible back but I note that once they were asked to demonstrate, they were deaf to any suggestion they forgo the exhibition and heard only the entreaties to go all the way. After about the sixth session with Loel, I mentioned having watched him do that and I couldn't have stopped his doing it again, right then and there, if I'd wanted to.

Loel went on explaining to Edie that after our rain-making, she's fertilized, though File will think the kid is his. And Edie muttered she was sure no one was going to miss my significance but she didn't see how she was going to put her pregnancy across to the audience at that stage of things. And that kept her busy with her own job of work and off my symbols.

But that was all two or three weeks later. We were only in

the early rehearsals that week between the windy Saturday and the Saturday I arranged a counter-discovery. Loel was surprised to find me—as much surprised as I had been the week before to find him—ahead of him in his private lair, stretched out naked. I made the repetition so like that he couldn't help seeing right off it was no coincidence and had the grace to laugh and come right down and join me. We climbed up there every Saturday morning until it snowed—just as I met Berty in the park when we were thirteen!

I'm sure now Cynthia knew all along. I'll bet Loel told her everything, even about those clandestine meetings in the furnace room of his house when he was supposedly fixing the furnace for the night. Loel loved to intrigue and play-act, pretending Cynthia would divorce him if she so much as suspected. Having to be circumspect because of Cynthia, we couldn't do anything really silly and get him fired out of his professorship and out of the whole teaching profession probably.

I wonder if old Loel is still there, posing as Jove in rehearsal and carrying on with delirious young actors—delirious but discreet, wildly desirous of another tussle with the olympian director and his king-sized cock and not daring to breath a word about their part-time apotheosis even to their faggy roommates, especially not to their faggy roommates. And I wonder if Loel ever met his match again. God knows it was not for want of looking if he didn't. And did he ever tell anyone else his name was really Hasselbauer? I hope not.

Did Loel ever think I really had acting talent or was he always mainly interested in me sexually? When I tried out for *Cat on a Hot Tin Roof* in my freshman year, he let me understudy Brick and hang around rehearsals.

And that year I was Brick. I didn't want to be queer, though I had that Skipperish thing going most of the year with Lloyd Stark. Just good clean All-American-boy fun. We must have spent twenty hours altogether in those shower stalls—we were clean, all right. Lloyd wasn't quite All-American but he was the best football player they'd had there in a long time. No one blamed him for swanking around a bit on the campus and I didn't really mind when he didn't appear to see me outside the dorm. I minded the second year when he wasn't living in the dorm any longer and I was becoming a campus figure myself and he was dating Lainey Palmer day and night and I was in love with both of them.

He gave me trouble the first month I was in college, more trouble than Jonny who was always making suggestive remarks and trying to get me excited with jokes and hoping to see me naked. From the first time I leaned back from my desk and looked out the side window and saw Lloyd Stark sitting at his desk about fifteen feet away from me, that beautiful big muscular body bare as far as I could see, I was hooked though I wouldn't admit it to myself.

Noreen was married and gone; my roommate was a bouncy cheerleading puppy with unappealing plans; I was in school to work and get an education. But I shifted my chair so I could keep an eye on Lloyd and prayed for him to stand up. The strong light of his desk lamp would illuminate exactly what I wanted to see. Of course when he did stand up, he had shorts on, baggy old track shorts. But I stayed at my post every night, getting quite a lot of school work done, too. And on the third Saturday night of the term, Jon home for the weekend, practically everyone in the dorm off somewhere, Lloyd and I were at our posts. Then he disappeared and my heart sank—he was getting ready for a date.

Indeed he was. He came back in a few minutes wearing a white terrycloth robe I hadn't seen before. He looked right over at me good and straight and opened the robe and showed me his huge semi-hard cock. He put it right under the light and pulled it slowly and steadily. I was never so choked up in my life—I certainly wasn't breathing. He gave it a couple of fast tugs, picked up a towel and turned off the light. I heard him going down the hall to the shower room and followed as fast as I could. I remember I was in such a hurry I almost forgot to take a towel.

He was in the last shower stall on one side. I went right into the last one on the other side, facing him. We indulged in a good fifteen minutes of exhibition, admiration and masturbation before we gave up and shot our loads toward each other. We never dared carry on that long again but we managed sessions often and in the whole year we never touched each other. It was poor Jonny who relayed to me the gossip that

Lloyd Stark had the biggest one on the campus and then later that he'd gotten drunk enough at a brawl after a football victory to let someone measure it. Reports on the actual statistics varied, however. I could have set them straight—his was almost identical with mine.

Lloyd was a junior that year. The next year was the Lloyd-Lainey year and I had only that one legendary session with him at the end of the year. He went off to med school and flunked out. I wonder what he looks like now. That big rangy type sometimes gets even sexier when they're a little older. He's probably coaching somewhere and showing it off to high school boys. If I'd had a coach like Lloyd Stark in high school I might not have wasted all those good years. And I'd have been a lot more interested in athletics too, probably. Is it possible there are fellows at the university now as sexy and all-American magnificent as Lloyd was in those two years we overlapped?

Or as beautiful as I was? Because oh God I was beautiful then. Physique-wise I was better set up five years after that when I was about twenty-five—the workouts and the extra weight helped. It must have been during my second year at college Jonny said I was like a sketch by an artist who had drawn the head lovingly and made it as beautiful as he could and then gone on to the sexual parts and made them as big and beautiful as he dared and then had just sketched in a body to hold the important features together. I wasn't very muscular then and didn't want to be. Lloyd and Loel and Orin were all three more muscular than I was but lanky compared to someone like Alex.

What a narcissist I was, searching out variations of myself. Or were they narcissists searching me out? Anyway we found each other. Of the three I was most emotional about Orin, yet I never touched him but that one time. And I actually got together with Lloyd only that one time, too, although all those times in the showers we were very much together in a way and usually came at the same instant. With Loel it never meant much after the first few times—the intrigue was the exciting part.

Jonny was short and stocky and never aroused me emotionally at all. Funny, I remember Jonny and the first year with him much clearer than the second—his yearning and pining and making leading comments and slyly touching me "by accident" and doing all that muscle-building naked, trying to tease me. It was funny Jonny didn't catch on to what was going between Lloyd and me—he even interrupted us a couple of times. The second year I was lonesome and lay back and let him have it—and he still went on with the muscle-building. He wanted me furiously without pause or diminution as far as I could tell but he wanted the musclemen too and evidently had a good many of them. The minute I finally said "Okay, take it," his whole aura changed—he was successful, invincible, no one could say no to him. If he wasn't lying, he didn't even have to ask them—they chased him into deserted corners and stripped off their own jockstraps or whatever. Nothing succeeds like seed sucked for a cocksucker.

I imagine it's the same way in business—good luck draws more good luck, everybody wants to be in on the magic. Probably it's that way in art, too, the commercial side—maybe even on the creative side. Once you've done something really beautiful, or someone claims you have . . .

Jonny was disgustingly grateful. I wonder if he remembers the second year we roomed together as better than the first? Or does he ever allow himself to recall either year now that he's married and has a couple of kids? It may be four by now; he'll probably have a dozen. When that year was over, did he just say to himself that he'd had it? He moved out to the Phi Delt house and starting dating Honorette that next fall and I started with Lainey. Even that last night of the second year he was saying goodbye in no uncertain terms.

If June and I had had a child—a son, I'd have had a son although she and Arnie had a daughter—would we have split up like that? Or drifted apart or whatever it was that happened to us? If I had felt tied down, would I have come to hate June and the child too and dumped them the way Sandy Utterman dumped Phyllis and Toby? Did my father ever resent my tying him down?

After Mom died, did Robby marry again so I would have a mother? I always felt he and May loved each other and never really cared much about anyone else. May did love me, off and on—more, anyway, than my father ever did. Or admitted he did. Was Robby afraid to touch me, to even think of loving someone other than May in fear that he'd stop loving May enough? or me too much? Or did Robby want me to be frustrated so that when I was old enough— No, he didn't deliberately plan. He didn't think at all, but subconsciously . . .

Orin. I haven't thought of him in years. But right now I want to remember Orin. It's my thirtieth year to heaven and in this rain of all my days I must remember Orin. And not other things. And I'll have to think about the future when I've worn out the past. I'll think of the future on my way back down the beach. I wonder if Caswell will still be there.

Orin. I don't suppose anyone thought he was beautiful except me, or yearned to kiss him. All that springy black hair and then, surprise, his eyes were utterly violet-blue, hydrangea-blue. And he was so quiet, I can remember his saying anything only once or twice. We must have talked a little at first in the chem lab. I probably talked a lot and was a real bore to him. I remember flirting with him—or at him—from the start. I realized I loved him only after months but I was challenged by his tender patient remoteness all along. Orin wasn't good-looking but he had sex appeal. Jonny was more jealous of Orin that year than of any one else so he must have felt it too. Orin couldn't stand Jonny but at least Orin tolerated me.

Girls were attracted, too, and couldn't understand it. I used to watch them looking at Orin and trying to get his attention. They were eager and speculative at the same time. He might be faithful and hard-working enough as a husband but he'd never make any money. He cared more about his theories and his work than he did about girls or money or me. Shirley Wein adored him and let him know it and offered him the use of her body. Then she used his decent gratitude to hook him into work for the Cause until his body and his time were no longer his own and he came to my room that afternoon and stretched out on my bed and laughed at the mess he'd gotten himself into and acted half drunk.

I felt like an old castoff mistress Orin had come back to and was as brazen as if it had happened this way a dozen times before—locking the door and pulling down the shades, rolling him flat on the bed and kissing him until we were both so hot we could hardly get our pants off. I'd sort of suspected he had a big one but then I'd completely forgotten about it and when I felt it bulging in his pants I was surprised. He took it out for me himself, which also surprised me. His engine was big, fish-shaped, with a huge head to deal with. I hadn't gone down on any fellow since I was fourteen but I'd been aching for months to jack off Lloyd and suck him off and here I had Orin, whom I had pined for all fall, his thick schwanz pulsating in my hand. I took it and tried to do a good thorough job. Much to my amusement he hauled mine out and took it in his mouth. We both came almost immediately.

I'm sure he'd never done anything like that before. And I prefer to believe Orin never did again, that being with me was a unique and very special experience, a wild little loop outside the path of his usual straight activity. Anyway we swallowed each other's gism and zipped up and he lay for a little while in my arms, both of us smiling and drowsy, saying nothing. Then he got up and went back to Shirley and I went back to waiting for a signal from Lloyd. I hardly even saw Orin on the campus after that and the next year he went to the University of Chicago. And probably was taken over by another Shirley Wein. Or Mike Kincade? Anyway, Orin knew what the choice was. And he may have been carrying on with the boys since he was ten. He didn't say Kincade was his first time.

My next mutual sex thing after Orin was more than a year later. And after that—Lainey. Lainey loved the idea of a flaunting romantic affair and sexual freedom and the two of us lost in our private ecstasy, quite a lot more than she loved actually screwing. Except at the climax when she went crazy frenetic. She hated all that introductory maneuvering and forcing we had to go through every time. She was tall and rangy but not easy to get into. Lloyd had been her first lover and I was her second—she hadn't realized all men didn't get that big when they were aroused, but I suppose she found out fast enough when she started sleeping around in San Francisco.

I don't think Lainey had a single female friend at school except Cynthia Hastings and Cynthia could very well have been under the same delusion if she were a virgin when Loel found her teaching art in the education school. I'll bet she was a virgin, though she may have had a few girl friends. She was a bit dykey in her supercilious fine-drawn fashion. She and Loel made a good pair, though God knows there was nothing feminine or effeminate about him.

My stepmother was dykey too but in a different way—blunt, raw-skinned, blundering, making trouble for others and herself and then suffering for having done a wounding and stupid thing. May always meant well and I wanted to love her. Dad was really very lovable—he was even plain cute at times. And he didn't want to be lovable, but he did like being cute. He was baffled by being loved. Only D. H. Lawrence could have done justice to that pair. If Robby hadn't stayed so far away and worked so hard at avoiding my loving him—until May was dead . . .

How much that afternoon in that strange hotel in that strange town was like the afternoon with Orin! It was more than two years later and Loel had come between and the resemblance didn't strike me at all at the time. But Robby wasn't laughing ruefully when he turned to me, he was crying the way I'd seen no adult cry. He had not shed a tear at the funeral or the cemetery or in the car coming back, even though there had been just the two of us and a minister and the burial people and the driver. But once we were alone . . . Even if I'd hated him I would have had to take him in my arms. I was so much taller and he was shaking so and seemed so pathetic and lost that I felt like the father.

That afternoon with Orin didn't really mean much to either of us—it just happened. But the afternoon with Robby meant a lot, I'm afraid. If we'd stopped after the first breakthrough of loneliness and need and not turned to each other again a few minutes later, as if we both knew what we were doing and had not fallen on the bed . . . That was what scared Robby off, our deliberately going to each other as if we'd waited for years to be free to do that. It was wonderful—we were so quiet and conscious of each other. His body was as smooth as mine but smaller all over, so sweet. I wanted to make him feel something besides loneliness, to feel himself loved, to give him everything I had, to make him feel I loved every bit of him. I wanted to go into him and if he had wanted to fuck me I'd have been glad to take him but I couldn't say any of that and he seemed to want a loving long-delayed sixty-nine and, after we'd taken each other at the same time, I held him and loved him up until he was ready for another one. And then I held him in my arms while he slept until it was dark and we bathed and dressed and ate dinner. And I went back to college and never saw him again. Robby, must I go looking for you like Telemakhos?

Must not a poet be eternally a child, wide-eyed and wondering, straying heedlessly into strange places or willfully darting in, deaf to admonitions? Who admonishes me or implores or even points out the folly? Julius Barnes wants to take over my poetry and tell me what to do but he is nothing to me—a gust in the Westport wind. He doesn't know anything, he doesn't publish anything good, he isn't interested in me or my work but wants to patronize me in front of Phyllis, make her see him as a bigshot, all-wise publisher, adept at dealing with presumptuous upstarts like me. He wants to impress her and lay her three or four times, marry her and then shift the whole relationship into a different gear—high gear for him, full speed ahead, business.

And she will be the silent partner in Julius's gaudy little press and the silent partner in their marriage, presumably satisfied with her house and her child and a couple of days a week of his rich company, the other five being spent on business, chasing budding Kathleen Winsors hither and yon. If I won't sleep with her, he's next best and at least she doesn't have to explain his car parked there for hours to her neighbors. But who asks Phyllis whom she entertains? Louise and Tommy Tomlinson don't, I'm sure. She could take the Italian who delivers the laundry twice a week and no one would know or care unless it was some other lonely matron down the route who was depending on Nick for her fast and furious little fuck before her tired husband dragged ass onto the suburban scene or the kids romped in from school to ravish the larder.

And that's just what Phyllis tells herself she'll never do. But if I don't take her to that opening of the exhibition on Saturday afternoon, she will have Barnes over on Sunday afternoon and get them both stinking on martinis and let him poke her with his ugly little circumcised excuse for a prick that probably pops with veins and squirts like a tomcat three times in fifteen minutes. And he'll light that foul butch pipe of his and puff and suck before he gets up to wash, but tickle her cunt with his tongue—never! No more than the laundryman would kiss her before he laid her on the entrance hall rug, although he, being a Latin lover, would give her a torrid cunt-licking fast enough and force her to go down with him while he was doing it.

I'd have trouble with Phyllis. She's aesthetic. She may not have looked at my cock yesterday when she was putting it back into my bathing suit but in a week she'd be staring at it and in a month she'd be licking it and making love to it and sucking it like a goo-gobbler at the baths.

Why do I do that to Phyllis? Am I subconsciously trying to make her unattractive so I won't be tempted to marry her? It's a cheap dirty trick, Kincade. Stop it. Be honest—Phyll is sweet and she might be eager to make love again but she would never let herself go idiot-wild and sensation-mad. She might go down on you because you have a beautiful phallos and beauty justifies oblation or because she thought you wanted that, were used to that and missed it, or she was pregnant or having her period. She would die before she would do anything of the kind for Julius Barnes.

How he reeked of tobacco crud and sex jealousy. Penis envy isn't confined to females. Half the trouble in this cock-eyed world is caused by little men hedging their holdings against the natural claims of the big boys, or getting their revenge on them just because they're there and enjoying their disproportionate endowments and it's damned difficult to deal Fate a really satisfactory kick where it hurts, so kick at Fate's darlings. Hence the tribe of the petty Napoleons and probably the original Napoleon as well. Josephine had been around and knew a tiny one when she didn't feel it. I'll bet both Hitler and Julius Caesar were hung like stud mice and poor little Alexander who had to be so great—pity. But Jesus had it to give away—"meat for the poor" as the swishy queans exclaim. And he had that red-hot sex appeal besides, which isn't the same thing at all.

That high-powered sex appeal can cause more trouble than phallic magnificence or inferiority even. The sex appeal that works on everybody—men, women, children and canary birds. And some men resent being aroused by other men and hate them. A few just accept it and bask in the warmth of loving another man but most are conditioned to fear and hate. God, what a culture we live in! A culture of fear, hate and envy and all the insidious ramifications and fortifications fear and envy develop. And the attendant deceit and pretense that all is healthy, well-ordered and rational, or will be tomorrow. No wonder the kids leave home. At least they've heard of ancient Indian tribes that lived in peace and love generation after generation. In health, too. And when they were old, they were respected and revered—they weren't obsolete nuisances at sixty-five.

Our world isn't even rational on little easy things like clothes. Why should an ugly-faced man with a beautiful penis be forced to expose his worst feature and hide his best one? Faces age faster than any other part of the body and deteriorate more disgustingly, yet we leave the raddled ruins out in the common view and muffle and disguise bodies worthy of gods.

When I see a man or a woman on the beach with a tired old face and the body of a twenty-year-old, I'm amazed they don't just get the hell out of here and go live some place where they can go practically naked all year long. I wonder how many women are suffering right now in the city, knowing they have beautiful bodies going to waste because their faces aren't pretty according to the current vogue. At least women's clothes reveal their bodies somewhat. Men's clothes are still utterly idiotic. Their first premise is that all males must look alike. If nature has handed out some special endowments and beauties, those must be nullified and forgone and the illusion maintained that what's inside the uniform is uniform too.

Some legs are much more beautiful than others. Arms, chests, midriffs and buttocks. What is more beautiful than shapely male legs and buttocks? A lot of men don't even suspect they have them. And some bodies are so ugly they should never be exposed at all; certainly a lot of cocks are ugly and should be kept out of sight but it doesn't follow the beauties shouldn't be right out there for all to enjoy—well, visually at least. Down with jockey shorts. What's in 'em isn't issued equally, ladies—they range from the pinky three-incher to the crotch-to-kneecap fifteen-inch colossus which is practically legendary and it's probably just as well. The biggest I ever handled was a thick thirteen and after I'd masturbated that a couple of times I was willing to pass it on. Once in his life he'd kept a lover longer than a month, poor monster. Well, he had a lot of fun in his fashion and it's condescending of me to pity him. I'd like to have one like that just for a week to see what it feels like.

I wonder if everyone, even the dinkies, wouldn't go back gladly to his original state eventually? And women wouldn't leave any adequate male for an exhibition piece—there's more involved in sex than size and shape. Most women don't even like big ones when they get down to letting in what can be got in comfortably. It's the dirty jokes that make it sound as if they did and their own ignorant imaginations. Even the most avid browning queans admit there are some phalli around they'd just as soon not be obliged to deal with. But those are the thick ones. Who ever started all this hush-hush about relative size, anyway? The same numbskull probably that invented pants for men and jackets and shoes and neckties. Pants for men! Ball crushers. Skirts are logical for men, pants for women—except that most women look like hell in pants, the poor myopic sheep. And nicely fitted pants do occasionally make it obvious what your friendly neighborhood grocery boy has got in them and wants the world to admire and desire.

Much as I loathe neckties in theory and practice I still wrap the rag around my neck when I have to. If I married Phyllis I suppose I would be expected to choke myself quite a lot of the time. Or would she go along with my refusal to be cowed by horrified conformists? Can that custom-carved, hand-tooled, college-polished, Westport-rubbed twenty-nine-year-old near virgin be taught anything or is she already rigid and elderly? Has she been handed a complete set of highly expensive, massively desirable images appertaining to her own behavior and her child's and her husband's and her friends'? And if the images can be shown to be nonhuman, inhuman, stultifying to the point of being death-dealing, can little Phyllis give them up or does her life's blood and whole spirit pour out if one of those images is amputated or tampered with? There's the respect that makes calamity of so long respectable matrimony.

For in that sleep of marriage what nightmares of conformity to dead and rotten dictates and decencies may come? Phew.

Is little Toby already suffering the damnation of dead and rotten decencies and is Phyllis, in her grim if seemingly blithe obsession to be not Jewish and simply one of the wealthy beautiful young people who are really rather special and actually know so well how to stay that way? Because she's less a brassy pushy know-it-all Smith or Vassar bitch than others I've met and met and met, is she really much different? And could she ever be different enough to be comfortable to live with? Comfortable for a free-wheeling faustian type like Mike Kincade who may not know what he wants but knows he doesn't want anything that's been in the refrigerator since Emily Post put it there in nineteen-twenty.

June pretended she wanted to grow, be different, jettison the family idols and ikons. Coming from a Bronx delicatessen, she didn't have much immediate choice—it was Bronx or Bohemia for little June and Bohemia looked glamorous but wasn't, and wasn't even comfortable when you got into it and one's husband had a way of being absent for days at a time. June would have given her right eye and left breast and ten years of her life to be in the fix Phyllis is in right now—house, defecting husband, father's fortune, quirky Toby and all.

But in a month June might find she was exasperated with that elysium, too, and head back to the good old Bronx because she was dealt a handful of engraved and holy images, too, and one of that hand she must play is a bulgy balding go-getter husband with hopes of making money, another is two bright kids to brag about and slave to get into a good private school even if the view from her picture window isn't a waterfall and woods but only the picture window across the street and that poor creature's hideous lamp.

Does June sing all the pop tunes in bed with Arnie? Oh God, she was cute once and so loving and slender-sleek and round in the right places. Just the sight of her made my cock gallop but I was always gentle because she was so damned delicate. But those delicate bird bones and fine flesh were cunningly conceived for fucking long and hard. At first. It was later the songs stopped and the complaints began that we didn't get enough sleep and maybe after she'd had a child or two she'd be able to take my big old thing twice in one day without feeling chafed and raped. I hope Arnie tickles her clit neatly on scheduled nights without wearing away the facilities.

Some whores say they can take thirty a night, all shapes and sizes, all fresh and rarin' to get what they've paid for, and feel no aftereffects. If any one of them was to retire suddenly into faithful matrimony, I'll bet she would develop qualms and queasies and start making rules and conditions about the bedtime activities.

Carlo and I always wanted all we could get of each other and laughed and were happy afterward—at least until that last month when I suspected he was only doing his duty and not even a good job of that. Duty is a cold fuck and a dangerous blow job—teeth are suddenly there that were never there before. Must sex always turn out to be insipid and unsatisfying eventually? I think I could have gone on forever with Carlo, with little forays now and then on the side—Ty when he was in town, Caswell, the Australian acrobat just once—like exotic meals that make the home cooking more satisfying than ever.

But I didn't foray, although Carlo said early he'd understand if I did sleep out, just not to say anything about it. If he had had a little affair with Hayden—even if I had known about it and all our friends had known about it too—I wouldn't have minded very much. All right, quite a lot, but I'd have lived and pretended I didn't mind and by now everything would be all right.

But Carlo couldn't do that. When he gave himself to me, he cut off ties with his mother. He did go out to see her regularly and dutifully and called her nearly every day. And just as dutifully he took care of my urges as long as he lived with me. Both of us hyper-romantic but in different ways. And now the romance is over and I yearn after him and weep for what got lost and he thinks of me once a week, maybe, and wonders if I'm still living alone and if my next will be a man or a woman.

Did he ever get the idea that I couldn't and didn't really love him after all those others I'd carried on with? That I was bound to go back to promiscuity and variety and explorations? That simple love was not enough for me? It was, it was. But would it have been in another year? Perhaps he felt I could always make out and drift along happily enough but he'd better grab Hayden while Hayden was eager or little Carlo would one day find himself out in the cold with no one all his own. And too proud to look available and not quite the classic Roman beauty he used to be. His father was a tub by forty and mama's a sylph by courtesy of Elizabeth Arden's regularly. Perhaps also Carlo and Hayden are simply more alike than we were and will go on forever and the very fact that I find their life dismal proves how wrong ours was for Carlo. If that's what he really wants or has decided to settle for—well . . . But Hayden will never love Carlo as I loved him and never see him as he was two years ago with the roses in his cheeks and Hayden will never write him sonnets as I did.

Carlo didn't divorce Mama Castella after all. She's still running his life remote control. If one's son becomes a New York decorator—and whose son doesn't these days?—then he should live the way Carlo is living now. She must have put up the cash for that new place they have—Carlo certainly didn't save any when he was with me. She has him tied not only with the silver umbilical cord but with the golden one of bank balance, the lasso generally associated with the father. The Montclair matriarch who always gets her own way. I wonder if Carlo's mom killed the old man, squeezed him off gradually with silent loathing and complete inattention.

The king must die. Everyone dies but kings die sooner, or at least more conspicuously. Some just find their crowns have been purloined and as kings they aren't any more. I have been a king in my day and I must die. What was my kingdom? A summer of being passed around like a sacred relic—touch me and you're really living, fellow. I didn't have to have a shrine like princely Saint Caswell's, I was carried about on a palanquin of envy. There was that being able to walk into any bar or bath or park and take my pick without any further ado. Just *les adieux* and you do me while I do you and we'll both love it because we were meant for each other and not for the delight of mere mortals, my fellow godling stud. O I was the cock of the walks and loved it. Is that what cock-of-the-walk means? I was the golden boy, the emperor in his old clothes whom everyone had probably seen naked at some time or other.

But I'm too young to be a king—I'm still the prince. Can I shine forth like bright metal when I'm a respected poet and call my sordid, somewhat silly past a foil? Then I will be a king.

Don't kid yourself, Kincade. You had a ball and you won't shine forth kingwise until you're too old to go on playing the prince game. And that's a long time in the future. You hope.

I could give up loose and easy living and tighten down to a common routine and thereby waste everything that is peculiar to me. Or is it just peculiar, period? Am I honest or am I just too lazy to lie? Am I manning the barricades for the beauty of plain truth—truth naked, the genitalia unairbrushed, un-G-strung, naked labia as clear and mysterious and stark as armpit and breast tip and ear lobe, phallos unfettered?

Well, the naked truth reminds me of something...

There were a lot of people around—men, gay guys, all drunk, bombed out of their minds and happy, happy, happy—and I wasn't happy. It must have been a party with poppers and pot, all the easy euphorics. In town? At the Island? Last summer? No, I didn't party then. That other summer. The orgy at Kelly's—they'd smoked all the pot before I heard the late-hour laughter and wandered in. Somebody popped me with a double inhaler and hauled out my cock and jacked it up stiff while I was on my way up. He kept popping me and fondling my balls while the others took turns sucking my lob that felt four feet long and made of pure flame. One guy had his tongue in my asshole forever and Eddy was popping beside me with his arm around me and I was jacking his huge black dick with one hand and had two fingers in finger fucking a little quean on the other side. For ten minutes it seemed like I poured a load down some marvelous cocksucker's throat but I didn't come down. They stripped me and laid me on the formica counter top where they could really get at my meat and kept popping me and caressing my nipples and kissing me right down my throat and they kept putting their cocks into my hands for me to jack them off and I had spunk up to the elbows.

Then somebody stumbled out, muttering he had something more important to do and someone else screamed, "What could be more important any time than sucking the biggest, hottest, most gorgeous young cock?" Everyone roared and applauded but I said out loud, very loud I suppose, one crashing soft word "Love." And the giggle died until Joe said, "I love you, Mike. And what I love most about you is your big, hot, gorgeous young cock!" And Eddy said, "I love being sucked. Take it, man." And whoever had been swinging on us went back to work, or to play, or to prayer, adoration, ingestion of the fabulous phallos, contact with the magic flesh of Dionysos, recognition and oblation of the rich gift Chance hangs in the elect loins and raises to remind men that they are not masters of their fates or captains of their own dimensions and propensities and though each may have his sac of seed, few are endowed with a foot-long engine for insemination, dissemination and battering the stars.

And what the hell good is the biggest tool in town except for being played with and fussed over like an extraordinary toy? And how many men who have played with and fussed over, one way or another, my extraordinary toy didn't say right out, "I'd rather have a cock like that than anything else in the world?" And add wistfully, "If I had one that big and beautiful, I'd play with it all the time myself and never let anyone touch it."

Which proves—as if it had to be proved—that men are masturbators first and anything else later. And how will I ever know if it's more fun for me to jerk off my big whang than it is, say, for Jonnie to jack off his six-inch pillar of fire? No more, no less is my guess. The magic difference appears only when you move over and fool with another guy's meat—then there are lots of reasons why the bigger the better. The delight on a lad's face when he finally gets you settled in the back row of a grope movie and slips in a trembling hand and hauls out that enormous equipment and it stiffens up as he jacks it in the flickering light. And you finally shoot off your gism onto your own chest with about fourteen envious hunters watching him work up that thick rigid tool to a walloping climax. And most cocksuckers and browning queans admit they enjoy the big ones, too, up to that certain unmanageable magnitude. And some of those big ones seem to have no nerves and stay hard and hot for hours. That notorious San Juan "hoss" must have trouble finding anyone, male or female, who will let him plow them with that ball bat and he probably hasn't had a real blow job since he was ten. And if it takes as long to whack off his ejaculation as it did that Scottish pilot's I had in my hands for two days, no thanks.

Most of the special photo collections in town seem to reach their climax in those six shots of Mac displaying his fabulous phallos but I haven't heard of anyone else who's had him except Eddy who brought him to me and Cal Vernon to whom I took him. But everyone who's been to Puerto Rico lately has at least watched the San Juan Superman carrying on.

I don't think I ever met a man who, having a real big dong, didn't enjoy showing it off. Of course there could be a million exceptions I never heard of and no one ever saw because they are too embarrassed or ashamed or rigidly inhibited to let anybody get a peek and how many millions more have exhibited their magnificence in army showers and back rows of Dakota movie houses and New Orleans whorehouse shows and Manhattan office parties when I wasn't around? There are probably a thousand in Manhattan alone bigger than mine. And how many of the big boys would want an even bigger one if he could get it? Well, at an orgy Eddy was asked what he wanted most in the world and he said, "Two inches more." And Gray Brylon once said he'd just like to be sure his was the biggest in show business. Where it all went when he was dancing I never figured out. He looked underdeveloped if anything. But when he pulled down his dance belt, his cock plopped out like a great pink cucumber.

What a little exhibitionist I was even in college. Loel wouldn't let me play Darcy in *Pride and Prejudice* but I stole the show in Bingley's pearl-gray tights. According to the pictures and Jonny's ecstatic report, it wasn't so much the unusual bulk that caused the audible gasps as the boldness of the relief those black shadows under everything produced. Loel had to explain to the president of the university that I did wear a supporter. In actual fact I wore a dance belt that held everything higher than a saggy old jockstrap would have, but he didn't tell the president that. I went on getting applause on every entrance and exit and that summer they tore up their fashionable new stage and put in footlights as Loel had recommended in the first place.

Then *The Rainmaker* with everything noticeably in its proper place and the all-male *American Dream* and all-female *Bald Soprano.* Besides having the obvious sex requirements, I'd put on about twenty pounds of muscle over the summer, slaving in that transshipping depot, and I was probably just bad enough as an actor to sound right as Albee's empty-headed beauty. And Milton Baker was funnier as Mrs. Barker than any woman could have been. I wonder if he ever found where his true talents lay and joined the Jewelbox Revue?

Then there was Dubedat in *The Doctor's Dilemma,* dying in Lainey's arms every evening in rehearsal and love-dying in them every afternoon.

I had resented Lainey the year she had Lloyd but I hadn't been able to keep my eyes and my thoughts off them. Then the next fall, after he had graduated and gone, I resented her because she was obviously looking for a substitute for Lloyd. I wanted the position but I didn't want to be known as anybody's understudy, not even Lloyd's body's. Lainey kept turning up in my road, waiting to be noticed so she could lift me up beside her and I played hard to get and gave her verbal love slaps instead of the smart crack across the luscious buttocks she wanted and I was busting to give her. And every time she gave me that why-not-now look, I looked deep into her Irish eyes and gave myself the luxury of wondering what she would do if someone were to tell her that minute about what Lloyd did in my room the night before his baccalaureate and about three days before they parted so sentimentally.

Julius Caesar must have come before *The Doctor's Dilemma* because we hadn't made it at that point. I was still teasing her and my fans with a promissory bulge in a leather loincloth in the first act. She was Caesar's wife and ordered to touch me to overcome barrenness. Or was I to touch her? Anyway I always managed a wink with my upstage eye and a ghost of a burlesque bump when she looked at me. Later that year I played Oswald in *Ghosts* with Cynthia Hastings as my mother. Lainey was too tall for Regina and too busy, anyway, getting ready to make a grand sweep of all the literary prizes.

Ghosts. Mrs. Alving's tragedy. Oswald is the "goat," the tragos, the tragic victim, but Mrs. Alving lives and suffers as the tragic heroes of all the Greek tragedies live and suffer. There was a scene in *Ghosts* that should have been a dinger but

Cynthia never got with it. I was jabbering on about wanting to have Regina to play with now I was dying or going insane or whatever—jabbering that the only way to fight off death, my only salvation, was in the joy of living and Mrs. Alving yelps out, "The joy of living? Can there be salvation in that?" Then Regina trots in with the champagne and the scene goes on about the joy of work being part of the joy of life and how dreary and depressing and unjoyful life has always been in the old homestead. Finally Mrs. Alving says she sees how it all happened and is going to speak when Manders pops in. Cynthia should have had a revelation of how she had brought on the whole tragedy by being so certain her rigid morality was right and denying her husband the joy of living, not only the wild sex fun he wanted but simple fun and work together. Dear Cynthia couldn't see it. Loel stormed at her and I tried to explain at odd moments... One time he and I suddenly found ourselves late at rehearsal one night saying the same words in unison and became very self-conscious and broke off. We never had an embrace later when we were together physically as close as that intellectual one right before his wife.

Loel and Cynthia posed as the delightful zesty captains of the local avant garde but I suspect their private life was pretty unjoyous. Perhaps they were both essentially homosexual in their inclinations or perhaps Loel was only homosexual because Cynthia was as cold and unjoyous as Mrs. Alving—unplayful, uncomprehending. Tolerant but willfully narrow and ignorant. The way I am about pederasty. Why any man would bother with a fourteen-year-old kid I can't imagine and don't want to.

Phyllis and Cynthia are a lot alike. It's that lack of real zest for the joy of living I fear in Phyllis. I'd begin looking around the way Loel did. The Italian laundry-truck driver would be amenable to a professional blow job once a month and the fat TV writer up the lane would be dying to be fucked with his fifth wife watching—the other four turned out to be lesbians and no wonder.

But Lainey was almost possible. She wanted me to marry her—she was sick with fear I wouldn't ask her and I didn't and she was ill all summer and I knew why. I didn't even answer her letter, I didn't want to know she was still sick and know why. That was another Lainey, not my Lainey who was life itself, dancing, boozing, fucking. O that wintertime-springtime afternoon fucking in my boarding-house room with Chance Tuscano's jazz records booming down the hall and the landlady we were sure was so sour and suspicious who wasn't thinking of us at all but of her cancer that carried her off later that April. And then her niece who took over the house and laid Chance and Dex for five a throw and treated Lainey like a rival prostitute and drove us oftener into the woods. Somehow we always ended laughing and that made the tears at the ending more bitter.

Lainey loved my poems—or said she did. They were different enough from her fine-drawn conceits so I was no serious competition: hers were the brand that always won the prizes. "Warmed-over Millay" I once called them and expected her to stalk away and never speak to me again. But she laughed her Looney-Lainey laugh and admitted there was a tiny bit of truth in my fumbling jealousy.

Would Lainey have laughed if she had been at the UMI that night last spring when I read my poem about her? In any case she would have strained to grasp what Deborah Booth was edging out so earnestly, forgiven and discounted her stage fright and shyness and bad legs. I'm afraid I didn't even try—young lady poets with heavy legs can only gush or protest or tat out Deborah-type attenuated sententious prose that poses as poetry and bores me stiffer than a gusher's unremitting vigor does. Yet Deborah Booth's meager output has been awaited and acclaimed ever since she dwelt in college halls. Why? I don't think she knows, either. She confessed she "was ever finding herself freshly amazed" at the reactions of others to her new works, though their reactions were always like the old reactions. As well they might be.

The auto-logo-intoxicated young professor didn't mean a syllable of what he was babbling. So many syllables per erudite word, so many words per hallucinated breath, so much bad Browning, poor Pound. He stood there and frenziedly masturbated his vocabulary and held off orgasm after orgasm until he finally got sore and weary and dropped the whole obscene project into a bathos of funereal celloing and deadly valedictory. And the silly little ladies in the audience applauded with elbows high to be sure they were conspicuous in the ranks of those who appreciate culture when it's flung in their faces and manipulated under a spotlight for their edification and empathic participation. They'd all had a good one.

I must have seemed a clod and a clown after those two earnest acolytes of the established church.

At least my delivery was good. All that acting experience isn't a dead loss. It was fun and I wouldn't want to do it again soon. The Utah Kid who followed me was an actor, too, a one-role, self-created, self-directed vendor of snake-oil magic, a big adorable lout with copper curls and Tom Sawyer freckles and a chummy twinkly delivery of such pomposities and sonorities and thundering commonplaces as would frighten the ghost turds out of the sky. If he hadn't been a trifle blubbery around the middle, I'd have been tempted to teach him to stride a few peaks New York-fashion and absorb a few mystical experiences through the membranes of his throat.

Where did I come off in that joust? A fast fourth if the applause were any gauge. And that was that.

But I went home that evening so sure of my relative worth I could hardly keep my loafers on terra concreta. I was sure I was the only authentic poet in the somewhat touted quartette, maybe the only good new poet in town—in love with my own voice.

No friends of mine had come to the reading. Carlo was off at the opera with Hayden and the ex-Zinka-claque clique, and out of the thousand I'd slept with and the hundreds I'd taught, you might have expected one or two to remember my name and drop by just out of curiosity. I couldn't have been more thoroughly ignored if I'd been singing Civil War recruiting songs at Carnegie Recital Hall or lecturing on George Eliot at the New School. For some reason I thought June might have seen the announcement in the Sunday paper and made a point of slipping down from the Bronx. I looked for her and waited a little.

And wouldn't you know that phony Julius Barnes yesterday insisted on reading out my whole *Laid in Jail* ballad in which I had deliberately—nay, doggedly—employed in strict alphabetical sequence every sex word in my vocabulary. Which is several. Including expressions like "shit chute" which I loathe. Phyllis certainly took it better than I expected and a lot better than he expected, I'm sure. At least she got the point that I had concocted the stupid thing to satirize the bald vulgarity of something else, in sorrow if not in anger, and saw my point that those particular confections were not to be considered a part of my serious work.

Barnes kept saying I was rejecting what I did best and could be another Ginsberg and I kept saying I'd cut my throat first and, if that was all he wanted, the coffeehouses on MacDougal were crawling with gaudier candidates than I. At least they pretend they're only semikidding, the babbling, howling bores. The antipoetry storm troopers in their pseudo-Nazi leather jackets and their pseudo-Left Bank squalor. It's one thing to be poor but something else to be impoverished and puny. Barnes kept saying he'd gladly put out a volume of the wild stuff if I'd go on in the vein but the rest was like forget it and he got Phyllis so angry she offered to pay for an edition of my good stuff herself just to prove he was wrong.

A lot came to light in that little session. She didn't bat an eye at all I obviously knew about homosexual variations—which surprised and disappointed my undeclared rival Barnesy-boy quite visibly. He was the one who stuttered and flushed and looked as if he'd been caught with his pants down and a cob up his ass. He snickered in the climaxes while we sat by detached and a little bored until Phyllis rocked him with the prospect that, if she should ever put money into his staggering venture, she might have a word or two to say about how it was spent. All three of us emerged with a few new dimensions in each other's eyes, I think. I certainly saw more to Phyll than I had suspected before. But would she fight for principles and points after we were married? That fiery bit may have been more a matter of intuitive flattery than natural disposition. And it was only an hour after she had been handling my hard cock—whatever Papa wanted, Papa could have at that point. Anyway, she saw Barnes floundering around with his pants down and if she marries him, she'll know what she's not getting, artistically speaking.

Hell, he's just a purveyor, he's not even a critic. He's way over on the other side in the eternal war between the artists and the culture makers. His kind mark the prices and hawk the produce and frantically hope they're picking the right star to hitch their wagon to . . .

In any case here I sit on a low wooden wall from which the sand was whirled away by the last storm and no officious guard blowing his whistle at me and me watching a bunch of kids throw a plastic discus around. I can hear their idiot laughter and I'd like to join in their lunging and yawping for about five minutes.

Meanwhile, back at the castle, the fortress—ah, keep your distance, Caswell Green. I'll think about you and your lovely, staring, appealing eyes and that husky little demanding voice and that lithe sexuality—later.

Back to my blooming, hyperluxuriant thorny perplexities. I, like Prince Charming deserted by Merlin, his fairy godmother and his good angel, am baffled by a thorny hedge. All I can do is break off bits and twigs of the bramble around the enchanted castle. Inside, the sleeping beauty waits to be reached, dreams of that quickening kiss, tosses restlessly mad to be had. And who is this Sleeping Beauty I rage to reach—or, in dull truth, desultorily break off bits of bramble to get at? Who is the fairest of them all?

Myself, of course—the lovely, wholesome, holy, carefree me that will be when I have solved all the human equations, found the very radical and root of happiness, burned the existentialist bramble barriers, faced down all the thorny facts, killed the dragons of Despondency and False Hope, the gut-tearing eagle of Arrogance, the harpy birds of unbridled Lust, forced my way into the somnambulant nirvana, roused out the purer part of me and with that kiss sucked out the soporific and gone to sleep myself. The old, evil, stinky, decaying Mike Kincade will be extinguished like a guttering candle, the old king will be dead, viva the cameo-pure new angel Michael, the shadow-shallow blissful spirit who doesn't want anything.

So the exasperated fury in the brambles is all—better off to Africa. "Look, I'm off to Africa . . ."

A line from a play? What someone said someone else said? A bunch of characters sitting around on a terrace—overlooking the Mediterranean—talking about a lad like Caswell who cried, "Look, I'm off to Africa!" and swam out and didn't come back. And then they wonder why he committed suicide and think they're talking about him but actually they're all talking only about themselves.

I could do that—leave my clothes here, plunge into the ocean, twenty feet out it's suddenly deep, swim as far as I could, gulp, be engulfed, try to cry out, thrash for a livid moment like Ikaros, drift into tenebrous thalassic oblivion, down, down. Who would care? When Hart Crane jumped off that ship, who cared? He had sung his song, the song was left—who needed the singer? I haven't sung any song anyone would care to remember, but so what? All the less reason for uproar. Crane was thirty-two. Maybe in a couple of years . . .

Dylan T. was obsessed with death and so were Villon and Donne and Dickinson. Why do I adore the death-obsessed singers? Death means nothing to me—it's only a gray thought in a hazy day.

But all the farewells, the departures without farewells, the betrayals without kisses or silver pieces—they are intimations of mortality, too. In them is the shiver-making brush of ineluctable wings, the faint but horrifying echo-beat of Old Bones a-riding, the swish of his scythe sweeping and nipping the napping. Enough of Old Bones. To Hell with him, to Limbo, to Lethe. Give me Brahms's autumnal grieving only . . .

The tide is out. These jetties are more exposed than I have ever seen them. I am something washed up here and left, effete, futile, scarcely breathing, as much dead as alive, gently stinking, good for nothing. My skull teems with maggoty words and wormy half-formed thoughts—and what would they signify to anyone else, what would they butterfly forth, even if they were fully grown, carefully assembled, arranged, scrutinized, ruthlessly criticized, pruned and planed until holohedral, stark and sound and shining? Eh?

So. What I really want is a beer. I don't suppose they're selling beer at that stand that appears to be, by some minor domestic miracle, open. And maybe the men's room is open, too. Nothing like the thought of beer to make you realize you have to take a leak . . .

Michael could see the youngsters fairly distinctly now. They had tossed aside the plastic discus and were dancing—at least the two girls were dancing and the taller fellow was clapping. He was probably older, too—his belly bulged a little. Behind him was a tall, gangling, blond boy in a white windbreaker and plaid bermudas. Beyond them a dark, dumpy, stumpy lad in a plaid jacket and old khakis and glasses. One girl was dark, sinuous in tight, flowered blouse and pants; the other had her head wrapped up in a rag over grotesque great curlers and had on a white shirt that flapped and pink pants. The tall man was taking off his t-shirt; he moved in a graceful, faintly familiar way. When he turned to throw the t-shirt behind, Michael saw he was nearly bald and as he straightened around, Michael recognized him—Luis, the Puerto Rican chauffeur.

Sequences of vivid images tumbled over each. Luis strutting in the steam of the baths, stunning and aloof, his small fiery eyes glittering between those extravagant sideburns in that too-handsome face. The sleekly muscled torso, the abdominals amazing in their sculptural definition. The large heavily veined dick swinging at half-mast, thin voluminous foreskin swathing the pendulous head—teasing, taunting, unattainable. Except to Mike who simply stops in his pacing and waits while the dark angel approaches and stands like a summoned slave with basilisk eyes that subdue and master all but the haughtiest of the golden gods. The revolving ghosts—the meager striplings, the lumpy would-be beauties, the imploring elders with flesh like melting tallow, drift to a silent breathless anticipation. Stare, envy, dare not touch but cast their humble libido into one of the magnificent males meeting, feel arrogance in a lifted head and demanding eyes, pride in the lifted swell of muscled chest, exultation in the enormous lifting, swelling, thrusting cock that yearns irresistibly toward its aroused and hardening counterpart. Mike stretches out his arm at shoulder height—Luis slips along it until their bodies clash. They clasp each other close and kiss, suspended. Luis slides down on one knee and slowly draws back the loose skin until his thumb is pressing in Mike's damp curls and his fingers cup his balls and his whole hard cock is displayed for the adoration of the supernumeraries. Then Luis licks it along the side and back underneath and takes as much as he can into his mouth and caresses it with his lips. Mike withdraws it and bends down, lifting Luis as he goes down so in one movement they are reversed and Mike oblates, masturbates Luis's rampant organ with both hands, licks the head, takes it and swings madly a moment. Then Mike rises and they kiss again and go out in a swirl of steam and lust and impotent envy.

Upstairs in the dingy disinfectant-stinking cubicle they battle on the bed, on the chair, on the floor, standing on the bed, rolling. It is an athletic meet, an endurance contest, an angelic agon, a ravishing delirium of muscular pressure and response, appreciation, comprehension. They find each other in delight, relief, delicious play of muscles and the miraculous plastic elastic hardness-softness of the other. Wet mouths slip over gleaming flesh and hair, suck at rigid palpitating sex and slip away to meet in breath-drawing kisses. Perfectly matched, they wrestle and writhe, bend and caress, tease, tear, adore, gasp and begin anew, pull, lick, lip and tongue, wallow, tousle, tickle, neglect no excitable zone, finger willing orifice, insert phallos in deep, banging belly on buttocks, pulling out that instant before rich ejaculation. Tumble, pant, twine merrily into weird positions, follow the leader, alternating in leading and following, forcing, taking, offering, urging, carrying every attack to the brink of rape and disaster. Rolling back dripping and laughing, dizzy, teasing, sliding into insatiable voracity and a raging sixty-nine. Finishing each other off riding the heaving loins and convulsing columns like sailors clinging to masts in their private hurricane. Then the calm after the flood with the sweet taste of spring woods and avocado and wet muscles going slack and loving . . .

The second sequence—the rented Rolls slowing down in the Park, the instant of surprise of recognition as Mike, on the walk, turns to face Luis seated, uniformed, winking, nodding with capped head toward the dusky interior. The slowly opened door and the vista of lovely leg kicking lightly, suggestively, the skirt draped up to mid-thigh and fluttered, the glitter of smile and jewels and the warm slow, "Well why don't you join me for a little drive?" The slow, muted sound and movement like an old black-and-white Cocteau film, the swift embrace and the slowing down at the side entrance of the hotel. The private elevator, the globular little buttocks of the Italian elevator boy deserving at least a lingering caress but getting only a surreptitious brush of fingertips. The expensive suite and the long, controlled but vicious fucking, the redhead muttering

Spanish hoarsely and grinding her teeth and biting. And afterwards, naked over whiskey and casual conversation about Mexico City, her career, her schedule in New York that allowed for so little real pleasure, her moment of dismay in the park when she saw how beautiful Mike was because he might be only a fairy. Her mocking laugh when he calmly replies he prefers men—revenge on the bitch for doubting his virility even for an instant. Her confusion in New York. In Mexico all was simple—men were men, fairies were only pathetic rejects, practically never encountered, thank Heavens.

Luis coming in without knocking and without cap or jacket to remind Señorita Salazar they must leave in twenty minutes. Her appeal to Luis who said he had visited Mexico City—did he ever encounter a Mexican fairy? "Dozens," he replies. "Any Mexican man can be had by any man who shows a warm interest and there are no women in sight. I never had so many beautiful men." Luis smiling like a little boy. Sylvia is furioso, fires him for lying, takes him back because she knows he is only teasing. A man is a man. Luis asks if she classifies him as a man in consideration of several whole nights of pleasure. She admits Luis is a man of men. Luis opens his pants and dangles his big cock in her face. "Suck it," he says. She shies away.

"Suck it, Mike," he says. Mike takes it, pulls at it with his lips, excites, it. Luis strips off his shirt, pants, shoes, drops his shorts and kicks them away, rolls Mike onto the bed and goes down on him. Sylvia beats at them, screams and pretends to weep, reviles them as they wave each other's stiff organs triumphantly and then give each other a real burn-down blow job. They exaggerate their ecstasy a little, pretend to come at the same time with great gasping and moaning. They pull apart and lick their lips and fingers. The señorita has turned to disdainful ice but she has not looked away for an instant.

Michael dresses quickly. Luis has gone into the bathroom to piss. Sylvia rolls out of bed looking about forty, stalks naked to the chair where she's tossed her clothes and purse, takes out money and thrusts it at him. Mikes slaps her beautiful bottom, hauls her up close and smooches her and says, "Thanks, baby, I had a ball. You're a great little whore—I should pay you." She relaxes and tucks the bills into his shirt pocket. Luis returns and he and Mike kiss wetly, sweetly, until she rips out in plain American, "Jesus, these fancy New York queans. You make me vomit." And slams the bathroom door as she exits. Luis says loudly, "Perth Amboy. Half Jewish. She don't mind who knows so long as they ain't in show business."

Mike recalled that he was playing in a Broadway show at the time. And was somewhat married to June. And that, in the elevator, he gave the elevator boy's bulging crotch a squeeze. The kid stopped the elevator between floors, went down on Mike and sucked off the load Luis had pretended to take. While Mike swabbed off with his handkerchief and zipped up, the kid finished jerking off his own fat putz and shot his gism into the thick carpeting of the elevator. "That movie queen sure gets the big studs. What does she do to you? I never took one up yet who didn't fuck me coming down or I didn't suck, hardly a single one. And the one I thought was a real square, the big bastard, sucked me off."

And there was Luis, half bald, gone to pot, chasing straight kids. The boys or the girls? Mike watched them for a minute, then turned away, preferring not to be spotted today by Luis. It would be embarrassing. It was only four years ago he met Luis in the steam. He might have been in his late twenties then, even in his early thirties. By now he was at the most thirty-five or so and look at him! When did he give up? Must I—never. First off to Africa, off the boat, cut my wrists in the bathtub, though they say the veins have a way of closing right up again. Get an artery. But if the deterioration is more subtle, sneaky and insidious, no one says anything, the beauties still stop and give you that you-interest-me-strangely, you-hypnotize-me look...

If we were to meet for the first time now, Luis as he was then, I as I am now—Luis might take me but I would have to ask, tease a little, be the first to kneel. The ego must die. I was king in my day. But king of what? Stretched naked and high on a bar in a Fire Island summerhouse for the delectation of a bevy of drunken faggots—was that my hour of royalty? Lying down on the beach away from everyone and waking up surrounded by watchful smiling hopefuls? Being bluntly propositioned by a drunken government big shot who knew he shouldn't have wandered down in the first place but was determined to have the best piece around to justify his indiscretion?

Being taken to the Royal Ballet and a celebrated discothèque by a college kid who spent a month's allowance just so he could say he had dated the fabulous Mike Kincade? Dear Brian got his money's worth—I took him back to my pad and fucked the shit out of him. Wonder if he told that part of the date when he got back to college? But I had a lot of fun and I have pictures to prove it. Motion pictures in technicolor. I heard Oliver Freelon—or was it Freelon Oliver?—who played opposite and over and under me in that epic, has been made head buyer of the furniture department in a big store somewhere. The two dancers who were in it with us became lovers and lived together until they died in an airplane crash. If Carlo and I had crashed coming back from Europe . . .

The gaudy times in baths and hotel rooms and elevators and on the boardwalk and the gang bangs come back too quickly. They crowd out the quiet times, the hundreds of nights Carlo and I slept with an arm under the other's neck and a hand cupped over the other's precious pleasurement. I'd wake with his arm under my pillow, his angel face breathing lightly beside my shoulder. I'd lift my hand and trail my fingertips along the rounded ridge of his thighs, he'd move in desire to meet my hand, his big beautiful cock stiffening and that winsome anticipatory smile coming even before he peeped out at me. Sometimes at night after we'd slept a while, sometimes in the morning. Sometimes he woke up first and gently tickled me with his tongue and took me half asleep. . . . There was that Sunday the first summer we decided not to go to the beach and only got out of bed to eat and mix drinks and put new records on the phonograph. By six o'clock we'd taken each other five times and then we went to see a revival of *Camille* and held hands and in the men's room the imp still made a hard-on for me. He was probably so amazed that it would come up again that he let me pull the skin down hard and show it to three or four strange fellows who were hanging around and even let me play with it a little until a couple of them hauled out their stiff pricks and moved nearer. As far as I know that was the only time he ever allowed a stranger to see it up hard, though he enjoyed their admiring glances when he changed to go swimming or strolled along the beach and he chose his bathing suits as carefully as any quean to enhance his intriguing treasure. In ten years he'll be blowing little boys in Puerto Rican movie house johns . . .

Enough of that. What would I come to? Especially if I married someone like Phyllis and felt bottled up.

Boobs like jello encased in thick cream under satin gauze. Very alluring but poets are peculiar—they'd rather be read than laid, published than provoked. They already get provoked and laid a lot—they don't get published very often. Fornication is ephemeral—publication is permanent, even if what's published ends up on the remainders tables or in those dirty heaps in Fourth Avenue back rooms. If I married Phyllis she would publish my poetry as a wedding present. Vanity oh vanity press—not that, not yet.

What I want is . . .

Well, hello, Caswell Green. Has that child followed me up here to this end of the beach? Does he have in his twisted little mind what in my twisted little mind I suspect he has in his?

"Hi, Caswell."

"Oh, hi, Mr. Kincade. I thought you would probably come back along this way and then I forgot for a moment to watch for you. I don't have my lenses in."

"Well, if you'll wait a few minutes more, we can walk back down the beach together. I'm going over to the esplanade to see if the men's room is open. Okay?"

"Sure, Mr. Kincade. I'll be right here."

CASWELL

Michael turned away and went across the sand to a very narrow cement walk that ran straight out across the beach from the esplanade steps nearly to the water. One of the more surprising vagaries of the layout, Mike reflected. There were a dozen idiotic aspects of the place. Most of them caused inconveniences—this one, the narrow walk, was merely puzzling. Who needed it? Could it possibly have been put there so wheelchairs could be rolled down to the water's edge. It certainly wasn't worth thinking about.

Caswell. His turning up in my path again was bit of a surprise. And yet not much. No doubt Alex went right over and crowded him. Alex had obviously been eager for contact. He probably staked out a station very near Caswell's crib, stripped off his clothes and made sure Caswell got a good look at his nice dong, put on his bathing suit and stretched out and proceeded to tease Caswell with a slow and steady erection. The question—did Caswell respond? Did he encourage Alex to stroll over nearer still, squat down for a little breathless casual conversation, a quick grope, a fast and thorough blow job with Alex against the wall where he couldn't be seen?

It probably didn't work out that way at all. Caswell avoided Alex, came right up here. Chasing me? Does he want me to go back with him to his crib? I'm certainly due for some action. It's been three days and then it was only a quick jackoff so I could get so sleep. No wonder I got up so fast when I was fooling around with Phyll. I was really up big, she had a tough time getting it back into my swimsuit. Funny how the actual size varies from one time to another. I wonder if there is a psychological aspect to the variation or is it merely a matter of general relaxation, suddenness of onset, elapsed time since last erection? Well, Phyllis knows now what she'd have to cope with. She didn't freeze up or go reflective and forgetful. Maybe her ex-husband was big, too. I can imagine a well-hung man would be all the more eager—no, anxious, determined—to get out into the competition, to show off, exult a little, get his share of the envy and attention due him. It's the little ones who try a homosexual affair or two and get only neglect and disdain, who become determined husbands and sometimes the bitterest faggot-haters if they don't get addicted to being fucked. Those that like fucking their wives and being fucked by other men—they have all the complications. Why can't three people be married if all three are satisfied? They could all three actually be in love with each other. It isn't difficult to be in love with two people at once, really in love. Who ever started the dull concept that two was the inevitable and only acceptable number for a happy union? The hippie group stuff doesn't sound like much for a lasting setup, but three? Or four? Or five? An extra man around the house. Trouble is there are as many women as men. All right, in some ménages, extra women around the house. A harem.

If Phyllis and Sandy had been invited into a therapy group like the one I found myself in last spring—an indeterminate number of men and women getting together now and then and no inhibitions allowed in, Sandy free to try other women, show off, get sucked, whatever, once every couple of months—would the marriage have gone on? Only Phyllis would never have let herself get into such a situation. So she could have stayed at home and lent them Sandy. If Sandy was anything they'd have wanted. There's nothing sadder than a grouper no one wants, unless he's a confirmed voyeur, of course. And when that slightly nothing guy is bypassed by two, the others seem to take intense pleasure in leaving him out, even shoving him out. Pecking system at its most vicious. One night at the baths I took care of seven of those left-outs in a row just because I was tired of seeing their dazed faces around. Two or three were hot little numbers and one got his *amour-propre* back and became the belle of the top floor.

If Phyllis could have it as she really wants it, would she have her ex and me? Or Julius Barnes and me—God forfend!

If I could have Phyllis and—Ty? Or Caswell! Hey, that would be sex deluxe à la king. Caswell likes girls, too, he said. Would I be jealous if he and Phyllis got together, shut the door and left me out? Well, a little, But I'd be happy, too, because I love them both and if I were sure they both still loved me... But how are you sure unless you're right there in their arms and they never look at anyone else? Their, they. Pronoun reference. We should toss the whole pronoun system out and get a new one. The queans who insist on calling any man who carries on with another man "she" don't help and neither do people who insist all cats are "she" and all dogs are "he." And novelists and playwrights who turn all their gay lovers into girls. Ugh. But I'll never believe *Virginia Woolf* was ever about two homosexual couples. And I prefer not to think about anybody who would use Virginia Woolf's name for his cheap joke. And if Leonard Woolf really did give his permission, what a critter he must have been all along.

Would Carlo ever believe how much I still love him if he had any idea how many people I've carried on with since we broke up? He does have a good idea and he doesn't believe I love him and he's glad. If he thought I still loved him and was wasting my life away in solitude, pining after him, he might be a little flattered but he'd be very unhappy too—we still mean that much to each other. No one who felt the way we did could ever just feel nothing for the other. Sometimes people who love come to hate each other but that could never have happened to us—he could never had done anything cruel enough to make me hate him, he hasn't that kind of meanness in him.

No one has ever made such a fool of me I had to hate him. I was betrayed, deserted, forgotten, but no one ever hurt me except by taking themselves away. I hope I've never really hurt anyone, either. I've wrenched myself away from a hundred people, sneaked away, faded away and maybe even been pretty brutal with people who wanted to use me. It's one thing to have someone enjoy looking at you and touching you and playing with your big lob and dying of ecstasy when you fuck him; it's another to be merely something to be shown off like a prize stallion or a particularly rare star sapphire. Cal Vernon was always thinking what an impression I'd make on his rivals when we were alone; even his fountain complex was part of a show-off urge. Well, maybe, as he said, next best to having it in your own pants is having it in your hand. Monique Vernon at least wanted me to give her a baby; she wanted my semen, too, but not just for display purposes.

There were a couple of old men at the drink stand; it was obviously open. The old white-haired auntie behind the counter, the poor sweet old thing that had been at the beer window all summer, fluttered by all the naked brown pectorals and biceps and astonishing baskets—was well-intentioned, utterly incompetent. But such morons had to work somewhere. The door to the can was open, all was well and miracles did happen even in city-run establishments.

Mike went around the blank drab-painted baffle and into the crepuscular depths of the men's room—the row of urinals along one wall, the booths on the other side, the basin at the end. No mirrors, no concession to vanity or neatness, no legitimate excuse to linger or peek, to loiter. No feet under the doors. Silence and not even much revolting pungence. Peace to piss in. A pleasure to take a leisurely, uninhibited, unexhibiting piss. To squeeze one's meat in innocent voluptuousness and flip it, to go right on and jack it all the way off if one wanted to spend it that way. Oops, company.

Caswell appeared around the baffle, wavering a little as he entered the gloom but not faltering. On silent bare feet he approached Mike and stopped at the adjoining urinal, pushed down his trunks and flipped out his thing. It was long, anyway. The tennis-ball effect was achieved by deft coiling in the tight pouch. He did not make any pretense of urinating—he held his long organ delicately with forefinger and thumb, pulling back slowly, sliding forward quickly to the head for another slow pull. It was stiffening fast. Mike was shocked, elated, aroused, caught in the pattern of Caswell's deliberate sensuality. Mike was aware that Caswell was staring intently at his big lob and Mike was also aware that it was no longer soft. He shook it vigorously to get rid of the last drops of piss and found it flexible.

"It's really big," Caswell said in an almost soundless gasp. Mike did not try to resist the excitement, the excitation of the youth's urgency. The older man lifted his hand and let his cock swell untouched.

Caswell gasped again, "Before it's too hard..." He moved toward Mike who retreated a step. In an instant Caswell had crouched before Mike and was taking his cock into his mouth and down his throat, almost the whole of it. Being taken this way, so quickly and thoroughly, was delightful, a sensation Mike had not often able to avail himself of, but he pulled out and whispered, "Not here."

Caswell knelt for a few seconds, staring at the still thickening and stiffening and rosy wet organ before him. "It's beautiful," he said quite loudly, as if unaware where he was. Mike tried to shove it back into his pants and turned away toward the wash basin. Caswell rose and got his back into his trunks, not a ball now but a long tubular ridge across his groin and right up to the edge of the little brown suit. He had to keep one hand on it to keep it from poking out. Mike, watching the operation, had an even harder time forcing his own unruly member under his clothes. He had to compromise by zipping up his pants carefully over as much of it as he could and draping his sweater over the head and three inches of bole. When it was out of sight, Caswell went to the doorway and peered out. Mike joined him and he asked Mike, nodding in the direction of the bathhouse building, "Is there anyone along there?"

Mike surveyed the scene carefully and said, "No." Caswell pattered briskly away without touching Mike again or looking back. After a few seconds Michael stepped out into the afternoon. The three around at the hot-dog counter were still jabbering away and were apparently oblivious of anyone else. The gang down the beach had retired even further away and were almost out of sight. Up the other way stretched empty beach and esplanade, deserted except for the slight graceful figure drifting along the esplanade. Caswell stopped about a third of the way to the main building and went over to the railing and leaned on it, apparently gazing out over the sand to the water.

Mike crossed the esplanade to the steps and went off into the sand. He couldn't remember when his cock had been so adamantly erect and hard. Every step was delicious pain as the waistband of his slacks pulled against the shaft and the light sweater caressed the head. He walked slowly, casually curving his trajectory. When he considered he was near enough so Caswell could see him well, Mike halted and pulled off the sweater so Caswell could see how hard it still was. Caswell stared as if hypnotized as Mike approached him and, when Mike was near, he abruptly indicated the sand in front of the spot where he was poised. Here the concrete esplanade was nearly three feet above the level of the beach and was at the deepest point of its long curve. The concrete wall made a protected spot, open of course to the beach and the sea but out of view of the food stand and of strollers who might come round the bathhouse building.

Mike smiled in simple complicity and well-being and stopped on the spot Caswell had pointed to.

"Take off your pants," Caswell said slowly and dreamily. Mike hesitated a second, only because direct orders, even gently murmured, always antagonized him. "Please, Mr. Kincade," Caswell added breathlessly as if he had sensed exactly the import of Mike's tiny hesitation. Mike unbuttoned the waistband and carefully slid the zipper down and let his pants fall. His cock sprang out, still aimed at the sky, reaching, wanting. Mike stepped out of his pants and laid them out on the sand along with his sweater. Then he knelt on them, still facing Caswell. "Take it in your hand and make the head shine, please," Caswell besought quietly as if in a dream. Mike pulled down hard and watched the big head go marble-smooth and shining. A smear of goo covered the taut little lips and as he watched another thick drop welled up. "I want it," Caswell was murmuring in that mad monotone. "I want to suck your huge beautiful cock. I want it more than anything in the world. I want to suck you better than anybody ever sucked you. I want to suck out every drop of your luscious come. I want it."

"It wants you," Mike found himself muttering back. He shifted and lay back on his clothes, rolling and showing Caswell his hard beautiful phallos from every angle, his fingers barely touching it so Caswell could see it all naked and complete.

Caswell gathered himself into a slight crouch and vaulted the railing, lunging delicately and precisely into the sand beside Mike, hardly disturbing the sand at all. He got his equilibrium and flopped down beside Mike, his knee against Mike's ribs. He took Mike's cock as if it were the Holy Grail and manipulated the loose skin up and down its length lightly and reverently, but after a few seconds he began to jack it vigorously and Mike bucked to meet his strokes. Then Caswell took it in his mouth, as much of it as he could, caressing it in quick strokes with tongue and lips. One hand wandered along Mike's belly and rubbed his chest and throat. Mike seized it and sucked Caswell's fingers. Caswell, with his other hand, fondled Mike's full round balls a little and then grasped the skin by which they swung and pulled down against Mike's upward thrusts.

Without a break in rhythm or slackening of force they swung together for what seemed to Mike a paradisiac eternity and he could stand it no longer. But he wanted to go on forever.

"I'll come," he groaned.

Caswell responded by sucking even more insistently and Michael felt his phallos burst into flame and shoot out jet after jet. Caswell took the heavy spasms, still lipping Mike's jerking organ and tugging at his balls. Then Mike faltered, sweating and panting hard. Caswell did not relax but went on torturing Mike's hard throbbing cock until the pain turned to exquisite pleasure and he was bucking and writhing again and shooting again, flinging his rigid legs wide and screaming in his throat, rocking and quivering as each fiery flood drained from deep in his loins, from his knees and his back. This time when the throbs lessened and died, Caswell let Mike go quiescent. But not limp. Caswell took Mike's aching, still hard organ and licked it before he let it swing over the man's belly. Mike lay smiling, inert, breathing more quietly for a little. His hand searched and found Caswell's knee and thigh. Caswell's slender hand caught Mike's and held it until they were again fused and full of respect. Mike felt Caswell's lips brush his hand and then Caswell rising.

Mike sat up, rolled to his knees and peeped over the edge of the esplanade. No one had appeared in either direction. He tumbled back close to Caswell's knees and shut his eyes. He wanted Caswell to take him again, slowly, luxuriously. Again. Caswell fingered the hard, wet, swinging thing, gave it half a dozen long deft pulls so it was thrusting up and throbbing again and then kissed and licked it slowly. Mike put out his arm to draw Caswell down but Caswell moved away. Mike took his cock and pulled it in a dozen long suggestive strokes. "Oh, it is beautiful," Caswell murmured. The sound was like a cool breeze on Mike's hot flesh. He lay for a few moments enjoying his slow masturbation and aching for Caswell. When he could not touch him, he opened his eyes.

Caswell was not about him or near him. On his elbow, Mike looked around. Caswell was off down the beach, drifting along toward the water as if nothing had happened.

Mike snorted and lay down again. For an instant he was tempted to jerk off fast, send that fiery third load zinging out into the blue. But that was not what he wanted. He wanted Caswell to take it again, even if he had to make him take it. For a moment, Michael lay back and rested; then he sat up and shook the sand out of his hair. There was still no one around. He stood up. The old boy down at the food counter was still talking to his cronies. Mike picked up his clothes in one hand and strode across the beach, down toward the water, his big aching organ still stiff and bobbing wildly at every step. He deliberately made it jounce and thrust—it felt wonderful. What he really wanted, he decided, was to fuck little Caswell. He yearned to hold the youth fast and fuck him long and hard, to thrust every iota of his love and energy into the lad, to capture and enter him and make him as ecstatic as he had been before in the other fashion.

At the water's edge Mike dropped his clothes and waded in until the cold water lapped his balls. It felt so exhilarating he was again tempted to jack off but he plunged in and swam.

Coming out, he felt clean and could hardly believe what had happened had not been fleet, highly colored fantasy. But it had happened and for an instant the futility and absurdity of it all clouded the afternoon and he was chagrined. His chin shook as if he were going to cry and he had to clench his teeth. His hair was trickling cold water down between his shoulder blades, he had probably lost his comb, wallowing around on his clothes in the sand. His cock was drawn up into a gristly spigot and ached a little. It needed a quick massage but the hell with that. Enough is enough. Who's to impress?

He went through his pockets and found his comb. Anybody else would fish out cigarettes now and smoke and avoid thinking. Anybody else wouldn't be in this situation in the first place. Exactly what the situation was, it was not clear, but Mike felt it was now a situation he had to deal with, whatever it turned out to be. And suddenly he felt it wasn't complicated any more. He carefully combed the water out of his hair, flinging it off in glittering arcs. The salt water would make his hair blonder than ever—golden blond. He worked until most of the water was out, combed his hair carefully into a smooth-lying helmet and spun the lengths that went over behind his ears into arcs that ended in points just behind his earlobes. They thought he didn't even know those intriguing points were there. Ha.

He sat gingerly on his clothes to dry off. From there he could see nothing but the long sweep of empty beach and the greater roll and sweep of placid water, its surf lapping so docilely nearby, its depths full of orange rinds and condoms, chicken coops and sharks and drowned sailors and all the symbiotic zoology and flora man could only spy on and never be a living part of. A loving part of.

Whom do I love? Carlo? Caswell? Tyree? Robby? Little Toby? All manner of man who wanders the earth, walking up and down in it. Phyllis and June and Lainey and Noreen, Cal and Monique Vernon? Alex and Luis, Loel, Orin, Earl, Lloyd—God, yes, Lloyd—and Jonny, too, and Mrs. Marigold, too, and even Alicia and Marcia and Charl. Charl!

I haven't thought of that brat in years. The tomboy rapscallion companion of my earliest pirate coves and Tarzan lairs. Black-eyed Charlotte, intensity in dungarees and cocklebur stubbornness in a cowboy shirt and hat. My earliest rival—what a lad she was for fence-climbing, fruit-stealing, strange-dog-chasing. What a little lesbian in the bud. Whatever became of Baby Charl? Does she, wherever she is, ever wonder whatever became of Ol' Mikey? We could stalk right by each other on Eighth Street and not recognize each other. Except I'd know her anywhere.

As a matter of record, what has become of Mikey? He grew up, he became beautiful. The mirror said so, the camera said so, friends grudgingly said so, enemies said it insultingly, lovers whispered, it, strangers said it in their sighs and stares. But beauty fades, though pray God there be fitful flushes of it now and then. At fourteen Mikey became aware he had something else to cope with—the kids in the showers called it his "flak cannon" and wondered what the girls would do if they knew. The girls suspected because he had a habit of wearing new dungarees once and putting them in the laundry and wearing the old ones that were short and tight and faded white over the beautiful bulge to the right of his crotch. May bought him jockey shorts but he swiped Robby's which were a size larger and allowed it all to lodge in a thumping lump along one leg, a lump he could casually drop a hand over and caress in study hall.

At home at night, if he hadn't had a chance to get off in the woods by himself or with Berty, Mike would undress right after supper, turn on his radio, stretch out on his bed and read, playing with himself off and on, the whole time. If there was math or something like that he'd had to bring home, he'd whack off first or he couldn't concentrate on the math enough.

When Mike was a senior, he and his family lived in a ground-floor apartment in a huge old house and his room was at the back beyond the kitchen. There was a porch outside and a steep hillside covered with brush, no neighbors on that side at all so he never thought of pulling his shade down. One night he was stretched out on his bed by the window naked, giving his now fully developed tool a slow workout when he heard surreptitious sounds in the shrubbery just off the porch. He immediately thought of the Manning twins down the block—eleven- or twelve-year-olds, towheaded and irrepressible, into everything. Mike got up to change the station on his radio and turned the volume down for a second, just long enough to hear sneakers on the porch boards and a whispered "Wait!"

He turned the volume up again and lay down again, nearer the window this time, and gave them a grand show, with bucking pelvis and spurting gism. After that, when he knew they were watching, he varied his effects. One night he even got up quickly and stalked out onto the porch and shot off in the moonlight over the railing. The twins were pressed against the wall in the shadow, right beside his window; he had to be careful not to look directly at them.

One night that same week their father came looking for them and caught them under Mike's bathroom window as they were leaving. He heard them tell how they'd chased one of their pet rabbits over there. Later Mike heard movements in the shrubbery by the porch railing and knew that Bart Manning was doing a little checking. Bart was a good-looking go-getter who was away a lot on business trips but, whenever his car was in the driveway, Mike knew he'd have someone to show off to if he'd hold off his workout until about eleven.

Mike laughed ruefully at himself for digging back for such trivia. But he hadn't really dug—it had popped into his cave of consciousness. And the stiff rod that had burgeoned again and was demanding attention might have something to do with the immediacy of that particular memory. And fantasy. How many times had the twins been out there—four, maybe five in all? And how many times did I wait in vain for Bart Manning to rattle those rhododendron leaves, my radio turned down just right, my whole being restless and thwarted. But he did come back two or three times. And the first time I was sure he was watching I discovered that, having let a couple of days go by, I was hot for a second orgasm a few minutes after the first one and that the second one was the real one. I'll bet he went right home and gave his wife a double.

Caswell knew by instinct that even though I shot like a demon that first time the best was yet to come and kept me right up there until he got an even bigger cannonade. But why do you shove yourself up there now, Prince Peter? Do you think Caswell hasn't really had all he wants of you and will really suck the sap out of you this time? What a suck-off artist that kid is, and it isn't just experience. It's pure instinct—every time the first time. If anybody else had yanked on my balls that way, I'd have clobbered him but he knew at that second it would drive me wild.

Ralegh Bronsten. Two beautiful kids from rich families and mad for nothing in this world but big hard cocks gushing hot semen into them. Ralegh's lust disgusts me and I reverence Caswell's. His is Dionysian. I'd like to take that little male home and pet him and feed him and keep him in my bed, let him have it every time he wanted it. And every time suck him off too, or fuck him and take him off in my hand so he wouldn't want anyone else, get over this sickness. He goes into a trance, he can't resist, he's compelled, obsessed, phallos-fixated, mad to have every big dong that swings into his ken.

But Alex said there was no obvious pattern to Caswell's choices last summer. It's even more complicated and twisted. Some psychic substratum has broken through, pushed up into the light of day, even into this calm October afternoon. It's weirder in the afternoon like this. In night and drunkenness it doesn't seem so abnormal, so erratic. Those drunken riproaring pot and popper high corybantes who held me spread-eagled on the bar top and oblated and fellated until I was moaning and oozing out orgasms of spit bubbles—they had the same psychic compulsion to go wild and free. I was their indisputable king, a king to be ravaged, to be had, shared, ingested, to be teased and pleased to the peak of human ecstasy and dredging seventh or eighth ejaculation. But it was just a party. It was ritualistic but it wouldn't happen again. Once was necessary but once was enough. My muttering "love" that way was so much beside the point it didn't spoil the party, not even for me or I'd have got down. I wasn't tied on that bar top. And no one can make you come more than once if you don't want to, tied or not.

Will I ever find myself enjoying the ropes and the chains or the whip in my hand cutting into human flesh, even into masochistic flesh that demands the whip? Five years ago would I have believed I'd let myself carry on the way I did last summer, fucking that skinny leather-clad neo-Nazi tied to the lamp post with a gang cheering me on, and then the boardwalk orgy with the cops ready to pounce? Well, all that is natural progression in a way—it could have been foreseen and accepted. But the sadism and masochism bit—that's an irrational jump I don't intend to make. Besides it makes sex secondary to a lot of apparatus and faked-up excitement. It's as silly to me as married sex that can only work if it's eleven-thirty on Saturday night in their own bed with nobody in earshot and the pessary in place.

Let them as like it, have it. Many a man's love is my utter boredom. And vice versa, I'm sure. So love in its myriad forms is equally natural but not equally delightful to all. Each to his own kind of polymorphous perversity carried through however many times it's still enjoyable.

Let loving be released from the bondage of vested interests of demanding church and even more demanding state and all the brittle propaganda they've promulgated for centuries to conceal their obscene power-grabbing. Let love be fun and easy and unashamed, VD eliminated and pregnancy a matter of choice. Let there be deep love, light love, love play—spend today, it will be back tomorrow, boys, and he who spends the most today gets back the biggest supply tomorrow, the body being the lovely obliging machine it is . . . If love were free and simple, would it be satisfying? And if love were ample and satisfying, would there be aggression and hatred and war? Would we still cling to war to keep the economy up and the population down? Especially those not very nice populations that offend us. Must we keep the economy up just to guarantee all those substitutes for what we would really enjoy if we only admitted it and permitted it and went ahead and reveled in it?

We? You, man, not me. I know what I like, I admit it. I embrace love, I love embraces, I lust after lust, I adore adoring—and even more being adored? I love love and all the appurtenances that appertain thereto. Yes, Caswell-Baby, I'm hot for your appertaining appurtenances as well as your languishing soul. I could love a lot of you—you appeal to me, cry out to me in that dionysian whisper and set me tingling with manifold dark and urgent desires.

I really wanted you last fall but I was married so I didn't even admit my desire to myself. Decency and all that, don't you know, at school—fidelity to Carlo all along the line. Since I was Carlo's and he was all I wanted, no other desires were admissible. I enjoyed being faithful. If I told myself that a lot of fun that was possible was impossible, it was a semantic trick and not a rationalizing lie. If I look back now and say I was faithful but what did it get me—I'm being unfair to the past. I let a lot of intriguing chances pass but those were the world well lost for real love. Unfortunately the love was only relatively real. Next time I'll keep that in the back of my mind so the letdown won't be such a jarring thud—love's worth everything while it lasts but it won't last forever. Love's never lasted for anyone else, so why should you think it's going to last for you?

I left Lainey, and June and I drifted apart. Robby had to leave me to go on being Robby. But Carlo? Why can't I hang onto someone?

Because you ask stupid questions and you're self-centered and are afraid someone will love you and you'll stop being your own Mike Kincade and be someone else's Mike Kincade. You're in love with your image of yourself the way you had a yen for that image of yourself on that screen in the movie you made. If you could see yourself as you really are, you'd be glad to be someone else's Mike Kincade. The worst thing about yourself you have to be told is—you're a self-pitying pig.

Which vice I will strive to exorcise. Pride I will allow in due season—self-pity gets the boot. In theory if not in practice. In all conscious dialogues in one's waking mind if not in certain furtive febrile maundering and feckless maudlin indulgence in autumnal desolation beside the lisping sea in the pallid aftermath of a double discharge, lying supine on my pallet by the sea, wan king of all I survey, absolute tyrant lording over a single, smirking, elusive subject—myself. Unruly subject, naked subject, naked lonely king, sterile kingdom—"In a kingdom by the sea..." Poor old Poe, how he got the literary shaft. Along with Longfellow and Whittier and Thomas Wolfe and Sinclair Lewis. Now that Faulkner and Hemingway are dead, will their reputations lapse too?

Not Faulkner's. No requiem for the high priest of the rolling, exfoliating redundancy and the tenebrous titillation, if you please. That's what life is—exfoliating redundancy and tenebrous titillation. Jettison Hemingway, chiseled journalism, Whitmanesque chest hair, death-adumbrated puritanism and all. And some of that all was rather rich, too—pure poetry of the commonplace. But so self-consciously richly commonplace. Like Frost and Sandburg and all the other condescending poseurs and deluded disciples of Matthew Arnold.

I like a poet who puts it on the line, shouts it out. Vachel Lindsay? Hurray for the purple patches. Hurray for the lavender patches and all the blond young men who ride off in the TV serial sunsets with beautiful dark young men. Or beautiful dark older men. On horses or in zippy little one-seaters to the cozy bunkhouse or motel or the back room of the law office while the ever-lovin', ever-wise secretary keeps her thoughts off what's going on back there by reading detective stories in which her hero hops into bed with every available female but wakes up with suspicious regularity alongside a strange cute male. Hurray for Chandler's Marlowe and Conrad's Marlow and Kit Marlowe and a small lavender raspberry for Miss Madam Marlowe. I'll take Ronald Firbank. God bless campy Ronny.

Speaking of camp, I remember those dykes Sweetie and I shared the Charles Street pad with—Cele and Edith and Judith. So smartly turned out when they clicked off to the subway in heels every workday morning, so slackly slovenly by suppertime every night, so roaring drunk by moonrise and on Sunday morning so ferociously hung over and mean. Dykes are so rough.

Beside them I feel so frail and dainty with the chinawear. Could it be I am only a delicate quean like all those other poor things and don't know it? Only pose as AC-DC bisexual, ambidextrous, normal, well-rounded—well-rounded especially around the heels. I don't really like spreading a broad's thighs, easing my thick piston into those consenting, relenting, cozy, oozy, embracing depths as far as it will go—which sometimes isn't far enough. For real hump do not a lad's rounded and flexing buttocks and bung offer greater leeway and more byplay?

The best would be a ballet boy, a student, not a virgin but not jaded and insatiable either. With a lovely dangle to handle and sweet little balls to kiss and a face like a scheming angel's. Wonder if Caswell would like to be a dancer? He responds so beautifully. He needs, deserves, implores someone's constant and devoted attention, someone to guide him and use him, need him. Caswell would never believe how much I need him—or someone like him—to love, to help, to be big brother, father, lover to.

At thirty I'm suddenly a father? I am no longer to be the son? I can say farewell to Robby—go your way, I'll go mine. The decree is final. Phyllis would give me a son, a slightly old battered one in Toby and a new one as well, one of my own.

The one June and I weren't ready for, had no time for, were a little scared of even in prospect and just as well we were. If Carlo and I could have had a son—honey, you're too much. Give up. . . .

It's up again as hard as a battering ram. If I went back up the beach and whistled to Luis, he'd leave those unprepossessing adolescents and zip down and take care of it. A few hairs off his crown and a few pounds on the brisket won't have diminished his ardor or the magnificence of his other equipment. Hell, I'd be willing to swing along on that big thing of his for a mad half hour and make him shudder off down my gullet for auld lang syne. And fuck him afterward, which is what he always really wanted, anyway. All that lovely sinewy bole and heavy ripe-plum head and he wants to be laid like a girl. The fact that he has one of the shapeliest, most entrancing and highly educated asses I've ever encountered is beside my ironical point.

I'm a satyr, a priapic poltroon and a sex maniac who doesn't know which way to turn and has been blown twice in the last half hour to orgasm and wild release and doesn't know when he's had enough. Go home. I want more, more sex and more than sex. I want, I need. It's the weather—the echo of summer and Fire Island, the last leaping of the blood before that winter hibernation. As if I were ever less horny in the wintertime. But I would like to shack up before the snow flies.

I gave in to Jonny in October. Lainey and I made it in October of the next year. Then after she graduated it was Loel in early November. Two years of teaching at Melbin Hall with celibate masturbation and a few quick pickups in Pittsburgh bars. The summer in the Poconos which was more boredom and pine woods than sex. Sweetie briefly that September, Dwight in October, June in early December. That fantastic Fire Island summer, the crazy Village fall and Carlo the following December. And for two more Decembers and Januarys and Februarys and Marchs. And half a third April. And now October again and me with all this beauty over me, crying after love. And if I thought I'd never be happily in love again, I'd walk right into that ocean and keep going.

Or stay here on land and become a great poet. If I'd just sit down and concentrate, sublimate . . . Maybe I should steal a car and get put in jail and hit a guard and get put in solitary; be deprived of everything, even paper and pencil, and have to hammer out poems on the anvil of remembered repetition until they were like metal sculpture. Or metal lace, if I know me. O I know you, Mike Kincade, you tatter and crocheter of verbal nonrepeating lace tape. If I only had one really good poem to display, to show myself, to prove I'd been serious or was at least susceptible to inspiration. The last thing I wrote down was that haiku sequence for Ty the week after meeting and parting, when I was still hoping he would call me.

Meanwhile there's also money to think of if I don't walk into the sea. Marry the girl today, give her the boyish laughter? Or play wise old uncle Mike at Quillquiar's and contend with the straitjackets, thumbscrews and duplicity thereof? There's still body modeling which is tiresome and pointless and ill-paid. Too bad the gorgeous mug in the photographs looks like a poet obsessed with death. Death doesn't bother me, it's death-in-life that harrows my soul, death of the spirit while the forked body still ambulates, vegetates, ruminates, fornicates. I am not fascinated by surceases or bournes from which no traveler returns.

What a noodle that boy Hamlet was. What a point misser. He'd just survived a rather unusual human experience at that point in the proceedings, a confabulation with the spirit of his dead father. Pappy babbled at considerable length about the exact hell he was going through in that bourne he'd just traveled back from. Shakespeare, poor scribbler, was rather messy sometimes. Well, enough, you prick, enough.

And what kind of slanguage is that?—labeling the dimmest dope or rascal by the term which also indicates man's most precious appurtenance. To call a woman a cunt or a twat is merely to emphasize her femaleness, but to call a man a prick or a tool is to put him down and despise him and spit on him. Envy? Rivalry? Hostility? The old old fear there isn't enough to go around and somebody's going to get left out. Minimize the organ and the urge, relegate it to the bestial half hour, in dark Lutheran-Calvinistic sublimation and disdain for the simple pleasures here on earth that make a heaven rather superfluous? Give up the pleasures of the body for the elevation and purification of the soul? Denying the body to purify the soul is like not eating to free the throat for freer breathing.

To sell oneself to that graceless bit of flagrant acquisitiveness implied in self-denial here for eternal bliss hereafter is too shoddy for the intelligent human being to stomach—it's *infra dignitatem* and all who advocated it should be treated like shysters running phony fire sales to catch the boobies. Think of all the bloodshed and misery perpetrated in the name of salvation—salvation that can neither be achieved nor avoided. Carve on my tombstone, "The beautiful carcase is here; the unalterable soul is where it always was." With which lapidary pronouncement I shuts up.

The soul is simpleness itself—the body is more demanding. Like food. I could have gone to Europe with Cal as his companion-secretary, looking after his pet piano and hotel accommodations and all that plus the usual, but Monique unfixed that when she pointed out I was the type who would feel I had to earn the fancy salary, and as soon as Cal was tired of messing around with me, he'd want me to go out and find other big ones for him to play with and I'd be obligated to do it. Messing around with me—jacking me off in front of mirrors all over Europe and assembled famous friends who'd be privileged to handle the secretary's fabulous phallos if they were very famous or very rich. Wot larks.

That playroom of his locked away behind his practice studio—the stud room I called it—with its crystal chandelier just overhead, the mirrored walls and the black and white linoleum, all spattered and laced with sprays of dried gism tricks of his had shot off. One mirrored door went into a big closet known as the gallery where intimate friends could sit and watch the fireworks displays through the specially installed glass that looked like ordinary mirror from the outside. I disappeared thataway one time myself after bringing up a very potent hippie type I'd discovered and had the fun of watching him exceed Cal's expectations and decorate a three-foot swath of mirror. Cal was so ecstatic he shot in his new pants and I shot my load onto the back side of the mirror for a change.

There was one spray on a mirror that went up nearly eight feet. Cal said one time it was the joyous ejaculation of a seventeen-year-old English sailor, drunk as a lord and proud as a lord of his huge machine. Battering-ram? Flame thrower? Catapult! Another time Cal said a colored boxer had been inspired to outdo all rivals at seed-slinging although he wasn't so triumphant in the ring. Anyway, Cal got me and a colored dancer into a drunken contest there. We were aiming for the chandelier. We did pretty well but the giddy quean went wild when I shot and did a dance of ejaculation and when we quieted down it was dripping off our hair and faces but none off the chandelier. It was like being in a crazy fountain for a few seconds. I hadn't seen so much joy juice air-borne since the night I pulled Lloyd Stark's big whang until he shot and three of the dorm kids let go the same instant and someone touched me and I went off like a rocking rocket, too.

I used to tease Cal until he had to finish himself off, telling him about that night and Lloyd's huge cream-skinned cream-shooting howitzer which I made three inches longer than it really was and twice as thick. Cal was all for making a trip to the Midwest and tracing Lloyd down and getting his hands on that hunk of manhood. Fortunately I never told him Lloyd's last name. And Lloyd would have spit right in his eye if Cal had made him a proposition. I think.

I could be posing now for Monique. About two hours of posing and one hour of love-making. She finished one figure of me in a big panel for a very tony decorating job but what she wanted was a baby from a young handsome man. I wouldn't have minded giving her the baby and that sweet, little pussy of hers was the original honeypot but she was too much the manageress for me. That delicate feminine elegance and flighty little flirtatious manner had me fooled for about a week. Like all those expensive neckties when she knew I didn't want to wear any and wouldn't dream of buying one.

It was my own fault—I had them both convinced I was a big hunk of trade, a dumb hot stud, willing and able to do anything as long as my fancy fee was forthcoming. Serge had said that pose would clinch my welcome when he took me to that first fancy East Side gang bang. Welcome! They were discreetly delirious with joy to see a new face and a promising bulge in the crotch of the old work pants I wore. I had to go up in the service elevator to make my entrance but it was worth it. A short ugly ad executive and his stupid, phony beautiful wife who couldn't kiss because of her caps, the aged conductor who only wanted to watch his Montana nurse-bride it would have taken a horse to satisfy. The cute little doctor and his cute boy friend who never carried on out of each other's sight. The gals who ran an employment agency and were, much to my surprise, a lot besides lesbian. The actor and his two ex-wives. The Congolese dancer and his Siamese wife. Were they all at the first one of those I went to?

It was at the doctor's the next week I met Cal and Monique and they were at that decrepit playwright's the week after that when I got so drunk and had a threesome with a pair who turned out to be a lawyer and his youngest son. They took their turn swinging on me but when I sucked them they both took it away at the last minute and gave it to the other. Very sentimental and sweet. At least Robby and I didn't do it with about twenty people trying to bust into the act.

I first saw Monique on her back, taking the Congolese for a joyride. When I saw what he hauled out of her, I knew she'd handle me with ease. Cal had been watching, too, and when he saw what the Congolese had, he took him into the bathroom and jacked him in front of a mirror for an hour. With the door open. The black giant had come four times and kept softening up but Cal handled him like a pro. I had Monique on a bed where I could see the reflection in the mirror.

After we'd met a couple of times, to put it euphemistically, Monique told me who she was and asked me to pose for her. I told her I had a daytime job in a factory and could only pose on Saturday as I had to go to Jersey to see my wife and kids on Sunday. Cal managed to get into the act and after a while I realized he was getting me up to his place in the late afternoon before I had a date with Monique the next morning. And every time he slipped me a fifty to let him jack out another load of my spunk onto his linoleum. The first time a couple of his friends came out of the gallery to lend him a hand I nearly split for good.

It was whoredom with a difference. I was tempted to tell Monique the truth about being a schoolteacher, a one-time actor and a part-time poet but I didn't. Our whole relationship was founded on the myth that I was a simple, hard-working animal trying to do right by his estranged family. My reticence was aesthetic—I couldn't break the image I'd labored so hard to maintain. It would have been playing the last act without the character makeup. Fortunately when I ran into them at the opera, I was wearing a dinner jacket and had my hair brushed back the way I usually wear it and was able to swish by them with Carlo and Alex.

Cal got twice as much kick out of handling my hard-on, thinking I was a primitive animal. I kept mumbling about dumping the whole scene and going where the big money was—Miami or Vegas or Hollywood. He kept telling me Hollywood wasn't there any more and I kept on not understanding.

My keeping up the role was more than not spoiling the illusion—it was fear. If Monique had ever had an inkling of my poetry and how much it meant to me, she'd have got into that. She might have found me a publisher but by the time it would have been printed it wouldn't have been the poetry I wrote. She was feminine as they come from the neck down but masculine in mental attack: she seduced and thrust in and mastered and planned. Wily Cal gave me impersonal adoration and kept me cozy and well-paid. I also suspect he'd done a little snooping before he asked me to go to Europe with him and knew he could pile a lot more on me than he could have on the Mike I pretended to be. He seemed to take it for granted I knew French and German, for instance.

Funny, with Cal I never felt like a whore. When Serge paid me to go with him to those parties and fuck him and everybody in sight, I felt like a real hustler. I even felt pretty tawdry when Monique hired me to pose for her and then took it for granted I was obliged to lay her, too. I felt the way the fellows felt who played houseboy to that leathery old basilisk at the Island. They had to get into the saddle and give her a good screwing once a week or out they went. They had a plushy setup—liquor, food, clothes, and spending money, invitations to every party, and they could drag in tricks day and night and throw parties once they'd done their duty. She even helped them get dates if they weren't aggressive. She tried to fix me up with the shy mainland mechanic she'd somehow gotten her claws on. I think she also had her eye on me as a replacement for the Italian cutie who was in arrears in his duty-do. She seemed to know by instinct who was broke and approachable.

She wasn't ugly—just sixty and plain and probably indefatigable. If I hadn't met Ty that day I might have stayed out there on her payroll—still be out there.

Three years ago or whenever it was I spent so much time out there, I must have looked an outright hustler to others. I was never there except as the guest of some unprepossessing host I had to make happy at least once during the weekend. I always tried to get that over with early in the stay—it made a cozier psychological relationship and left me freer to do whatever offered. Of course it was hoped I'd drag beauties back to be shared by the kind host. The ones who were interested in that deal were mostly the other five or six mercenaries working the Grove that summer and some of us made the whole circuit. In a couple of houses we were auxiliary to the regular lover or keepie and once I was simply there for a guest from the Coast AWOL from wife and kiddies. We almost started a love affair but decided it was too complicated. I was still married to June and didn't quite know what was going to happen next in my own bailiwick.

I knew I was reacting against June's passive possessiveness. And I was flattered by their adulation. I told myself I was doing exactly what I wanted to do. June knew from the start I enjoyed carrying on with men as well as women and I never said I'd change. When Dwight signed me up for the Broadway show, June and I really set up housekeeping and I bought her everything she thought we ought to have. But I didn't promise her exclusive rights to any part of me or all my time. Even after she left the apartment and we abandoned all pretense of being married, I still wouldn't make love with a girl until June and I were formally divorced. At the Grove I had a few fancy offers in that line, too. Some of those wives who were so patient with their husbands' aberrant meanderings in the dark were eager for a little action in their own bushes. And that big Italian dyke nearly raped me.

Looking back it sounds messy but fun—rather innocent, mindless fun, scandalous, of course, but that was part of the panache. And, although I was having a ball, all along I was pretty disgusted and considered the whole place a snakepit full of loonies. That's why I wouldn't go back until last summer and then only briefly. Maybe those orgies in river-view duplexes wised me up to how relatively unfrantic the Island really was. But at the time I was an adolescent prig of twenty-five or six, a holier-than-thou intellectual doing it merely for the money and the experience, a brain-washed Bible-belt refugee gone berserk. I went through the motions, all of them—I laughed like a fool and was the first to strip and I jacked off strangers in the water and on the boardwalks I groped everybody I could reach and got them into the action and, if it was a nice hand-filling, mouth-filling piece, knelt to it and sucked it a while. Including the cop in mufti who was looking over the scene and planning a raid.

It wasn't more than ten o'clock and everyone was still eating dinner. The cop was leaning on the railing of the Bridge of Size, lighting a cigarette when I came up. I knew he was a cop in mufti and when he offered me a cigarette I told him I didn't smoke. His hand with the match was shaking and when I got close I could feel his knees were quivering. I groped him and he pretended not to notice. He had a thick one and I kneaded it in his pants until it began to get hard but when I touched the zipper he gasped. I unzipped him and flopped it out and went down on it before he could get his breath and in about thirty seconds he shot. And thirty seconds later he was still pouring it out—he reminded me that way of the only other cop I'd ever had. When he finished I tucked it back and zipped him up and kissed his ear. He said, "Okay, okay, but next time don't do it. I'll have to arrest you." I grinned and said, "Yeah, I know." And I strolled off. At the house they thought I was making up that last part. Maybe I wanted to be arrested, felt I ought to be. Maybe I was testing my luck, seeing how far I could go, how audacious I could be. I saw him around in uniform after that and let him know I recognized him. He looked stony but once in the middle of the afternoon I found him alone back in the corner of the grocery store by the book rack and rubbed his basket until we heard someone walking around. He stared at my cock getting hard in my pants. He probably has a house out there now.

It was harmless fun and a lot more casual all around than I preferred to think it was. I really thought half the madness was deliberate defiance of the attempts to hamper the action—that if the police were called off and the fat-ass young politicians on the mainland, so determined to build up images of themselves as clean-up crusaders, just shrugged and said to let them carry on however they want as long as they don't hurt anybody or anybody's property, and no one were to write snide stuff about the Island in magazines, then the whole crowd would fold their beach chairs and dismantle their gazebos and go somewhere else.

Now I know they wouldn't. Last summer I realized most of the people there weren't much involved in the sexy doings at all. They had nice houses and liked the quiet and the sun and the cool breezes away from the hot city and the costume parties where they could wear drag if they wanted and could drink themselves into a stupor without bothering anyone or bring out a favorite student they wouldn't dare be seen on the campus with. I discovered half the physique types were college professors and the other half were hairdressers and several of the hardest-working waiters were Florida hustlers in the wintertime but were having emotional love affairs among themselves and the whole fad of parading beauties you'd paid to visit you had faded like the decal tattoo fad and all the others. Guess I hit that wave at its crest. It certainly didn't take me anywhere though.

I could rarely think of myself as an ordinary hustler, partly because I was operating in the chic beach houses and luxury apartments instead of squalid hotel rooms and movie-house toilets, and partly because I didn't try to work the john up and blow him or flop for a quick *schtuck* job to get his nuts off and leave myself all sexy for the next customer. I made it clear what I wouldn't do and I delivered solid satisfaction. If he wanted to be screwed long and hard, that's what he got, and if he wanted to do me for trade, he got a big succulent clean dick to swing on and a full load of spunk—no pretense that his own drool was my joy juice. And if he wanted it mutual, he got a thorough blow job from a professional and the privilege of taking my load first and making me work for his in cold blood. That's whoring—sucking off some dreary little india-rubber diddle when you've already been sucked clean yourself or pounding some woman who still wants it long after you've given her your final puny contribution and would rather talk about the stock market or the Chinese question.

Oh, I was a good geisha boy but no more whoring. I don't have to and I won't do it. If Cal comes back and I go up to see him and he has a few friends who want to watch me jack off my nice one and I feel like exhibiting my big dick and volleying my spunk at his chandelier, I'll jack off and shoot down his chandelier—and if I don't feel in the mood, money won't make me. And if there's a good-looking new guy in the bunch, I'll let him jack mine if he'll let me jack his—no more of that letting the drearies do it just to please Cal. Of course he may not call me when he comes back. And Monique probably has found some younger stud and is trying for the pregnancy jackpot with him.

This winter I will write. At least in that game I am young yet, I can ignore phonies like Barnes and do as I please somehow. I'll go on collecting rejection slips. Maybe I'll write a play in poetry. Shakespeare did it so why can't I—said Schiller, Byron, Tennyson, Fry, Eliot and I. Schiller and Eliot almost made it.

Dwight always said he'd produce any play I wrote. I should hunt up the mad Dwight. I'd be fresh and new after all these years—three? five? Six! Well, he'll be a little tattered, too. I was certainly fresh then, fresh in town, fresh from the Pocono hills, tooling through Washington Square in my tightest Levi's, pushing what I was so proud of like a perambulator along the walk until I spotted that gaudy creep catching it with a movie camera. Pretending to focus on pigeons and kiddies and aiming right over them into my laden loins. I pretended, too, ambled right through the swirl of startled pigeons and infants as if I were lost in reefer clouds and strode right down the walk into Dwight's camera, making my basket rock as I approached the lens. I must give him credit—he didn't flinch or pretend it was an accident. And in twenty minutes I was sprawled on his filthy bed, dripping, drained, and he was grinning in his van Gogh beard. Well, I got the part in *Sons of Villon* out of that bit of sexual vaudeville—not the part I wanted of Villon's soul son, the neophyte rogue, but the real son, the bland aristocratic by-blow. I could play that soul son now. Or would he want me to try the leathery angel, Villon himself? Not that I'd ever be as good as Devera was.

I wonder if Devera ever told his jealous girly little lover how many times we had each other in that cul-de-sac offstage left while we were waiting for our last-act entrance. Dev took too long one night and I had to make an entrance with a quivering erection threatening to let go in blue silk tights. We had a new kid playing a guard—a tall skinny blond with big eyes and those eyes nearly popped out when he saw what I was trying to hide with my sleeve. I had to say his line as well as my own.

And June, out front checking the performance for Dwight, saw what had happened and made a note of it.

I wonder if Devera remembers that episode when he's making those horse operas in Arizona—and all those Indians and cowboys? And if he gave up Patty Shea when he got married? And whatever became of that wonderful woman who played my mother? That neurotic ride and brilliance put off most directors but Dwight knew how to harness it. She was ushering in movie houses and dying her hair different colors I heard. Such a waste of talent—she's never gotten a good part again, on or off Broadway.

I was never a good actor. I'd never go back to that. In college I was as good as anyone Loel could find, in more ways than one. But Dwight frankly gave me the role because having me at hand was a convenience and kept him from wasting time cruising the streets and bars. No more whoring of any color. No giving in to easy aggrandizement. Or to easy flaccid living—death in life, dying by layers, going numb and uncritical, uninvolved, sleepwalking, deathwalking, mechanical and uncaring. I'll go home and clean my apartment for a change. No Alex retreat, no Westport letdown, no Quillquiar's stultification. What I really want is—my apartment clean and Caswell in the bed.

Does Caswell care? Is his seduction mechanical, obsessive, his lust a gust that whips him like a sheet of paper in a windstorm? Does he choose to be the Caswell he is? That fierce tender fanaticism is appalling but it's enthralling too—one wants to give him what he wants, to join him, to share that tender determined dionysian ripping away of inhibitions, of decencies. Not to give and take but to share, participate in the frenzied ritual, the purgation, the exaltation. But if it means he's numb to everything else and callous, sleepwalking, when he isn't actually pursuing his quarry, stalking beautiful birds in his fantasy rain-forest...

How many people do I know who have any vitality to mention who aren't equally obsessed by some pursuit?—hooked on making money or running a house smoothly or making a perfect painting or poem or dramatic production or just being the best lay in town? Not any.

On the other hand, too many don't have any vitality at all and aren't interested in anything, much less dedicated or obsessed. All those Quillquiar drones. What perfection did they ever strive for? All they ever tried to do was fool the kids into thinking they were infallible, the masters. And all those busy busy parents, so blithe, so gallant, so assured, so ruefully independent—every one of them a time-server, swept along, eddied, caracoled by every fad, ad, flashier personality, political novelty, until they piled up into trends, bulged graphwise, constituted manipulated electorates and monstrous high-handed pressure groups that were hardly aware of what they were pressing so obdurately for or against.

Which is less human in the long run—Caswell obsessed by the pursuit, capture, and subduing of beautiful phalli, or the pleasant man next door trying to do all the right things: get a raise, get a newer car, send Harold to college, keep up with the news so he'll have something to gas about at the obligatory coffee break? Neither hurts anyone.

But Caswell's physical pursuit will undoubtedly grow tedious and even he will admit its long-range pointlessness and its short-range fatigue. He must concentrate on college and not depend on rich relatives any longer. Comes the revolution, he may need that degree, though of course some randy commissar will spot him and put him in a chic uniform and keep him around as a consolation and a toy for visiting commissars and inspectors-general. I would if I were a commissar. But comes any revolution, I wouldn't be a commissar—I'd be shot as deviate, degenerate, supercilious, disruptive, bisexual, wanton and poetical. A deposed aristocrat, a grand-duke of the Eagerdongs.

I probably spend even more time thinking about sex than

Alex does, even if I don't much like talking about it. And I'll say for myself I don't just think about it—I do it, too. And I'm equally concerned with poetry. True no one alive thinks I'm any good but I know I'll write a real one some day soon.

Bless me, O Robby, with your fierce tears. Or were all the fierce tears mine as they were with Carlo? If Robby and Uncle Lawrence did have an affair, were lovers at twenty as that photo I found of the two of them with their arms on each other's shoulders might suggest, especially as Uncle Lawrence appeared to have a rather impressive erection in those tennis pants—I'll bet Uncle Lawrence suffered.

There isn't always suffering at parting—neither June nor I suffered. We were both more than a little relieved, I think. And at the end of our year Jonny was unflatteringly glad it was over. Getting me soused and turning his giddy little dorm sisters loose on me, daring them to undress me, was his final derisive gesture.

How did Lloyd Stark get into that drunken orgy? Who brought him to the dorm? Did he just wander in or did Jonny find him and bring him in as a farewell present to me? Did Jonny suspect, all that other year? I never questioned until this minute how Lloyd got there. He was drunk and ready for anything but I didn't know he was within a mile of the place until I realized the luxurious insistent fellating had stopped and the bloodshot blue eyes staring up at me were Lloyd's and it was his close-cropped curls I'd been caressing. If he'd never carried on that way before he certainly knew by instinct how to do a wonderful job of it. There he was sprawled on his belly on my bed, drunk, ravenous, libidinous, determined we were going to do what we'd pretended wasn't in our minds when we'd jacked off together and even come all over each other the few times we could get close enough.

I made him kiss me, which he did so wholeheartedly I undressed him while we were kissing and rolled him over on his back and displayed that lovely big white cock to those panting dainty ones before I went down in it. When he was about to come, he hauled me up and sucked me again and batted off the ones who were trying to handle and lick his until I was ready to give it to him as I'd dreamed a hundred times of doing.

But he put me down beside him to kiss and let me jack him again until he reared up, my hand riding his bucking loins and holding the skin down tight, his great wet tool shining like a monument and his semen shooting out in glittering arcs, the other kids shooting their stuff all over us and someone giving me one heavy pull that released my load into the air, too, and before I'd even stopped throbbing out spunk I swung around and took Lloyd's still jerking and spouting cock in my mouth and sucked it hard.

He grabbed mine and took it and we sixty-nined until we gave each other our semen the same instant, as we'd both wanted to for so long.

Jonny mopped us off with wet towels and Lloyd held me tight in his big arms and stroked my hair with his big sticky fingers and giggled and whispered over and over it was the first time and he'd wanted to do that for two years and Jonny was to be sure to clean the ceiling because he'd shot his first load all over the ceiling and was sorry, it was an accident, he'd meant to give it all to me. The ceiling was about ten feet high and unspotted but the floor was a mess. Jonny turned out the lights and Lloyd and I slept in each other's arms for an hour and then we went in and showered in the same shower stall for the first time.

It probably was the first time Lloyd ever touched another male, as he kept saying. It was the first time I ever carried on with anybody with an audience watching. But it wasn't the last time. And that fall after the Fire Island weekends, when I didn't care what happened or who I let have it, somebody was always taking it out in a bar or in the movies and playing with it.

That fall I was a real beatnik or something—drunk more than I was sober, not sleeping in my own bed for a week at a time and never in the same strange one twice. I was sick of restrictions and conventions and bucking against restrictions and conventions. I didn't care about anything. June was gone and I wasn't ready for Carlo. I didn't write. I didn't want to do or say anything. Maybe I'm only a poetry appreciator, a culture-hungry harpy after all. Maybe aimless drifting is my destiny.

First I would slit my throat or take up woodwork.

I can't expect another Mrs. Marigold Clattahan to die and leave me a thousand dollars to go on with. There can't be another Mrs. Marigold although there are a thousand droopy nieces named Alicia. How cagey Mrs. Marigold and I both were about showing our poetry, both so sure the other would hate every word. And we would have—Alicia knew that at least. I suppose Alicia and I were the only intelligent people who ever treated Mrs. Clattahan as if she were a poet and took her attitudes and ecstasies seriously—or pretended to. No, I wasn't pretending and neither was Alicia. We both knew good poets didn't have to pose that way but we both knew Mrs. Marigold did have to pose that way—to her it was an essential part of being a poet and kept her going. I was bored to death that summer but I didn't pretend.

Stuck behind the reception desk of a Pocono hotel for old teetotalers, swimming with kids too much younger than I was—what an energetic, unimaginative, lanky, dinky lot they were and poor Howard was in love with them, individually and collectively, but didn't dare touch a one of them. And I was determined he wasn't going to touch me, either, since he had lied to me about the place when he hired me. Far from being a country club it was the last stop before the mortuary. At least I could write, perched up on that stool, and pretend to flirt with anemic Alicia down at the tennis courts.

I wonder if she suspected I left her early to go off into the woods by myself and the last part of the summer to go to the Hiway Rest a couple of miles down the road. Two beers and maybe a hand job or something and back to the bunk. It was makeshift but fun in a grab-it-while-it's-here fashion—the fast sixty-nine with the truckdriver and him nuzzling me afterward and claiming he'd leave his wife and kids if he could meet someone like me every night. The sweet little farm hand with the tow hair—Earl. Did I ever know his last name? He looked so shy but grabbed me when we went out back in the woods to pee and stood tight against my back and jacked me off with both hands. I could feel his hard cock in his washed-out Levi's against my bare ass. He wouldn't let me touch it until that last night under the umbrella I'd borrowed from Howard.

The second time Earl was there and we went out back, Old Max the bartender followed us very quietly and stood and watched Earl jack off my big piece. I suppose Earl told him what had happened the time before. Max must have passed the word to the truckdriver who came back and groped me and asked if I'd like a lift home.

One night it rained hard and Earl and I both got drunk and giggly. Max gave us a couple on the house and we let him watch while we jacked off into a beer stein. Earl had a nice one with a biggish head and I'd have liked to suck it but he wouldn't even let me touch it until that last night before he left. And there was the cute stage manager from the summer theater on the other side of the mountain. He had cute ideas, too—he blew me in the glare of his headlights with his two actor friends watching. Then he told me they were straight. Straight, hell. I'd already been groping one's hard rod over the back of the car seat and the other came around the next week and took me to a motel. He was a tall pretty thing but he wanted to get rough and I had to beat him off with a sneaker and walk five miles home.

And the Monday highway patrol cop. He pulled up to the bar on his motorcycle just as I was leaving. When I stopped about halfway back to the hotel to piss out my beer on the highway he overtook me and said if I were going to do something like that he knew of a more private place. It was at the edge of a field off the road a few hundreds yards and very romantic in the moonlight. He was very proud of his big lob until he saw mine up hard. He did have the biggest balls I'd ever seen. I blew him and he came by the quart. The first time it was seventeen distinct spasms. When he was ready to leave he kissed me again and took my cock out and looked at it and asked if he could take it the way I took him. I was more than willing and, when he finished me, he said he'd never done that before but now he had, he was going to do it to his kid brother—no use missing all that fun. Wonder if there is any correlation between those big balls, which I remember as being like shelled boiled eggs, and the copious flow of semen? And which quean on the beach is that kid brother he was so hot to get at. I hope he taught Bubby-boy to kiss the way he did, like a hot girl. The cop was the only person I kissed the whole summer. We kissed and carried on two more Monday midnights after that. Him, Earl, the stage manager, the actor—it sounds like a busy summer but it wasn't. I spent a lot of time wandering alone in the pine woods.

That was the real beauty of that summer, being poetic in the *schwarzwald.* How I posed and yet how innocent and honest I was in those days. And stern, too. One of the lanky work-crew kids had a cute smile and a big teasy bulge in the crotch and he was intrigued by me, too, I think, but I would have nothing to do with them—they were too young. I even steered clear of the maid Marie with the muscular thighs and the high tits. She made do with a couple of the kids and several of the guests if I didn't misread the signs.

Would old Marigold have left me the thousand if she'd known what I was doing, or hoping to do, after I dumped Alicia every night? Yeah, she would have. She wasn't concerned about sex at all—just imagery and her asthma. Did she know she was going to die soon when she stuck me in her will? If she hadn't died, would she have given me the money anyway? I'll never know. You were a good old egg, Mrs. Marigold. A golden egg. And wouldn't it be ironical if some day her little verses turn out to be as much acclaimed as Dickinson's?

I can cavort here and no one sees. The beach is a desert either way and wonderful in its desolation, miraculous as a mirage. I wonder how far I can walk without putting on my clothes? Can I walk right up to Caswell's crib?

I am a gypsy at heart, a woods and water sprite... Is that why I quoted Dickinson to Alex? He loathes poetry. I suppose I had to say something. I always feel so much older than Alex—responsible. And I can't go live with him—my old Simon and his old Sophie would never get along.

Carlo never loved Simon though he pretended to. Simon knew better. Maybe Simon reminded Carlo I'd been married before to June. Does Carlo call Hayden his husband? Hayden couldn't be anybody's husband.

Why do I grind out my days among these clodpolls? Why don't I cut my elegant Richard Cory throat? Because I'm too curious, that's why. And because I love my life. My life. Is this my life? This? Yep. This Is Your Life, Michael Kincade. The only one you're going to get and if you've made a mess of the first thirty years... well, haven't you? Nope. Well, a little messy. But fun. Is fun all you live for? Yisss. But now will you settle down to Work? Work? Or let it slip uselessly away? Well, probably. And if I do, who will care? What difference will it make to anyone what I do?

Whichever way I turn, whatever word I say may start some strange concatenation I know nothing of and cause a death or a marriage or even a train wreck. But one can't just stand naked on Riis Park Beach afraid to breathe because one might cause a train wreck if one stirs in a certain direction. In fact, just standing here naked I might cause some woman with a spyglass to leave her husband and dash over to her lover in Babylon, heedless of the warning-bell. Then—smash-crash, messy wreck at the crossing in Patchogue. If Patchogue comes between here and Babylon and I am as exciting to susceptible married ladies as I like to think I am, in my Greek-god-plus nakedness. Of course if that babe has a really good spyglass, she will also see the wrinkles seeping in before my ears and anyway these days women don't get their ovaries in an uproar over naked faggots parading on beaches. It doesn't take one to know one these days.

My God, Kincade, are you saying you're queer? You never meant to be one of Those. Now I sound like June. The girly boys she didn't mind so much—they couldn't help themselves, poor dolls. But men who looked like men and carried on with other men—those queers like Jan and Ugo upstairs over us on Riverside Drive—how vicious she was about them when it finally dawned on her. They were trying to fool her by being heavy and hairy and wearing loose pants and windbreakers and fancy shirts like real squares. But we could hear them staggering around drunk and chasing each other and squealing and panting and they never cared who was around if they felt like a nice long smoochy kiss.

June knew I liked men, too, and resented her snide jibes but she couldn't, or wouldn't, restrain herself. She was as neurotic as I was. Which doesn't mean anything because, of all the weirdos of this world, I am the only one who isn't the least bit neurotic. Thee and thee and thee, but not me, girl. I won't camp—much—or wear drag or let you fuck me. I am just broad-minded, athletic, eclectic, and, in downright chips-on-the-table reality, a lazy bit of rough trade. And the fact that I swing once in a while myself and penetrate an inviting ass is beside the point. Right? *Ja ja ja*. I just don't have much character and don't like to say no and besides, being from Kentucky, I am naturally polite and have an affinity for KY and lots of horsin' around.

I wonder if Caswell has ever been properly fucked. Wouldn't it be funny if Sexpot Caswell Green were just as adamant about none-of-that-thank-you-very-much as I am?

How old Twitchell used to stamp his little feet in rage and scream that Caswell Green was "weak, weak!" because he wouldn't do his history assignments. And I'd drawl, wide-eyed, "Weak, Mr. Twitchell? When he won't let you bully or blackmail him into doing what you want him to do. Weak?" And Twitchy would scream, "You know what I mean—intellectually weak, shiftless, irresponsible. We shouldn't be asked to deal with his kind. It's an insult and an imposition." And I'd say, "Perhaps it's a matter of personalities, sir. He does everything I ask him—and more. I find him rather refreshing." Then the real scream. "Refreshing! He's just plain fresh. And lazy. Such idle boys should be made to do what they should do. They should all be fired right out into the street, all those stiffnecked idlers who will work only for one master." And I'd murmur, "Oh, but I'd hate to see Simmons fired out. He never does any of the reading I require but he does do your history, I hear. He's even your brightest star, I hear. Even your pet." What a blithering fool Twitchell was. Go back to that? I'll wait on tables first. There are some indignities up with which I will not put. Thank you, Winnie-poo and e. e. too.

And I won't go to Key West with Mark Atwill to lure home sailors for him. He keeps saying I must come down and spend the winter with him and we'll both write. It's a temptation, a shrewd and devious snare. The famous Mark Atwill, that corrupt, weather-beaten and gin-raddled menhir, coruscating, fulgurating intermittently in the marshes of my private landscape. The only critic to mention me in a review of the Broadway show I was in. Scathingly. "As the local baseball star who struts in and waltzes off with Bernie's girl, Michael Kincade neither struts nor waltzes and certainly gives the impression of being more at home at Gilbey's than on a baseball diamond."

When I reminded him of that jab, he smiled his well-known

wry smile and asked if I'd have liked it better if he'd written what he actually thought: "Of all the heavy-hung beauties that mill around in minor roles reserved for the passions of directors, stars, producers, et al., Mike Kincade is definitely the most beautiful and appears to be the most lavishly endowed and who cares if he doesn't look like a baseball player? When he tooled in, every clitoris and half the cocks in the house stiffened in desire . . ." Or something like that. Rubbing my leg and fumbling with my zipper while he murmured his sardonic apology.

He was my second host at the Island that summer and his house was in the Pines, of course. What a quaint little tussle that weekend turned out to be. When he made it clear he expected me to get his breakfast and wash dishes and tidy up after him—him and his dribbling cigarettes and drabbling clothes, he couldn't move from one chair to another without shedding something and dropping it on the floor for me to pick up—well, he got maid service but that was all he got until he relinquished that position. At least he didn't make me ask for my tip the way that quivering neurotic songwriter did. What an inferiority complex poor Vicky Boy huddled under. Victor was sure the minute he paid me I'd be out the door and never darken his bed again. And I was and I didn't. And he did, eventually, one year and fifty callboys later, what he was always promising to do and left his tiny fortune to an old flame who had been married for twenty years and must have had a sweet time explaining that souvenir of Vicky's to his wife.

It's a wonder more people don't commit suicide than do, just shuffle off the mortal coils flesh is heir to. But millions go dead and spiritless without ever making up their minds to leave off living—mill around in a prefabricated world that doesn't elicit any response from them more vital than which apartment to take, which restaurant to eat in, movie to go to, car to buy, girl to marry or boy to make out with. Most homosexuals are half dead, mechanical. God, how I hate mechanical jokes, gay birthday cards, gay bars, gay bar chatter, gay clothes. It's all about as gay as a ride on the Long Island railroad . . .

Caswell's sand castle, half washed away. Fortress. Walled to keep what out? what in? The tide, the casual, lisping, mocking, irresistible tide has licked away one wall. Lord Caswell, your ramparts are vulnerable. But Alex said Caswell made a new one every day. Bids for attention? Compulsion to be busy? Creative urge to better yesterday's edifice? All three working slyly together like hags in the blood? It makes me shiver. It's a cry for help, this lopsided, phallic-featured, crumbling, childish work of two beautiful, useless, pleasing, graceful hands—like a wave of farewell from a drowning boy, carried out by the tide, not off to Spain because he wants to go but because he can't stop what's carrying him away. Caswell, come back!

I can't see him from here. Just the end of that barricade, crib, he's made. Pants on. No need to shock some nice daft old lady admiring the golden afternoon from her hospital window.

Up here on the brow of the blufflet I can see the shape of the crib but I can't see into it. It may be empty, the bird may have flown. And he may be there like Sleeping Beauty, waiting for me. He came to me first, now I must come to him. Fair enough. What a fantastic construction he has piled up. He could sell that to a dealer in far-out assemblage sculpture.

There's Alex further down the wall and he's found company. Whoever he is talking to must not be very exciting—Alex has his bathing suit on. Although the other guy appears from here to be completely in the buff. A long hairy type—bony knees and hairy legs. If he'd shift that leg a little I could see his schwanz. Ah, thank you, sir. Didn't realize my telepathic equipment was working so well. That's a nice long dangle you display. Now your face, please. Oh, he fingers the dangle. It was good, he wants more. Alex helps him handle the dangle. He wants more, too.

And now Alex spots me. Hi! Just passing. Oops, he's dropping everything and getting up and coming to meet me. I'd forgotten how sexy Alex looks in that butch little black bathing suit. He's a sweetie in or out of his suit. Pity my old Simon and his Sophie would fight so catly and dogly.

I still can't see if Caswell is there in the heavy shadow. He may have gone home right after blowing me. I usually want that second trip fast but when did I ever want a third one so much? And if I knew for certain it would never be more than once per go with us ever again, I'd still want him. If I walk further that way, they'll think I'm cruising the naked number. Alex will glower. I do want Caswell, I want to hold him close, closer than Carlo ever really was. We could be closer, we have more in common, we wouldn't have to try to reach each other . . .

"I see you found company," Mike said.

"Yes, other people had the same idea we had," Alex said. "You know Ron Barrett?"

"No. At least what I can see of him doesn't look familiar though it's quite impressive. Shall I continue on down the beach and let you finish what you were starting again?"

"God, no, we're both past all that," Alex said.

"Oh," Mike said.

"No, not us—Ron and me," Alex said. "I was finished off by your little Cas Green before I'd spread out my shirt, much less got my pants off. Then I took a nap and when I woke up he was gone. I walked down to the Rockaway fence and when I came back, he had Ron in there. I watched while he took Ron twice. Cas knew I was watching but he didn't seem to mind. Then he threw Ron out and motioned for me to come in again. I was tempted to ignore the little bastard but I couldn't deny him the pleasure. Besides I was aching to tumble in there and get that special treatment again. I don't know how he does it but that kid makes you feel like you're all cock and a yard long. I was going to pay attention to how he did it but he got me so worked up I didn't know what was going on. I didn't care if a thousand people were watching. As a matter of fact Ron and his roommate were."

"His roommate?" Mike asked.

"Yeah. Dick Spenser. He's in there now. He's been in there about an hour. Either he's got a leather cock or Cas is getting weak."

"Or he's seeing how many times he can make Dick come."

"That's doubtful," Alex said. "Ron says he begged Cas to go on but he wouldn't. Two per customer seemed to be the quota. Let's see if they're still alive."

Alex turned and walked quietly in a curve, stopping about a dozen feet from the double barricade of flotsam doors, a chicken coop, boards, a chunk of log and two big black tin barrels set like bastion towers. Mike followed, not sure he wanted Alex to look, very unsure about wanting to look himself. And see what he had to see. The idea was a little nauseating. It was Caswell in there. And a stranger. Mike snorted to himself in disgust, disgust for being so sentimental, so soft in the head. A hard cock and a soft head—what could be weaker, more open to disaster, conducive to despair, sillier in a grown man, to be seduced by a cynical self-obsessed little psychotic?

Alex halted before the open crib. Mike came up and stood beside him. Half reclining in the far corner against another chunk of log, spread-eagled, was a thin red-haired man of about Mike's age—Dick Spenser—his freckled white skin whiter in contrast with Caswell's olive shoulders and back and legs. Dick's head was tipped back, his mouth was open. His naked pelvic section writhed and thrust up to meet the youth's deliberate dips which took in about half the hard penis's length. As if he were aware they had come to see the show, Caswell let the long, inflamed and wet organ swing free. Mike saw with a pang of jealousy that it was nearly as big as his own—even longer perhaps, not so thick though. And the head was astonishingly large and deep red. Caswell inspected it, pulled the loose skin down slowly and firmly, lifted his head to gaze vacantly at the ghosts outside his castle, turned back to the shining organ and masturbated it thoroughly and slowly, licked it from base to tip and down again, poised over it and took as much as he could of it into his mouth and resumed slow insistent fellatio.

Mike turned away. You're jealous, he thought. You wanted to be the only one, or at least the one he took twice, the one he lingered over, the biggest one, the best one. He's found another one just as big, he's making it last longer, he's in love with it. Why are you trembling? You knew this was what he did; it was bound to be this way. You had to look though. But that stare. Not just myopic, contact lenses lost. More than that. Animal stare. The stare Simon gives me when I interrupt him in his pan. Subhuman. Not even catlike, not animal—machinelike, ghostlike, nonconscious, weary, helpless. Why did he look at us at all? That turning to us meant so much. As if to say, "See what I can get. I don't need any of you, any one of you. I don't even need this. I don't care what you see. I do what I have to do, no one can stop me, nothing can stop me until..." And I want to stop him. Not just out of jealousy, I don't want Caswell to want me alone. I wouldn't let him touch me, never again. He's polluted, all the pollution is gathered on him. His touch would be like a slimy snake's. I might chill and slip into his demented twilight. Demented? Caswell, come back! God, I'm crying.

I haven't cried since—well, I cried after Carlo but those tears didn't burn my eyes this way. Not my tears for my lost Robby or my errant Tyree or those I've suddenly wept for sweet little Toby. Earl and I wept when we said goodbye in the rain outside the Hiway Rest but those were sweet tears—these are horrible tears of rage and helplessness. I don't love Caswell, I couldn't love that, but I have to do something about him, make him love me. Make him love you? What a fool you are, Kincade. That's the most dangerous business in the world—it's deadly, making someone you don't love get worked up and in love with you. Psychiatrists do it. You're no psychiatrist, far from it.

But I do love Caswell in a way. And he already loves me, in the same way. What happened this afternoon is over. We had to get past that, through that gate; we're in another land. Now we can make love—mutual love or I won't have it—or not make love. It would never be simple lust again, I swear. I'm sure it would always be more than that for him as well as me. I love Caswell, and, because I love him, what I do will be right and it will help him. Help him?- Bullshit—don't let superficial nagging and niggling ruin this. You need Caswell as much as he needs you. He'll be helping you more than you help him. He can go for years this way but what are you going to do without him?

He's invulnerable? About as invulnerable as that sand fortress and you know it. He only seems invulnerable and heedless. He's too bright to go to waste this way and he knows it. No one knows that as well as Caswell knows it this minute. When I said he was being carried out by a tide, I was right. He knows that. I'm young enough, he likes me, I can still get at him. No one else can get at him—the psychiatrist failed, his aunt hardly tried, Proctor's crew made the routine motions but they didn't care...

There's that awful female in the tight green outfit sitting down on that log. What is she doing down here? Has she caught some hint of what is going on? Is she hoping to get a peek at the fairies at play? She probably hopes there's a man in the lot who will take her behind something and lay her, poor desperate critter. She's got the bounce, she's hot, willing, discreet, relatively clean, she won't ask for money. Sorry, lady, there isn't a good fuck left in the lot of us and, if there were, you wouldn't get it. You're a weird barbaric foreigner. We want ourselves, no exogamy, ourselves to hold and kiss and come with, ourselves as we might be, have been, could be. Immediate and thorough response, total knowledge, total abandon of Self in Self, ecstasy without mystery. Reassurance.

Women are always different, mysterious, who knows what they want? And if any of us wanted a woman for a change of pace, you wouldn't be the lucky one, ma'am. We can easily have the best. But to a lot of men you'd be as good as any—bouncy, juicy, hot and free and no names mentioned. I'd better distract her now she's getting up again. God knows what she might do if she happened to turn around and glance into the crib right now. I can see it—she shucks off those preposterous casings, slithers up like a panther woman, pounces, tossing Caswell aside like a used towel, straddles Dick, grabs his huge hard rod and rams it all the way up her juiced-up pussy and jounces them both off like they've never had it so thoroughly. She goes skipping down to the sea to wash and Dick, who's never been had by a woman before, loves it so much he changes his gait and goes ape over tight little teenyboppers.

Good, she's drifting oh-so-gracefully down to the water. I'm supposed to follow casually as if I didn't notice her there. Okay, sister, lead on. And keep your stupid face turned away. It's not your best feature, you know. And neither are those flabby rolls encased like loose sausage. I'm afraid your best feature just isn't out where it can be observed. If you knew how I loathe red hair. Your dyed red and Dick Spenser's rusty curls. But Caswell's hair is reddish. Dark purply, gold and rust red, rich, blending with that olive skin. How beautiful he is undressed, how healthy, so zestful, springing, enticing, drifting away like a wild little animal. And untiring. It takes concentration to suck a cock like that, handling a big one is work. Muscles ache. But he goes on and on.

Chet Andrews—Anderson?—Anders?—told me that during one whole spring and summer he had a special bench in a park near the entrance to an army camp and every night he'd suck off twenty or thirty guys when they came back from downtown. Some stopped by nearly every night. One kid really loved it and got curious and took up a station beside Chet and took care of three or four himself to see what Chet did it for. He said it wasn't nothing to him at all except a lot of hard work. Chet said if he stopped he was so tired he could hardly sit up, but as long as he was in continuous action he could do a good job. He swore in all that time no one ever made a pass at him and he felt no urge to masturbate while he was doing them or when he was alone. Sex is funny. I'd better lead this tramp back toward the bathhouse. Yep, follows like a lamb. But she looks more like a pregnant ewe.

I want Caswell to stop that. I want to see him laughing and happy and normal. Queer normal, that is. Hell, even ordinary normal if he wants that. He said he'd been carrying on with a girl up at that country school. Evidently he liked that, too. He can't imagine how much alike we are, really; I wonder if it's better he knows it or only wonders, guesses. Senses. Bright kids like Caswell go ahead on hints so fast. But that same intensity and drive that makes it possible for them to learn fast can make them go off so far in weird directions that they can't get back without help. As long as he's getting what he wants, he probably can't see how far off he's going.

Doesn't anyone ever talk to him? He probably avoids being told. Those stories of his revealed he wasn't entirely off in a dream world about himself. The ones about the Middle Ages bothered me a little—that Kafkaesque realism that went quietly into the absurd, but he knew it was absurd and laughed about it himself. And Salingeresque ones about the messes he got himself into—he knew they were messes. He knew he had a lot working against him but he wasn't begging for pity and he didn't think it was all a plot. He isn't paranoiac. But he is off and this afternoon he certainly doesn't show any glimmer of humor about anything. I wonder how he sees himself, or if he dares to look.

When Caswell's there in front of you, demanding, begging, the sheer strength of his need and his will carries you along. Especially if you have a need, too, that matches his or you know he's going to take care of you. And it isn't just the prospect of getting thoroughly sucked off he offers. It's a whole new level of experience. He offers the only chance you'll probably ever have to participate—body, blood, breath, seed—in a dionysian rite, to make the ultimate magic with him and appease the otherwise implacable gods. Sacrificial. I felt sacrificial. That damned redhead looked sacrificial, initiated. And yet it is Caswell who is the final sacrifice, the tragos. I wonder if it meant anything to Caswell that two of his victims or fellow revelers, male maenads, phallic kouretes, whatever he sees us as subconsciously, had the biggest whangs around and a third one is evidently a long one and the fourth is well above average in size.

If I stop to wade a bit, that ought to shake the redhead off—that kind loathes water. I hope she doesn't hunker down and wait for me to get through playing. The water here is almost warm but out a little it's damned deep and cold. No more swimming this year. She's going on past. Keep moving, lady; keep right on swinging all those things in the slow seductive bovine amble. You know I'm a real bull and hot for the juicy little treasure you have tucked way back in there, I'll follow you right out to your car. Only I won't. I'm heading back to my baby. And thank God that Spenser character is finally coming out. It's a pretty good body if you can stand those big white-skinned ones. Rather like Loel's. Or Lloyd's without the heavy muscles but enough ass to swing that big dong and that's what it's all for anyway. He looks fairly pooped and well he should. I wish he'd put some clothes on. He looks still lost in the dream. Wake up, man. Move on, go lie down. I have to get Caswell out of here, out of his fortress before the tide comes and carries him away.

And now to rescue Caswell! Courtesy of an ex-English teacher Caswell teased for a while and finally made out with between other engagements on a warm autumn afternoon at Riis Park. Trick number thirty-seven for the month of October, who's had the full treatment and will now kindly fade into decent oblivion if he has any manners at all.

Well, aren't they cute—Reddy Fox Spenser and the hairy Barrett, their arms under each other's necks. Caswell's nothing to them, just an episode they shared one idle October afternoon. Cocktail party shock-and-giggle stuff, two more knightly guests of Caswell's castle. There will always be someone who's heard how it was at Fire Island, too, someone who was admitted once into the unholy fraternity or claims he was. Imagine the nudges if you walked across the lobby at the ballet with Caswell or through the men's department of Bloomingdale's on a Saturday afternoon. Well, I've been talked about in my time and stared at and giggled at. And in clothes he's almost as beautiful as he is out of them and we'd make a pretty picture. The combination ought to send no few eyebrows zooming up where the hairline used to be.

Imagine Twitchell's face if I went back to Quillquiar's this fall and casually mentioned I was living with Caswell Green. And the Withered Poon—he wouldn't be able to shit for a week.

Caswell, Caswell, listen to me. I have a feeling I am your destiny and you're mine. Come down from Beaton every weekend and we'll show the town a thing or two. Between private engagements in our bedroom. Yep, he's still in there, naked, lying on his face, all limp like something discarded. He looks dead! But of course he's not. Spenser isn't a maniac. It's just my imagination. Caswell's breathing, he's probably asleep. And of course Alex wants to talk.

"The party's over, it appears," Alex said. "Ready to go back to town?"

"Sure, I suppose so," Mike said. "It must be almost four."

"The air is beginning to cool off. In another hour it will be chilly out here. Dick's taking a nap. The kid took him off three times and still didn't want him to leave."

"Three times? Are you sure? Did he say so?"

"Yes," Alex said. "But we knew anyway—he grunts and snorts like a crazy man when he shoots off. That makes seven rounds little fragile Caswell went in about two hours."

"Nine," Mike said.

"Nine?"

"Yes, he followed me up to the other end of the beach."

"I should have figured that when he was gone so long," Alex

said. "He certainly wasn't going to overlook anyone like you. But I thought maybe because he knew you . . ."

"That doesn't seem to make a difference," Mike said.

"I don't suppose I have to ask you how you liked it. This time I know for myself. I must say all the reviews are very enthusiastic. Four men—every man on the beach."

"Oh no, he missed Luis and his friends. Couldn't see them, I reckon."

"Your Puerto Rican friend with all the charm? I haven't seen him around for a year or two. He is up there?"

"Yes. The charm has begun to slip a little. He's added a belly since we saw him last."

"I never actually met him," Alex said. "But from what I've heard about what he's like in the sack, I'd take him, belly and all, any day. Beginning tomorrow. Just now I've had beaucoup. I'll put my pants on and say goodbye to Dick and Ron."

"Caswell seems to have quieted down, too," Mike said. "He looked as if he had passed out."

"Well, if it's possible to get too much of a good thing, I guess he's had it this afternoon. I've known Dick Spenser for years but I never suspected he was hung like that. When your little friend was swinging it around, I felt like taking it away from him and finishing it off the next time myself. I'll have to fix myself up a date. I've already got one with Ron. He's quite a man but he doesn't bat in the same league with you and Dick."

"I wonder how Caswell got down here. Did you talk to him at all?"

"Not much. But he said he was alone and didn't have a car. He must have taken the bus from the subway. Well, if he's had you, he's probably ready to shut up shop. If he wants to go back now, he could ride with us."

"That's what I meant," Mike said.

"Ask him while I change. If he hasn't really passed out."

Alex went back to where he'd left his clothes beside the other two men. Mike stood a moment looking over the wall and storm fencing at the blank shining windows of the hospital. Not a face at any of them. The old people no doubt long ago became accustomed to the silly shenanigans of the boys on the beach and nothing ever happened out in plain sight anyway except someone strolling around for a minute naked as a jaybird. Right now Alex had stripped off his trunks without turning his back to the hospital and was putting on his jockey shorts. So what? It must be pleasant, Mike thought, a real relief, to be old and cool and unflurried by sex, not even teased, much less tormented and tyrannized.

Mike moved over to Caswell's crib and stopped before the open side. Caswell was still lying as if flung from the heavens and dead, his body from the knees down lost in dark shadow. While Mike watched, the youth rolled his head a little and the hand visibly clenched. Mike quietly stepped up close to him and knelt. What a little fallen angel he was, so beautiful, so bleak. Caswell seemed to be whispering. Mike leaned over quite close and his shadow fell across Caswell's face. Caswell turned his head almost involuntarily and opened his eyes wide to stare up. Then he closed his eyes again and the clenched hand relaxed. Mike felt it against his knee. For an instant Mike was sure that Caswell had seen nothing, was lost still in that dream, the womb he had made for himself.

But Caswell said, "Hello, Mr. Kincade. I'm sorry."

Mike was shocked but had to keep Caswell talking. "You're sorry, Caswell? What about? I'm glad. At least about us."

"I shouldn't have left you that way. I couldn't stay. But I wish I had stayed with you."

Mike was at a loss. The child wasn't being coy. He wasn't even being terribly polite and considerate. He meant he wished he had stayed there with Mike. But Mike was afraid to let Caswell go on in that vein. It sounded too much as if he wanted to begin again where he left off, take Mike a third time as he had Spenser. Keep him there.

"You had fun, didn't you?" Mike asked. "I mean here, too?"

"Fun? Oh yes, of course. Please..." He lifted the arm nearer Mike and rubbed Mike's knee.

Mike looked at the smooth sweet young body stretched out so unresisting and ready, the lightly muscled back, the thin waist, the neat bottom that invited fucking. He put out his hand to stroke it but stopped himself even though he felt a quick stirring in his pants. While he held himself suspended,

Caswell turned his head blindly to Mike and rolled over onto his side, opening himself up to Mike. His hand stroked Mike's thigh. Mike was surprised and rocked back, caught his balance and knelt, looking down. Caswell opened his eyes but did not look up to Mike's face; his eyes did not lift their gaze above Mike's crotch and the hand slipped up there and sought Mike's expanding organ through the cloth of his pants.

"Before I go . . ." Caswell whispered. "You don't have to do anything. Just let me. I mean if you don't want to give me anything, any more of you . . . But just let me, for a few minutes . . . Please, sir."

The brat's insatiable, Mike thought. He doesn't care who it is, me or that redhead. As long as it's a big one. No, it isn't that. That's what anyone else would say. I must say more than that. Caswell is saying more than that to me. He knows who I am. He knows what I'll think right off. And he isn't trying to see whose will is stronger.

"It's so beautiful, sir, It's important to me and you'll like it, I'll be good, I'll give you . . . I'll stop whenever you say but I want it again just once more. It's all I want. It's getting hard. If you'll just let me . . ." Both his hands were caressing and beseeching.

Mike found it difficult to resist and even more difficult to go on thinking clearly. The boy's words were like a call in code, one call disguised as another call. Not lust, not sex even—need, warmth a moment longer, an hour if he'd stay. Caswell had begged Spenser to stay, too. The excited whisper was hypnotic, commanding, and the eager hands stroking his hardening cock were seductive. Caswell didn't attempt to open Mike's pants—Mike had to do that himself, willingly. It would be easy to let the boy have what he wanted for a little until it was really raring, then clasp Caswell and spread him down on his back, roll his slender legs into the air and enter him gently—he'd love it, they'd both love it. That was what Caswell needed—to be used, wanted, needed, taken.

Mike's heart pounded. He had to resist and do something else right now. He flung himself down, half covering the youth's body with his bigger, heavier, clothed body. He slipped one arm under Caswell's neck and nuzzled and kissed his cold, moving lips. With his other hand Mike sought and found

Caswell's cold thin cock and rubbed it. He kissed Caswell's eyelids and forehead, his mouth again. The boy went limp and distant, seemed hardly to breathe.

Mike slipped down, kissing Caswell's chest and smooth soft little belly; he nuzzled into Caswell's pubic hair and took his cold organ in his mouth and warmed it, caressed it gently with his lips, tugging a little, trying to bring him to life. There was no answering warmth or reaction.

Mike's hands touched Caswell's face and his chest, rubbed lightly but insistently all along his body, clasped his narrow hips. The boy did not resist in any way Mike could feel but he seemed to have gone away. Mike realized Caswell did not want just that, just sexloving, either. Mike let Caswell's cock slip out of his mouth and kissed the lad's loins and stomach and chest, throat and face, finally his lips again. He put his lips to Caswell's ear and kissed it and whispered, "Caswell, love me. Please, I'll do anything but it has to be us together because I love you."

Mike was a little shocked—he hadn't intended to go so far, but it was true and if he had to beg Caswell to love him, if that asking would make the difference . . . "Caswell, I've never asked anyone to love me before, ever. But I want you to."

Caswell rocked his head away, writhed in Mike's arms. He was trying to escape Mike—Caswell hated love, rejected it, feared it, of course. People were always saying they loved him.

"Right now I love you, Caswell. Maybe tomorrow I won't. But I will because how can I not love you? I've been looking for you. I need you. Do you hear me?"

Caswell smiled and said, "Yes." He didn't even whisper it. But he didn't turn toward Mike, either. The new face of things was more puzzling to Mike than the old. He could only blunder on, do as he felt he must or could. He put his lips close to Caswell's ear and went on whispering.

"I can't help loving you because you're myself. Only different and new. We're two of a kind. You're the brother I never had, the only kind of a lover I need. When we talk, you'll know what I mean. You may not like my poems but you'll know what poetry means. I wanted you last fall but I was clinging to someone else, trying to make a go of something that was already falling apart. He didn't know what poetry was all about and he thought sex was only physical. I've had you now and I want you, every way. But I want more than love in bed. That and everything else." He massaged Caswell's genitals gently, felt and fingered and caressed them as he whispered. "You're beautiful and sweet and everything I want. And so damned sexy I can't resist you. Come on. Come home with me, please."

Caswell turned his head, his eyes still closed, and Mike kissed him gently. Caswell's whole body moved closer to Mike and in the boy's hand Mike felt movement, surging of blood and stirring toward life. Caswell put his arms around Mike but, as he drew close against Mike, he began to sob. Mike held him so tight that he knew he was hurting him. The sobbing was dry, nervous and soon over. The crisis was over—Caswell would go back with them, he would not stay behind until it was dark and walk into the water, go out as far as he could and never come back, as he had planned to do, Mike knew. They both knew but it could never be spoken of.

Mike was aware Alex had approached the crib and was standing out there watching them curiously, but Mike lay a little longer, holding Caswell close, keeping him warm, letting their pulses beat together and their breath mingle. Alex would be curious and would try to figure out what was going on but there was no way to tell him all the truth.

ALEX

When Arnold said, "Brunch at twelve," Alex had made a mental note to arrive at one if he didn't want to be there before they got up. But it was now one-twenty-seven and it might take another twenty minutes to find a parking space at this rate. Alex drove slowly through East Ninety-first Street. He was already five or six blocks from their apartment house and getting further away at every turn. Two kids ran out of an apartment-house door with flight bags in their hands and climbed into a car at the curb. Obviously that car would be going out soon. Alex stopped. The kids remained in the car but no one else joined them.

A slender languid trick in a duffle coat and dark glasses ambled out with a huge poodle on a leash. Rather cute, Alex noted. There was a flash of gold at the wrist, where he held the lapels of the coat clutched together at his throat. Probably kept. Well kept. It was an expensive-looking apartment house and he was an expensive-looking doll. A taxi horn behind Alex startled him.

Cruising around the block, he thought he saw someone he knew coming toward him—a stocky figure in tight plaid pants and a short brown leather jacket and a black leather cap. But it wasn't Jake, although the basket the plaid accentuated was as big as Jake's. The bony face under the low-pulled cap was strange. Alex halted beside a hydrant space to get a good look. The guy didn't miss. He glowered at Alex but stopped to light a cigarette, his big basket pushed out and tilted up for Alex's inspection. Alex licked his lips suggestively. The guy licked the cigarette, puffed, rocked his pelvis slowly. Then he moved to the hydrant and stood with one boot-clad foot on it, showing

Alex his shapely ass. All that meat and he wants to be fucked, Alex thought. Or, more likely, to be beaten. Or to pound on me like that bastard Jake who I thought he was. Alex drove on without another glance...

Jake at the gym... Hairy, hard, rather heavy, with smoky gray eyes dreaming out of long lashes, heavy eyebrows, a thick cock dangling out of all that underbrush. They'd gone to his place, a ratty tenement railroad apartment with ugly Salvation Army furniture and a mattress on the floor—rye in cheese glasses. Little talk, a lot of waiting and rubbing through the pants. Finally the undressing, the nuzzling, the nipple-biting. Alex didn't react favorably to that but understood he was to reciprocate and he did. Then the fingernails digging into his back and shoulders. As Alex muttered, "Take it easy," the other guy, Jake, muttered, "Go on, make it good," and Alex had realized what kind of a mess he was in. So he dug with his nails a little and slipped down to blow the joe fast, massaging his buttocks roughly to accelerate things. No erection. But Jake hauled him up and sucked his now somewhat reluctant prick until it was no longer reluctant. Then he pulled Alex down as he rolled down and back and ordered, "Now, man. Ram that big thing into me. Fuck that ass hard, man. Make it good."

So Alex fucked hard and heavy and it wasn't bad at all. Jake hooked his thumb under his capacious foreskin and beat his now hard thick jock as if he'd tear it off.

"Hit me, man. Slam those balls right into me, fuck me hard with that stallion cock, I want to feel you!"

Alex really let him have it, eager to shoot off and pull out of the whole damned mess. He'd never fucked so heavy right up to a climax before and found it so wonderful he got carried away and banged the bastard full force until he was shooting before he knew it.

Jake rocked and whimpered and spurted a heavy spray all over his own face and chest hair. In an instant Alex was up and had wiped his cock on Jake's undershirt and was dressing. Jake lolled back and lit a cigarette—probably pot—and winked at Alex and said sternly, "Next time, man." Alex was pretty sure there'd be no next time but those last few minutes had been pretty exciting...

He was almost despairing of finding a parking space and depressed by the hustlers and callboys and sadists and the general dirtiness of the streets on this raw gray December afternoon. And Christmas was hardly two weeks away. Less—ten days. Crazy phony Christmas.

A car pulled out from the curb and he raced to the spot, maneuvered the little Peugeot in deftly and walked to the corner to see where he was. Only six blocks from brunch. And half an hour late. New York.

He was still the first guest to arrive. Arnold Kohlman and Roger Peters had a split-level flat like a million others in New York. Everything was chic and pretentious, nothing of any interest whatsoever. Except a tall blond lad, more or less in white silk pajamas, reclining full-length on the sofa against the far wall. Rog, who had opened the door and was taking Alex's coat and muffler, shushed Alex and belatedly directed Alex's attention to the recumbent figure, in a whisper, "Ralegh Bronsten. Slightly hung over. We had a night."

Alex's subtle nose detected the unsubtle stink of poppers and he noted a movie screen rolled up but left standing in a corner. Alex loathed poppers but even more he loathed being blatantly reminded that he hadn't been invited to see their new dirty movies. He'd seen so few.

"Arnold's in the kitchen," Rog said. "Go get a drink and goose him up if you want any food today. He's half asleep, too. I'm going to shave." Rog was in a rumpled silk dressing gown of cerise and black squares on a cocoa background. It hung open and the hair on his chest and in his groin was as marvelously golden as the fluff on his crown. His heavily veined penis hung broad and limp. Alex lifted it and rolled back the drooping foreskin from the blotched red head in mock-serious inspection.

"You did indeed have a night," Alex said.

"God, yes. I bet I couldn't get up and off in less than twenty seconds this morning. Unless you squeezed a little."

Rog was known to achieve full erection seldom and to enjoy hours of manipulation without ejaculation. There was a rumor he was over sixty but Alex was sure the two of them were about the same age. Alex knelt and took it all in his mouth, the soft length, and let it slide out. As he drew back, he saw what he expected to see—motion on the sofa. A hand fumbled in the open pajama pants, drawing out and caressing a long organ almost as thick as Rog's. Alex stood up and patted Rog on his silk-covered plump ass as he stumbled into the bedroom. Alex quietly closed the door behind Rog.

Alex waited a minute. Ralegh Bronsten's knees swung wide and his strokes definitely became lazy slow pulls on a hardening organ. Alex went silently down and across to the sofa. The slow pulling continued a minute and stopped with the hand holding the skin down taut. It was an extraordinarily large cock and he was a lovely lad lying there with his eyes closed and his tongue licking his lips in deliberate invitation. Alex knelt and sucked the swollen thing adroitly. The youth's hand fumbled in Alex's crotch and opened his fly, dragged out his half-stiff piece to play with.

Better than brunch, Alex thought.

Only he had carried on so excitedly with the athletic premed student he'd picked up at the West End last night that this party was a little forced and he was even a little relieved when Arnold, who had been watching from the railing, called, "How about a drink, you two making love on the sofa? Besides, Tyree'll be here any minute and you know what happens if he comes and finds you carrying on, Ralegh honey."

"Yeah. I get fucked. That bitch wants into everything. This man sucks good, Arnie."

"She should, she's been at it even longer than I have. We both had Adam before he found out about fig leaves and girls."

Arnold was as decidedly dark as Roger was fair and the general effect of the thick black hair and carefully shaped eyebrows against the white skin was oriental. A whittled-down-to-a-button nose and long slits of eyes added to the effect. In his hairdressing salon he was called Mr. Arnold-san and affected little enigmatic *moues* and bows.

"Incidentally," Arnold said, "in case you care about such things, let me remind you the dick you're swinging on is Ralegh Bronsten, AWOL from Philadelphia and the bedpost he's usually kept tied to."

Alex acknowledged the introduction by bowing down and taking all the young man's slackening cock into his mouth and down his throat. "And the one down there—all the way down as I am amazed to observe, wish I could do that but my throat's so dainty—is dear Alex. We were sisters in the Navy and stood many a watch for each other."

Ralegh shook Alex's cock politely, dropped it and withdrew his member from Alex's mouth and stood up rather shakily. Alex rose with him and they kissed. The boy's mouth tasted like old buffalo shit. Somehow the silk pajama jacket had slithered back to the sofa and Alex had his arms full of languid limber nakedness, smooth, tanned, feverishly hot and sweaty.

"Oh no! Not twice before breakfast! Twice is not decent. No. No." Arnold stormed like a tenement mama.

The pajama pants were on the floor and Alex put his mind to doing a thorough job of caressing the warm damp flesh, as smooth and softly swelling as a girl's, Alex supposed. But Ralegh dropped to his knees, hauling down Alex's pants and shorts as he went, and took Alex's cock into his mouth and teased it up hard.

"Oh God, that one's on her knees again," Arnold moaned.

"Do be a dear, Alex, and give her what she wants in one good gush or my Creole brunch will be ruined. Rogah!"

Roger came out naked with lather on his face. "See," Arnold bawled, "that Hungry Hannah will swing on that big dick until everything's cold. Do something. Rim Alex so he'll get all excited and shoot. No, guess you'd better not, honey—your lather would get all over everything and all up everything and you'd all be sick."

The chimes mingled and moaned. Roger swooped over and opened the door. Ty O'Neill swept in, followed by an even taller young man with a huge English sheepdog on close leash.

"Well!" Ty gasped. "Aren't you dears in a state! I presume that's Roger behind the suds." He grasped Roger's famous organ and held it across his palm. "Yes, it's Roger. Roger, meet—Oh, I am sorry, I don't think you told me your name, young man."

The young man was stunned, too surprised to step into the room, too fascinated to step back into the corridor. The sheep-dog lunged past him and snuffed at Roger's penis and licked it.

"Gently, boy," Ty admonished and stepped between the dog and Roger, "One thing at a time. Your turn will come. Roger, uhhh?"

The blushing twenty-year-old mumbled something. Ty rattled on. "Norris. Or Morris or something like that." He turned. Alex, not sure of the situation, had done nothing and Ralegh had not broken his rhythm.

Arnold screamed and fled in tiny steps into the kitchen.

"That was Arnold," Ty continued blandly. "Shut the door, Norris or Cornelius as the case may be." The tall youth hurried to do so but without looking away from the scene in the living room. Ty strolled elegantly into it and drew along the stranger, encumbered by embarrassment and rollicking *canis*.

"The kneeling angel of mercy is my lover Ralegh Bronsten," Ty said. "The other sodomist is unfamiliar to me. Everything is sodomy in New York State. So imprecise. And I've heard some judges give the working party ninety days and the worked-on only thirty. Because—well—even judges and cops occasionally stand still for a little loving, I'm told." With one hand Ty caressed Alex's round bare buttocks and with the other he drew the tall youth nearer.

"I'm Alex," Alex said formally and extended his hand. Ty's lad shook it briefly.

"There," Ty said. "I knew the awkward moment would pass. I picked up this young man at the tobacconist's on the corner—or his dog picked me up. It was a bit confusing there for a moment and the place was so intimate. I persuaded him to come along for a drink."

"I think I'd better—" The young man managed to utter and then broke off, stumbling back against his dog. "I mean I'm not queer and evidently—well, it's a mistake."

"Don't fuss. We were all young like you once upon a time. And don't give me that quaint shit about not being gay, dear heart. You picked me up. I remember only too happily."

"Yes, I did speak. I recognized you. I was at the opening night of the show in New Haven. I recognized you, I mean. I just wanted to—well, converse or something. I had no idea..." He looked wildly at Alex who tried to look upset and commiserating.

"I suppose you're a design student," Ty sighed. The boy nodded. "And you're six feet three, twenty years old and never been blown. A likely story! That hard-on in your pants tells me what I want to hear."

"I mean I'm not queer. Of course I'm gay. Everybody's gay. It's just—well—"

Alex was in love again. The lad was indeed six feet three, a walking dream, and there was a considerable hard-on in his snug Levi's. Ralegh turned to look, letting Alex's rigid wet cock swing out in full glory. Alex was delighted to note the boy looked right at it. But how to get him out of this nest of vipers?

Naked and charming, Ralegh stood up beside the tall youth. "I'm Ralegh and he is not my lover. My lover is an older gentleman in Philadelphia and I'm in New Rochelle visiting my sick sister." He patted the boy's bottom chummily and with the other hand rubbed briskly along the burgeoning bulge.

"Oh, God," the boy exclaimed and looked up at the ceiling. Then he made an effort again to ecape but his dog was pushing against his legs. Ralegh used both hands to zip down his fly and draw out his cock. Alex got a look—it was eight inches long already and thick and had a big head—before Ralegh went down on it.

Ty shrugged, tossed his chesterfield onto the sofa, swung Alex around so they could both see what Ralegh was doing, and went down on him. Roger came naked and shaven from the bedroom and stood with one arm around the lad. He had shut his eyes and seemed for a couple of minutes to have withdrawn in spirit from the occasion. But his hand slipped from between his thigh and Roger's naked one and sought and found Roger's big organ. He grasped it and squeezed it spasmodically and jiggled it in little two-inch jerks like a kid with a peewee. Amazingly, Roger's soft organ stiffened and thrust until it was harder than any of the other three had ever seen it. The kid handled it roughly in little jerks and bucked and grasped in rhythm and Ralegh sucked furiously. Alex found that even after last night he was eager to come again but he wanted to suck the new kid off first.

Then Roger announced in a whisper, "I'm going to shoot." Arnold said in a hushed tone from the railing, "Good Lord." The youth pulled away from Ralegh and knelt beside him and took the head of Rog's great cock in his mouth and jerked at it wildly with both hands. Roger arched back and went rigid and moaned. The kid choked but didn't give up until Roger was quiet. Then the lad stood with his eyes still shut and found his handkerchief and wiped his slimy face.

Alex ached to break from Ty and take the boy but Ralegh was back at work before the older man had completely straightened up. Hungry Hannah, Alex thought. Another Caswell Green. Or Caswell as he was last summer. Caswell now was quite different.

The dinner party of last Saturday night flashed momentarily in Alex's vision—his own surprise at seeing Carlo and Hayden there, the two married couples chatting cozily. Hayden better looking than Alex remembered but still not Alex's type—too effete, too passive. The place looked beter than Alex had ever seen it. Caswell had withdrawn from Beaton College and hardly went out except to shop. Caswell, glowing, content, a perfect young host; Mike, equally glowing, so proud, hardly seeing Carlo or Hayden or Alex or Bobby Dallett who was the fourth guest. Alex had known Bobby and his bookshop for years—they dished merrily while the others sedately conversed about Europe.

Caswell had been to Europe when he was ten and again when he was twelve. That was the time his father didn't come back, Alex knew. Drinks, but not too many, Mike decided. But still everyone had one or two more than they should have had and there was a vin rosé with the veal, and not a very good vin rosé. Alex offered to teach Caswell about wines. But there were artichokes in butter, the roast, baked potato with sour cream and parsley, slightly candied carrots, salad with a good dressing and chocolate mousse . . .

Alex was brought back to the messy present by the lad's sudden loud breathing and quivering. Alex didn't want Ralegh or anyone else except himself to have him. The older man kept his gaze on the boy's blank face until he turned it away as he zipped up. Alex was rather surprised to find he was still being quite ardently done by Ty. A hell of a state when you could lose all consciousness of a thing like that. And for a moment, recalling Mike's and Caswell's dinner party, Alex had even forgotten the boy he'd fallen in love with a moment before.

Alex had to smile wryly. He certainly wasn't much in the mood for sex if his thoughts could wander off so easily to a party that happened more than a week ago and neglect this new doll as well as the much gossiped about and glorious Ralegh Bronsten and the theatrical butterfly Ty O'Neill whose name was now frequently in the papers. Ty might be a great social figure but his technique was nothing to write home about. He lacked rhythm and that other sense that made all the difference—that imagining into the other man's emotional state. But maybe Ty wasn't concentrating. In fact it was apparent he was trying to see if his pickup trick was leaving. He was.

Alex felt like singing out to Roger, who was walking the lad to the door, "Get his name, his telephone number!"

Ty halted but Alex could hardly go bounding over. Ty rose and waited. They were at the door. The young man turned and waved, a bit as if he were still blind, and bundled the huge dog out. Roger closed the door, leaned against it, slumped and sat flat in the foyer, his eyes crossed in mock amazement.

Ralegh was still kneeling, naked, by the coffee table. Now he peeped around with big mock-solemn eyes and Ty laughed. Alex tucked in, zipped up and plopped on the sofa. Arnold leaned on the railing.

"Such a morning," he screeched. "You should live till I tell you. This is a brunch?"

Ty turned crisply. "Have I delayed things awfully, dragging that Yale undergraduate and his outlandish dog along? I am contrite. Now you say something, Ralegh Bronsten, sitting there smirking like the cat that's had all the cream."

Ralegh responded by smiling like a cherub and licking the corners of his mouth.

The brunch was much too rich but the drinks had so much rum in them that everyone forgot calories and incipient gastritis.

Alex was frustrated and depressed but ravenous. Perhaps so ravenous because he was so frustrated—compensation, classic case.

Roger had merely asked the young man to come by again sometime, reminded him of his name and Arnold's, had not asked the youth's name or gotten his telephone number. Ty was glum—the Yalie would look him up and want to talk scene design, be a pest now. Alex wondered who of his teasier young tricks he could offer to trade to Roger—in case the young man should turn up again. But if he did come, it would be for another swing on Roger's extraordinary tool—the lad had hardly noticed Alex at all.

Arnold had the stereo going madly with old show tunes. Conversation was about pickups. Everyone had had experiences with sadists and with masochists and with leather-clad beauties who turned out to be real ladies. Alex became aware Roger liked the rough stuff a little and Ralegh was fascinated but fearful of disfigurement. Everyone knew someone who had had to go to the hospital for a couple of weeks to be sewed up. Or unsewed.

Then the hustlers. Ty admitted he looked for them, paid them, got a kick out of calling AO to see who'd come. As often as not it was some haughty beauty he'd seen in a bar or at the theater or a waiter he'd had his eye on for weeks. Once he was sent a cute trick he'd had at the baths a week earlier—they'd both gone on as if they'd never seen each other before. Some were surly and stupid, some tried to please but were dull. One or two were stunning. One was nearly forty but a real stud—his cock was so long it could be shoved up his own asshole. Alex had never paid a hustler and hated the whole idea. He wondered if Pierre had ever hustled.

Then the thieves, the ones who weren't honest enough to ask for money but took rings, watches, rifled billfolds, stole keys and came back and hauled out typewriters, expensive clothes, cameras. It didn't do any good to report burglary to the police—they never got anything back smaller than a car. Where did the stuff all go?

Alex had been robbed. Someone had picked his lock or had made a key from a furtively taken impression. The shy college student, studying to be a law librarian? The sweet haughty youth from Caracas who was so determined no one should think he was Puerto Rican or Mexican or Cuban?

And there was the beautiful klepto Lee. You just had to go to his lover and he'd see you got your jewelry back. Alex had known Lee and Pixie for years and had heard nothing of all this. Alex wanted to protest it wasn't true but knew it probably was...

They all sat glumly a moment while the music made hysterical whoopee. Arnold and Roger both made money but were always in debt. They tried to stay out of trouble. Most of the time they led very quiet commonplace lives, going out little, buying new clothes—but something always happened. Roger had a police record—twice he'd been caught being done in subway toilets by men he'd hardly glanced at and wouldn't have been aware of at all under other circumstances. Arnold's family rode him for money. They had troubles—legitimate and incessant troubles and only Arnold made more than he spent. Ty's taxes were in a mess and his last show had closed in Philadelphia. The new show didn't challenge him—his designs would be awful. Ralegh was well and closely kept. He'd met a dozen beauties in Philadelphia but had to share them with Edgar who hogged them first. And, Ty reminded Ralegh, there was the one that got away last summer—Mike Kincade.

Ralegh retorted that at least he had taken Mike away from the famous Ty O'Neill. Alex perked up.

Ralegh had tried to call Mike yesterday but had gotten no answer. Maybe today—he'd have Mike again sooner or later.

Suddenly Alex hated Ralegh, Ty and even his old friends Arnold and Rog. They were petty, nasty, drearily evil. Mike and Caswell had to be protected from such people.

Arnold was telling Ty that Alex was a long-time friend of Mike's, and Ralegh wasn't missing a word of it. He immediately began quizzing Alex who decided the less said, the better. Arnold and Rog knew Caswell's summer reputation and would make a fuss about that if they found out.

"Mike has a new lover," Alex said, "and they hardly go out at all. Mike's cool to everyone. I hardly see him myself. Sometimes I suspect they don't answer the telephone—don't want to be bothered with anyone else at all. It's rather touching. What show is that from?"

Arnold listened a second. "*House of Flowers.* Wait. We saw Mike this fall, Rog, remember? Where was it? And he was with that awful little faggot from Fire Island, the one who sucked everybody who came along."

"Everybody but you, Arnold. And a lot of others. He was very choosy—took only the best."

"Only took the big ones is more like it."

"Big ones?" Rog asked. "Jim Darcon? Al Moore? Rayman? Honey, don't be a bitch just because he never would take you. Why, he wouldn't take Starr Schwarz, either, and Starr has the biggest one this side of Brooklyn."

"Okay already," Arnold said. "Still she was a whore. Is that who Mike Kincade's shacked up with, Alex?"

"Cas? Yes, I think it's the same boy," Alex wearily admitted.

"So you'll have to wait another month," Tyree teased Ralegh.

"I wouldn't count on that," Alex said quietly and wondered how he could change the subject without being too obvious.

"I'm counting on it," Ty said. "I met Mike in the Rack at four o'clock. By four-fifteen we were in bed having a real ball. He said he'd never been so excited in his life and it was one of the best bed sessions I ever had. Then you dropped this sugarplum into my lap and I was distracted but I'd like a lot more of that wild Kincade stuff, if you don't mind."

"I don't mind a bit if I can swing on that gorgeous dick of his for about two hours first," Ralegh said. "I don't mind your having anything that's left. Did I ever tell you about that same night on the boardwalk?"

"Yes, you did," Arnold interjected. "And every time you tell it, it gets wilder and funnier. You were stinking drunk and high on pot besides. Sheer fantasy, the whole tale, I suspect. Mike had not only been in the hay with Ty all afternoon—that was the night he fucked Mac the Zipper against the lamp post with several of my most reliable spies watching. He fucked Mac to a fare-thee-well, you should pardon the expression. Anything that happened later that night mostly happened in your little pot-happy head, honey child."

"It was the most wonderful hour of my life," Ralegh purred. "I wouldn't expect it to be that good again but if it was just half that good . . ."

"Mike has something—" Ty began.

"Of which Roger has more, for God's sake," Arnold interposed.

"No, you'd be surprised." Roger smiled. "But it isn't that, anyway."

"You too, viper?" Arnold snorted. "When? You never told me."

"Long ago. He was in a play in the Village Stairs, and I had a hard-on whenever he was on stage. I went backstage and met him."

"We saw that play together," Arnold said, "and we went back and met my dear friend Devera, who promptly took you into the can and blew you. Right?"

"Right. But the third time I saw the play, I went back upstairs and had Devera introduce me to Kincade. We had a few drinks while they took off their makeup and the rest of the cast cleared out and then we had a three-way session with mirrors. We were pounding down the home stretch, Dev doing me, me doing Mike, when I caught a glimpse of another body in the doorway. It was one of those kids who played the guards in the last act and he was whacking off a piece of meat the size you wouldn't believe. Mike motioned him in and jerked his load off all over Dev's back."

"So what was so glorious about Kincade?" Arnold asked.

"That was another time, a week or so later. Here."

"Here? Oh Roger, how could you et cetera. Where was I?"

"With your family in the Bronx you told me," Roger said.

"Hmm. Very pretty," Ralegh said. "The guard with the incredible schwanz. You didn't just let him fade out of the picture I hope."

"I should say not," Roger said. "He was only sixteen at the time and wouldn't even let you lick it but he did let everybody photograph it. You see his pictures in all the best collections."

"Show me yours," Ralegh said, "Right now. And that Starr Schwarz, do I know him?"

"He's a mess, honey," Arnold said. "She wears net pants to all the parties to show off that huge thing and then gets real butch indignant if you try to put your mouth on it. Hands yes, mouth no."

"Whoa a minute," Alex said. "Question, Roger—this Starr Schwarz, how old is he?"

"Why, about twenty-two or three. Have you had him?"

"No," Alex said. "I've seen pictures of him, of course. And I think I watched him get jacked off in three different movie-house heads last winter but he always had a hat pulled down over his eyes so I couldn't be sure."

"A black hat? That's Starr," Roger said.

"One more thing," Alex said. "Was Starr the kid at the Village Stairs?"

"Bingo. That was going to be my big surprise."

"Meet Miss Pinkerton, girl detective," Alex said.

"You spoiled it," Ralegh whined. "I though there were two more to add to my list and now it turns out there's only one."

"Never mind, dear," Roger said. "There are always new items coming along. I read where a London whore said all the young ones were bigger than the old ones. Too big, she said."

"Poor thing," Ralegh said. "My box aches for her."

"As a matter of fact," Roger went on, "Starr said the boy who played the other guard at that point appeared to be equally well endowed but no one ever got a good look at it. It just got hard in his pants when he played with Starr's, but he was like your Yale friend—not queer. A blond Italian—Angelo Bruno. And to save you time, there are about a hundred Brunos in the telephone book."

"What is Mike doing this fall?" Alex realized Ty was asking him. Alex wished everyone would forget about Mike and Caswell but he told Ty how Mike had gone back to Quillquiar's. Alex didn't feel obliged to tell how much Mike had disliked the idea of going back but he and Caswell were both broke.

"What does Caswell do?" Roger asked. "Shouldn't he be in college or something?"

"He withdrew," Alex explained. "He's learning to cook."

"For his husband. How sweet. I suppose he has plenty of money of his own. The scuttlebutt last summer was his family was loaded. I hope he's seeing a good psychiatrist."

"He went through a bad period but it's all over now."

Ralegh was still looking thoughtful. "When is Mike's vacation? I have to go back to Philly tonight but my sister could have a relapse about Wednesday and if I could lure Mike down to my hotel room for a Christmas drink—no one can refuse a Christmas drink at three in the afternoon. Thursday Edgar and I are leaving for Acapulco."

"Mike's vacation doesn't begin until Thursday. All the private schools let out Thursday. Tough," Alex answered absentmindedly.

He was wondering if Caswell really should be seeing a psychiatrist, as Arnold had said. The summer phase was over but there had been a while last Saturday night that wasn't very pretty. The glimpse of silent fury and struggle in the bedroom with Mike trying to calm Caswell. Mike had succeeded and they'd come out of the bedroom and gone on with salad and dessert and been pleasant and polite though even more wrapped up in each other than before. But the scratch on Mike's face had begun to bleed again.

The rough time had started innocently enough with drunken effusive compliments on Caswell's cooking. Actually Carlo and Hayden overdid it a little—nothing had been that special or difficult and Cas was a little embarrassed. Mike had gaily diverted the fulsome flow by announcing that besides being a wonderful cook, the kid had the most beautiful legs in the world. And he'd swooped Caswell up, stood him on a chair and divested him of his pants in a trice. Caswell hadn't minded a bit, posing there in his short shirttail and red silk bikini that bulged neatly and roundly.

"Even more beautiful than Alex's," Mike had claimed. Of course the two sets of legs were too different to compare.

"But not more beautiful than Hayden's!" Carlo had insisted. Hayden dimpled prettily and said Charles was prejudiced. Charles, as Hayden insisted on calling Carlo, led Hayden over beside Caswell's chair and pulled his pants off. Hayden's legs were a lot shapelier than we'd expected—sleek and a little heavy, like an English actor's, fabulous in tights and Levi's and in bed. But besides the lovely legs there was something else to feast your eyes on. Hayden was taking long peeks at Caswell's amazing basket there under his nose and was getting a fine erection-reaction which Alex hoped Carlo-Charles wouldn't discourage for a few more minutes. Alex yelped out that if there was competition afoot he had a right to be judged on the evidence, not on hearsay, and shucked out of his pants and shoes. Bob Dallett, of course, couldn't stand all this since his gams had been a feature of every C G Follies for years, and he was out of his togs in a drunken swoosh, only somehow he absent-mindedly stripped off his underwear with his pants and his bouncing three-piece set added to the merriment and accelerated Hayden's erection as Bob had figured it would. Carlo was a little drunker than most of them and he went after Mike's pants, yodeling something about the most beautiful legs in the world being right there if he remembered correctly.

While Carlo was on his knees removing Mike's shoes and pants, Mike stripped off his shirt and made muscles for us in his jockey shorts. Hayden shifted his drunken attention to Mike's crotch and Carlo looked up and caught him at it and giggled and stage-whispered, "Here's your chance to see it at last, lover," and he pulled Mike's shorts down. It was there all right, beautiful as ever, but Mike pretended not to be aware of what was going on down that way and went on making exaggerated muscle poses, riding down hard on his pelvic section and thrusting it all out toward Carlo's face.

Hayden muttered something complimentary like, "And I thought you were exaggerating," and moaned in a properly campy fashion. Then he moaned again, slightly in protest, when Bob hauled his stiff cock out of his shorts and started masturbating him. Carlo muttered Hayden hadn't seen anything yet and started giving his ex-lover's lovely dong a fast workout with both hands. Mike, the eternal exhibitionist, thrust against Carlo's strokes and the thing rammed out big and beautiful. Alex was sure Carlo would at least lick it and Hayden was sure, too, and escaped Bob to come up close. If Carlo licked it, then he could, too—he'd really swing on it, Alex figured. And Mike would let them.

Then Mike and Alex thought of Caswell at the same instant. Alex looked up. Caswell's face was almost unrecognizable—swollen, staring, bleak, his eyes like slits in a hideous mask. He wasn't looking at anybody and he hadn't moved a muscle but Alex had never seen such a figure of pure despair. Then Caswell's legs started twitching and he kind of doubled away. Mike grabbed Caswell by the legs and tumbled his rigid body down into his arms and huddled him off into the bedroom.

Everybody gasped and then Bob giggled gleefully and began handling Hayden's still stiff cock. Carlo staggered up and snatched Hayden away and they rolled onto the sofa in a drunken embrace.

Arnold and Roger were discussing an invitation to a Christmas party at the Pines. A friend had an all-year house and was giving a big holiday blast. There would be nothing to do but drink, gab and carry on . . .

Alex and Bob curled up and gossiped for a bit. Then Alex went back to the bedroom to check. The door was ajar and Alex glimpsed the turmoil. The record player was blasting out Tijuana Brass or they'd have all heard. Caswell was writhing on the bed, slashing at Mike, hitting him as hard as he could, biting, kicking, pulling his hair. There was blood on Mike's face and the bedcover. Overcoats and hats had been kicked into a corner. Mike was trying to restrain Caswell, pin his hands and legs down. Caswell kicked Mike viciously in the stomach and started up. Mike grabbed him again, ignoring the scratching and kicking. They were both panting and crying and Caswell kept himself turned away as far as he could. Mike was whispering, pleading. Caswell was still shivering convulsively whenever he was held rigid for an instant. Poor Mike, trapped with that, Alex had thought.

Had Mike realized then how badly Caswell needed help or did he just see it as an isolated incident, an accident that he had carelessly allowed to happen and had to suffer for, would wisely avoid in the future? But could it have been that crazy and still meant little, even though fifteen or twenty minutes later they came out calm, washed, even smiling a little? Could the nausea, the vertigo, the utter helplessness Alex had felt have been only surprise, dismay at unexpected violence, not the fear a normal person feels when faced with madness? Caswell had been so lonely, he was so young, he had already changed a lot, he could snap out of it. Viewed as a single relapse . . .

* * *

"Snap out of it, Alex," Arnold ordered. "So he got away. I saw you looking lustfully at the young trick. Was he a good cocksucker, Rog?"

"Awful. Like a girl, But he was mighty handy with those hot little hands."

"I guess I can stand seeing one fellow handle another one that way though it seems an utter waste of time to me," Arnold said. "What makes me puke is seeing somebody beat his own meat. At home they should do it yet if they're still that adolescent. That movie last night, when the stud pulled out of the pussy and jerked off for five minutes. Yuuk."

"I love those parts the most," Ralegh said. "I love to see that goo shoot out. I guess I am a little queer, Arnold. My brothers let me jerk them off any time I want to. But their wives are really queer. They all want to handle my meat. And my brother-in-law! He says Nadine's had enough kids. He wants to have the seventh one himself. He says if I—"

Ty stood up and yawned inelegantly. "Ralegh will spin out those infantile fantasies for hours and I must work. Alex, don't believe a word of it. He's a simple country mouse from Fort Lee who's determined to make the city mice notice him." He walked away with Arnold and Roger, speaking without lowering his voice of a party they were invited to at his place the next week.

Alex felt left out as usual, but he was also sure this elegant snob wanted another session with him but was too proud to show it. If Alex should offer to drive him home right now—but Alex balked. Tyree O'Neill was famous but there was something about him Alex loathed. His self-conscious manner was one thing—he satirized it himself. But under that was another phony layer and under that the real—what? Selfishness? Who wasn't selfish if you dug down a little? But if Tyree called—still, he wouldn't call; he'd expect Alex to call him. Well, he'd wait a long time for that call. Alex thought. And when they met in public, the greeting would be very distant. Alex knew he might as well cross this one off.

ROY

They rode up in the small neat elevator, a bit drunk and weary, smiling at each other in quiet mature anticipation. When the elevator stopped at the tenth floor and the door slid open, Alex led the way out. They crossed the wide empty corridor to a big white door. Alex inserted his key and went ahead of his guest.

Inside in the semi-dark Roy could see they were in a large room—the wide windows in the far wall overlooked the river and a glow came up from the streetlamps of the Drive. Alex closed the door and Roy turned to him. They kissed in an almost ritualistic way and stood for a moment pressed against each other, swaying a little, smiling, silently enjoying their peace and security and what they knew was to follow. Alex removed Roy's topcoat and his own, pressed a wall switch and two big lamps came on. Alex put the coats in a closet.

The room was squarish, quite large and rather barren. There was a sofa with a low table before it and there were big chairs at the ends of it. There was a love seat and there were more chairs and tables. A tall chest stood against the wall near them. Across the expanse of carpet there was a window seat under the three tall windows and on each side of the room a wide opening to another room.

"Shall we have a drink?" Alex asked.

"One more," Roy said and followed Alex as he moved through the opening at the right. The dining room had a simple mahogany table and four rather square-built chairs around it. Against the far wall there was a red lacquer cabinet and over it a big painting.

"The painting is familiar," Roy said. "I think I've seen it before." Alex touched the wall switch and the overhead light came on. The painting was a contemporary oil but the effect was almost of watercolor—blue, gray and white in soft masses and sweeps. Out of them, as if out of a fog, a few forms emerged or promised to emerge—buildings and a bridge perhaps. "Yes, I saw it in John's exhibition two or three years ago. I wanted to buy it but we didn't have any extra money. September is always a teacher's worst month."

"Do you know John well?"

"Yes. We have a couple of his smaller pictures. He comes up to dinner sometimes. He's one of the few gay friends I've introduced to Nina. You knew I was married, didn't you?"

"Yes." Alex looked at Roy curiously.

Roy was not as tall as Alex and was even broader. He was thirty-five or so. His short, light brown hair was beginning to thin, and he wore glasses. His clothes were very conventional. He might be a commuter to Rye or Scarsdale, an editor in some big publishing house or another architect. But through his upper-class ordinariness shone an exuberance, a zest that was rare. He seemed to radiate health and vitality—they shone on his lips and cheeks. It was impossible to imagine him depressed or bored.

"Somehow I never can actually believe anybody who is married is really gay."

"You'll find out," Roy said grinning. The light played on his full red underlip and his white teeth. His mouth enchanted Alex.

"I know but I still don't believe," Alex went on. "You know Mike Kincade, don't you? When I found out about him I could never see him quite the same way again."

"Mike Kincade is married?"

"Was. Twice, he says. Maybe he'd say three times now. Once to a girl and then to Carl Castella and then to Caswell." Alex flicked off the light and went into the kitchen and turned on the light there. Roy followed him and stood by while Alex got out glasses and ice and scotch.

"I haven't seen Mike for months," Roy said. "What is he doing now? I don't really know him but I used to see him around when I first moved into New York. I had a big letch for him. Then I heard something about what happened before Christmas."

"He's—waiting."

"Waiting? The boy died, didn't he?"

"No," Alex said. "He's still barely alive. It's been two weeks and a day now."

"Oh," Roy said. "Somehow I got the impression the boy died a day or so later. Are you a close friend of Mike's?"

"Yes, I think so. Mike called me from the hospital that day, to bring him some things. He didn't even have shoes or socks on. And later he asked me to feed his cat. I brought Simon up here when Mike wouldn't leave the hospital. He's around somewhere, probably on my bed." He handed Roy a drink.

"Thanks. Shall we go dispossess him?"

"Easier said than done. I find him curled up behind my knees nearly every morning. And on those lucky mornings when there's someone else in the bed, he's between us."

"Lucky Simon-Pierre."

Alex led the way through the dining room and living room into the library. A cat was curled up in a wing chair, a sleek black and white cat, with his paw over his eyes. Alex paused to pat an ancient dachshund who whimpered in her pillowed wicker basket. "The big room's fine for parties but I hardly ever sit in there. I read and work in here and watch TV. Sophie loves television. Simon ignores TV, Sophie and me when I'm awake."

"It's certainly a nice spacy place," Roy said. "You're lucky to have it. You should see what Nina and the kids and I jostle around in."

"I asked Mike to share it with me last fall. There's another bedroom and bath beyond the kitchen, with a separate entrance. But that was the day he ran into Caswell again. Did you ever see Caswell?"

"No, but I heard he was—is very attractive."

"He came back into town that day with us. He sat in the back like a little kid in his striped t-shirt and dungarees and sneakers. Mike had his arm over the back of the seat and I knew they were hanging on to each other—they both seemed afraid they would lose contact. Then Caswell knelt against the back of the seat and Mike put his arm around him. It couldn't have been very comfortable for either of them and I suggested to Mike he get into the back seat but he said it wasn't necessary. I couldn't see it would look any funnier, the two of them necking in the back seat, than Caswell in the middle of the car that way. But they didn't hear much I said. I'd never seen Mike that hypnotized by anyone though I'd heard how he and Carlo practically carried on at parties, even after they'd lived together a year."

Alex turned on the light in the bedroom and set down his drink and pulled back the covers of the big bed. Then he took off Roy's jacket and started with it toward the closet.

"Don't put it away," Roy said, "I can't stay. Remember? Just put it on a chair where I can find it."

He started to undo his tie but Alex came over and untied it for him, unbuttoned his shirt and slipped it off him and put them on a chair over his jacket. Roy was taking his t-shirt off over his head when Alex returned. Alex kissed Roy's chest, knelt and untied Roy's shoes and slipped them off. Roy stood quietly while Alex unzipped his pants and pulled them and his jockey shorts off together. Before he rose to put them on the chair, he took Roy's thick stiffening cock into his mouth briefly and swung on it. Roy smiled and caressed Alex's bristly round skull and little ears. Alex rose and put the pants and shorts neatly on the chair. Roy lounged on the bed, flipping off his socks and drinking and watching Alex undress.

Alex put his jacket and shoes into the closet, then his tie, shirt and trousers. Roy eyed the wide muscular back, the heavy arms and thighs and calves, the neat ass. Without turning, Alex snapped off the light.

"No fair!" Roy cried.

Alex snapped on the bedside light—a double lamp that threw one strong clear beam across the bed and a dimmer orange glow upward. In the orange radiance he made muscles for Roy, grinning, flexing his biceps one-two, one-two, rubbed his basket suggestively and stripped off his shorts and hopped into bed beside Roy. They clasped each other's naked firm bodies in eager arms and kissed and caressed for a while. Then they broke to sip their drinks.

"Warm enough?" Alex asked.

"God, yes. But I have high blood pressure even without

anyone like you around. Man, what a body, It's almost as much fun to feel big muscles like that get hard as it is to feel a big cock get hard."

"Almost but not quite?"

"Almost but not quite. And when a guy's got both—sheer heaven, I say. I love women but oh, you beautiful men. Yum yum. I'm a simple soul—I just love the best of everything. Mmm, good scotch too." And he took a big swig.

"You know Ty O'Neill, don't you?" Alex asked, almost too casually.

Roy put his drink down. "Sure."

Alex went on. "You mentioned him at Murray's tonight. Those Garland records were so loud I couldn't hear all you were saying but I gathered you knew O'Neill pretty well. I've met him."

"Got a yen for him?" Roy asked.

"No. We had a small do once and I had the idea he wanted to go on with it a little further, but that's not the point. When Mike asked me that day to get his things—his clothes and all—he said he'd left Ty O'Neill in the apartment and he might still be there though he didn't imagine so. I went right down to Ninety-fifth Street but he wasn't there."

"Yes, he'd have gone long before that."

"Look, what happened?" Alex asked. "Mike wouldn't talk about it. I couldn't very well insist at that moment and ever since then there's always been a nurse or a doctor in the room."

"I guess no one person knows exactly what happened—all of it, anyway."

"All right, Mr. Pirandello, no one ever knows everything. But here I am half involved and more than half in the dark. I still can't figure it out—there are pieces missing. I thought maybe Ty told you about it. After all, it isn't the kind of thing you run into every day and if you're on the same kind of terms with Ty I am with Mike—although Mike doesn't tell me a hell of a lot when you get down to it."

Alex looked at Roy who turned away from his questioning look to drink. Alex went on. "I've got Simon here. I paid the rent on Mike's apartment yesterday so his stuff won't be thrown into the street for another month anyway. I called his school and told them Monday they'd better get a substitute for a while. I didn't know whether to tell those bastards about Caswell and I certainly didn't want to hear them pretend to be shocked and grieved and gloating right through their grief. Maybe they already knew and had the decency not to say anything. It was in the papers. Look, Roy, what was Ty O'Neill doing there and Mike undressed? If he had anything to do with the accident, I'll—"

"You'll what?"

"I think I'll kill him."

"Then kill him," Roy said. "You've got my permission."

"You do know," Alex said.

"Ty called me as soon as he saw what had happened. He'd stood at the bedroom window and watched Mike tearing down the street after Caswell. Ty saw Caswell run into the West End traffic and he saw the cab hit him and the crowd gather and Mike push through. When the ambulance came and Mike didn't come back, Ty phoned me. He hadn't moved out of the room. I'd just come from a faculty meeting and was taking off my shoes. Nina was out picking up the kids. Ty said, 'I'm standing here stark naked and Mike's out there with Caswell and Caswell's dead and it's my fault.' No, first he said, 'Roy, I've done it again.' I couldn't imagine what he was jabbering about—he sounded drunk or something. I didn't know where he was or who he meant by Mike and I'd never heard of Caswell and anyway Ty had a tendency to overdramatize anything he's mixed up in. I tried to get a few straight facts out of him but he said he was coming right over as soon as he dressed. I came to and said Nina and the kids were there. I heard the ambulance siren over the phone, as it left, I suppose. I asked how about a bar. Ty said it wasn't anything he could talk about in a bar, for me to take a cab down to his place and he'd do the same. So I put my shoes back on, left a note and hurried down to Charlton Street. On the way I recalled what I'd heard about Mike but I couldn't recall any Caswell."

"If you were out at the Island last summer, you might have heard of him as Cas. He was talked about a lot."

"I've never been there and from what I've heard—"

"Take Nina and the kids to the Pines for the summer," Alex said. "It's full of ambidextrous papas. Half the population is schoolteachers. But when you got to Charlton Street—what?"

"Nothing. Ty was home when I got there, having a brandy and dressing to go out again and well over his urge to tell me all. He finally said he'd been at a friend's and the lover came in and misunderstood the situation and ran out and got knocked down accidentally in the traffic. And it wasn't Ty's fault at all by then. He hoped no one knew he'd seen as much as he had, he hadn't seen enough to testify and he was much too busy to get mixed up in a lawsuit against a cab company."

"That crud," Alex said. "I knew there was something sleazy about him when I met him that one time."

"Congratulations," Roy said. "Most people get the impression he's a darling little devil and the cruditude comes as a shock later."

"He said he was stark naked? Mike jumped into his pants and pulled on a sweater before he ran out. Hell, if he'd run right out, he might have caught Caswell. That's irony—Mike's the biggest exhibitionist I know and he stops to put on his pants. You can bet he's thought of that often enough."

"Anybody'd take that much time. After all, he was only going to chase the kid up the street."

"That's true," Alex said, "he didn't know Caswell was suicidal. But what was Mike doing in bed with Ty O'Neill? That's the part I really can't fathom. If you'd seen Mike and Caswell together this fall—"

"It happens," Roy said.

"No. Caswell was in love for the first time. It was the first time he'd ever been loved, too, I'm sure. But Mike was just as much in love as Caswell was—I'll swear to that. And even if he hadn't been, the last thing he'd have done was hurt the kid that way. At a dinner party they gave, Mike made a false move when he and everybody else was drunk and when he realized how it must look to Caswell, he was horror-stricken. Caswell wasn't just a new playmate. The day after he took Caswell home with him from Riis Park, he called the head of the school he'd resigned from and agreed to go back to them and I know how he loathed the place. Caswell didn't want to go back to college and Mike didn't want to have him out of his sight so he helped Caswell formally withdraw and they planned Caswell would start his freshman year next semester at Hunter or some place here in town. Caswell hardly set a foot outside the apartment except when he went out with Mike or to the grocery store. Mike must have known Caswell would be right back. I can't see Mike taking a chance like that, even if Ty O'Neill was the most irresistible male in the world."

"Maybe subconsciously he wanted Caswell to walk in on them," Roy said. "Maybe he expected Caswell to join them. It seems to me half the beauties I meet want me to go home with them and have three-way sessions with them and their lovers. It's usually a ball."

"Well, they might have got around to that in a year or two but Mike knew how upset Caswell got if he looked at anyone else. Mike said he was even a little jealous of me. I was flattered but I was also not expected to be around so much. I tell you they had the real thing going—Romeo and Juliet, Tristan and Isolde... It was love. And they didn't just love each other, they were becoming each other. By the end of the first month, I could hardly tell which one I was talking to on the phone. And when I was there, one of them would start a sentence and the other would finish and I only realized later what they'd done—I don't think they realized at all. And somehow they always managed to sit and stand so you could see them both—they were one unit, you couldn't have one half without the other. Mike wouldn't even let me gossip about people Caswell didn't know yet but they went out to the theater and a few parties and Caswell was getting to know a good many of Mike's old friends. I gather Caswell had almost no friends of his own."

"Complete identification," Roy said. "I've never been sure I wanted that. You can't go that far with a woman."

"I certainly wouldn't want to," Alex said. "But I've never managed to get very far with another man, either."

"Then you didn't want to," Roy said.

"Not enough anyway. Have you?" Alex asked.

"No. If I'd met you about ten years ago—but I didn't. I settle for little spasms of identification, I guess. Sometimes when the other man comes, I feel it so strongly I'm not sure whether I came too or not and literally I have to check to see."

"I've never even gone that far," Alex said. "There's so much I hold back from. Well, Mike never holds back. He always lets himself go. He dares risk whatever it is I won't risk. And wish

I had. He and Carlo had that same kind of identification, but not to the same degree because he and Caswell were more alike to start with. Mike was older, of course, and had been around more and was a lot more sure of himself, more stable. But Caswell was so quick and he loved Mike so much. He trusted Mike—oh, my God. I cannot imagine what happened."

"Maybe Mike will straighten it all out for you some time, Alex. Now lie down, relax. Or better still, lie down and stiffen up. You've relaxed too much."

"You're right. Thinking about it isn't going to help. And all my chatter can ruin what promises to be the most fun I've had in a long time." He ran his hands appreciatively over Roy's firm, smooth chest and midriff.

"Thanks," Roy said. "What are you smiling about?"

"How hot and smooth your body is!" Alex turned off the white light and they lay in the orange dusk, gently loving each other. Suddenly Alex rolled away and sat up. "What did O'Neill mean, it was all his fault?"

Roy sat up, too, and drank a sip, "I don't know, Alex. I honestly don't know. As I said, he dramatizes. I suppose he meant Caswell ran out because Mike was in bed with someone—he was the someone—ergo—"

"Then why wouldn't he talk about it?"

"Ty says I'm his best friend, his oldest friend and all that crap but he still pulls stuff like that on me. He did tell me he and Mike had a fling at Fire Island last summer over Labor Day and kind of picked up where they'd left off."

"Yeah. That time I met him at Roger's and Arnold's he said the session with Mike was the most exciting he'd ever had. But I doubt it was so special for Mike. Frankly I found your friend Tyree a rather poor cocksucker."

"No, he's more adept at being a good lay, I gather," Roy said.

"Oh? Then that might account for something. Mike was somewhat hooked on him, even wrote him some poems. Do you know a blond kid who lives in Philadelphia—named Ralegh Bronsten?"

"No," Roy said.

"He was in on the Fire Island doings," Alex said. "And even hotter to see Mike again than Ty was."

"Oh?"

"He also claimed his round with Mike was the climax of his career, so to speak," Alex said.

"When was this party where you met Ty and the Bronsten kid?" Roy asked.

"It was Sunday—brunch—the Sunday before the mess-up on Thursday," Alex said.

"Yes," Roy said. "Ty's show closed in Philadelphia the weekend before that and he's working on a new one he knows isn't any better. He's been pretty frustrated all around. If the Bronsten kid raved about Kincade that way, it would have been all Ty needed to set him afire to get into bed again with Kincade. He'd probably filed the whole Fire Island bit away as past history until Bronsten made him realize what he was missing."

"And Caswell or no Caswell—"

"He'd certainly never let anything like a new lover stand in his way."

"But how did he manage to get Mike to do it?" Alex asked. "There's the real catch in it all."

"He managed. That much we're sure of, aren't we?"

"Yes. But how? How? You have to remember Mike was as much in love with Caswell as Caswell was with him. What could Tyree O'Neill have done or said? He couldn't have blackmailed Mike or bought him or forced him, for God's sake. Mike was naked in that bed with O'Neill because he wanted to be."

Roy finished his drink and grinned amiably at Alex. "What I have begun to suspect—but please don't tell me if I'm right—is that you dragged me home with you tonight less because you wanted my hot body than because you heard me mention Ty O'Neill."

Alex looked a little chagrined but managed a weak placatory smile. "Stinker," he said. "Suspicious brute. Married man."

"All right, I'll accept your fervent denial of ulterior motives."

"Either reason would have been enough, you vain critter," Alex said. "Two was icing on the cake."

"Hm. Which is icing and which is cake? I'll believe the one I want to believe if you get a proper hard-on the next time I kiss you. Meanwhile, Mr. D.A., honey . . . " Roy rose and went to the chair where his clothes were.

Alex bounded up in alarm. He'd gone too far. The dreamboat was preparing to blow the whistle and pull away from the dock. Or was Roy going to produce some evidence—a letter he had in his pocket or something. Roy took out a pack of Parliaments and put one in his mouth and lighted it. Alex sighed deeply but silently and moved an ashtray to the table beside Roy's part of the bed.

Roy rolled his pillow into a bolster and reclined against it in reach of the ashtray. Then he slipped his free arm around Alex's back and drew him close. Alex snuggled up, his face against Roy's shoulder and one arm down around Roy's waist, the other hand roaming over his chest and belly and fooling with Roy's genitalia as the younger man talked.

"You're a sweet butch-looking angel, Alexy, and you've managed to survive very well but I think it's time someone told you about a certain kind of people—people like Tyree O'Neill, who is only one of a few million of the type I'm lecturing on. Tyree O'Neill is selfish. He is also just about as smart as a snake. While he was still at Yale, I arranged a dinner party for him and a youth he was intent on seducing. Tyree had tried a number of approaches but none led him into the pants so he begged me to set him up for a sure happy ending. I borrowed a friend's apartment because I was still living out in the country at that time. I invited a couple of others so it would look very innocent and social—even had an odd number. I cooked, I went to no little expense. Ty and stalwart friend did not show.

"I called the hotel where Ty had said they would stay. The hotel had never heard of them. I called New Haven and was told O'Neill was in New York. At eleven we ate the soggy meal and fled to the Ever Hard.

"The next week I had a sad soggy note from Ty about being ill in the infirmary all weekend, so ill he was under sedation and too much asleep to have anyone call me. A year later when I mentioned I'd called and been told he was in New York, he gaily regaled me with the truth—or what had become Ty's truth about it all.

"He'd taken the Milwaukee hussar to a fancier hotel, made a

pass at him in the shower ten minutes after they'd checked in, had his will of the lad for a couple of hours thereafter and had been so impressed by the hussar's long lance that he had fed him, drunk him, and waltzed him off to the baths to show him off in the steam room for an hour, allowing only the loveliest to swing on the hussar's unflagging but thoroughly drained equipment while Ty relieved those special lovelies of their turbulent spunk. Anyway, we never saw the Milwaukee marvel and Ty stood me up as he had before."

"I hate people like that," Alex said, "I don't see why anyone has to lie."

"You don't lie?"

"No," Alex said.

"If I tell you why O'Neill lies, will you keep it to yourself? He's becoming a little famous and it's tempting to quote what his old friends say about him."

"I won't quote," Alex said.

"The dull truth is, Tyree O'Neill is almost," Roy said.

"Almost?"

"Yep. Almost—almost anything you can name. Bright, talented, the darling of the talented set. His family out in Pennsylvania is almost in the social elite—almost but not quite. And Tyree is ambitious and envious. Emulous. He never has enough."

"Sex?" Alex asked.

"Sex, money—anything. He doesn't quite have a big cock or a lot of sex appeal. He is not quite a real beauty and he is not the flashing genius of a scene designer he'd like everyone to take him for. But he gives a damned good show—he acts modest, makes flattering appeals and works like a dog to make a brilliant impression. And he stops at absolutely nothing to get what he wants or to outdo someone. I've known Ty for ten years and I've come to think of him as a bundle of aching needs."

"Everybody needs."

"Sure," Roy said. "But you and I don't need anything the way he feels he needs everything. He doesn't believe in anything except his own immediate desires and the next step in some long-range project that will get him what he wants. He's so busy scheming and maneuvering he sometimes doesn't even have time to enjoy what he finally gets. He's a chaser."

"That's a type I'm familiar with," Alex said.

"Man, there are thousands of them. And most of them aren't gay, either. It's a basic human weakness. Or strength, if you admire that kind of ruthless initiative and aggrandizement. What can you say to them? What does one ever know certainly except what he wants to do at the moment? Do I know what you want right this minute?"

"At least I know what I want. And I'm getting it. The lowdown on O'Neill and a hot body in my mitts. And I know what I'm going to want in about two minutes and I'm going to get that, too."

"You're queer," Roy said. "But even if I act as if this is exactly what I want, too, how can you be sure it really is what I want? Maybe at the party tonight I really wanted Patrick Long and you really wanted that Negro editor with the suave tailoring that both concealed and accentuated his shoulders and other nonintellectual assets."

"Answer—Pat Long's a lousy lay. He's got equipment to spare but he hasn't got the ass to swing it. He also has a lovely ass and he hasn't got the balls to keep that rolling. And I don't get started with Negroes."

"You're almost as difficult to argue with as Tyree," Roy said.

"You said you've known him ten years," Alex said. "Was he a student of yours?"

"Yes, I was teaching in a little college in Pennsylvania. Just married, first baby on the way, and bright-eyed for somebody to play with until Nina was available again. And there was Tyree in my humanities class—shy, lovely, and ready for the plucking. We glimmered hopefully at each other but were inhibited and did nothing. He thought I was an unimaginative married man and I thought he was an innocent virgin. Example of how far wrong what you think is right can be. I also was flirting with a sturdy blond devil in one of my other classes and he kept my hands full—literally—for a while.

"When I didn't take steps to waylay Tyree, he gave himself to a fat shrewish art teacher who made passes at all the boys who got in arm's reach and connected in about six cases out of ten. From fat old Leon, about three months later, Tyree learned

I was gayer than I chose to appear. Ty came right into my office and sat on my desk and told me he loved me and we'd both been fools and he was never again going to try to figure out what the other man was wanting or thinking—he was going to take what he wanted if he could get it, no matter how many wives and kiddies swarmed in the offing, and he wasn't going to be stuck with any more makeshifts like Leon, either. Tyree had told bitch Leon he was in love with me the first minute Leon had laid a hand on him and it had taken Leon three months to tell Ty he had a chance with me. In a way I felt involved in the genesis of Ty's philosophy if not exactly responsible for it. And I've heard him repeat that policy of operation any number of times since then and seen it in action even more often."

"Doesn't his need to repeat it to you sound as if he weren't too sure it was right? He knows you don't think it's right."

"He knows and he says I'm a fool to consider the feelings of anyone beyond my immediate family. No one considers my feelings. I waste my time trying to help people who don't want my help, don't need my help or consideration, would be better off if I left them strictly to their own devices. Maybe so, maybe not. All I know is we have a wonderful time without scheming and grabbing and shoving any one else out of the way, and Nina and I have a lot of nice friends and Ty has no one he can tell anything to except me and he's pushed himself into some messes that would turn my hair white."

"Hey, don't hint," Alex said. "You told me he informed you on the telephone he'd done it again. What did he do before?"

"You're worse than my students. Theory bores them, they want the lurid details about Lord Byron's sex life. Well, a lot of the early chapters of Ty's loves and crimes were in the papers though I don't think his name was mentioned. And a lot of people know what the papers didn't dare say because what everybody knows is going on is still hard to prove in a libel suit. I helped Ty get into Yale as a graduate student although his record at our little lyceum hadn't been very promising. I knew a couple of people and all that. The second year he was there I went to teach in a fashionable private school in Connecticut that about doubled my previous salary, so I was nearby and the natural recipient of his periodic confessions, so to speak. Propinquity if not affinity. Like some tumbles into the hay."

"Man, if we were to be more propinquitous it would probably hurt a little and the affinity can wait another minute."

"How about an affinity for dishing absent acquaintances?"

"I'll go along with that, too," Alex said, "I'm all ears."

"Liar," Roy said. "There's one part of you that isn't listening at all and is just waiting to get on to more interesting affinities. Patience, John Thomas, you'll have your inning."

"Do you mean—"

"No, not unless you insist or something," Roy said. "Meanwhile back at the campus. Ty had an affair with a local socialite—an ex-dancer, the darling of Broadway for a few seasons, tall and slender with butch little ginger curls tumbling into his huge blue eyes and a thick cock you can still see in photo collections with a dinky little coke bottle beside it for comparison purposes. His name was Philip Hastings. He became a producer's assistant and, in the course of raising backing, ran into an ugly heiress with a rubber-goods fortune of her own and fat settlement from her first husband who'd used her capital to become the king of the toilet-seat manufacturers or some such. That husband left her, Dorothy—I can't recall her then last name—for her prettier girl friend. It was a triangle—the wife and girl friend carried on girl fashion until the girl friend discovered the husband could be detached and reattached without damage to his fortune. So deserted Dorothy married Philip Hastings who back in his modeling days had been Philip Hasselbauer. Philip was a shy sentimental charmer and perfectly honest.

"He really was shy and honest. I met him after he fell in love with Ty and they'd been meeting quietly for a while. Philip was afraid if anyone found out, Ty's academic career would be jeopardized. But our Ty knew the purse strings were in Dorothy's hands so he played up to her. He slept with her a little and lied to her a lot about not being Philip's lover. Philip took it for granted she knew and Ty saw to it no questions were asked but when Ty found out her lawyers were adamant on the subject of no more investing in New York shows, he dropped Dorothy and let her know what a fool she had been.

"Dorothy saw she was bound to be the loser every time and

committed suicide very discreetly. But she let Philip know what Ty had done and she let Ty know how his lying had caused all the trouble. And Tyree confessed to me and thereby purged himself, I suppose. And somewhere along the line he convinced himself Dorothy led him on with hints about producing a show he wanted to design until she'd got what she wanted from him. I may write a book about Tyree some day. If you still want to kill him, I could work that in, too. Your killing him would be very poetic—pure, detached justice."

"It's very illustrative," Alex said. "And I won't tell it and spoil your book. And if I run into Tyree O'Neill again I'll be tempted to commit that murder. Maybe choke him to death. But he's just the kind that would go down biting and clawing. The thing to do would be to find someone else I loathe as much and get Ty O'Neill down on him and hold his head down. But I don't loathe anyone else that much and never did. And I'm in this mess, too. I let O'Neill know how happy Mike and Caswell were—he had to prove he could break it up."

"I expect that was part of it but I suspect his main impulse was even simpler," Roy said. "When he heard how hot that younger demon was for Mike, he suddenly developed an implacable desire to have back what he'd tossed aside months before. The silly part of Ty's behavior is he doesn't even know what he wants until someone else has it or wants it. He can't bear to be left out."

"I wish the bastard could see Mike sitting there in that hospital right now," Alex said. "The doctors said Caswell wasn't so badly hurt he might not live. But he doesn't come back to life and he doesn't die. And Mike sits there waiting."

"Everybody is waiting for something. Guess what I'm waiting for."

"This." Alex drew Roy closer to him and kissed him. For a moment they lay holding each other so tightly each could feel the other's breathing and heartbeat. Then they slackened and lay back smiling. Simon chose that moment to hop up on the bed and creep between them but he was allowed to snuggle with them only very briefly.

MIKE

Gray light.

Doctor Brady checking the chart, straightening up, holding his nose. His glasses in the gray light looked blue; they became more intensely blue, they expanded and contracted, pulsated. Why is he holding his nose? As if he knows something here is rotten. Rotten flesh, rotten dreams, rotten mortality, rotten morality. Nothing here smells bad, it's in his nose.

It isn't Doctor Brady, it's Doctor Zeeman. Brady is at least polite. Zeeman pretends he knows more but Brady knows his nose pulsates. Zeeman thinks he knows but he stinks, he's the expensive expert on internal sabotage. Caswell ate his sabot but it was Ty's sabot like a taxi bull—exactly at five in the afternoon.

The cabdriver Strauss is in the doorway behind us. He sweats. He is silent, accusing us. He screamed to the cop, tried to scream away a world that crashed. But now he isn't saying anything. His eyes are pale blue eggs, the iris floats in the white almost indistinguishable. Doctor Zeeman shoves right through him and clatters off down the *corrida*. His pipe vomits a low-rolling gaseous noxious obnoxious train-trail that winds like entrails, expands, dissipates, corrupts the rose. Tobacco is good for roses but this tobacco wilts these roses. These are the rarest roses. They will not bloom again.

The cold wave rolls, it rolls away, cold, cold. The roses will not come again. Unless there's warmth in the earth, in the center, the unstill point as the earth turns, the warm glow. The stalk grows, wetted and warmed—the stalk grows in throbs, horny-thorny. The blue-green leaves, heavily veined with purple, wrap the thickening stalk—like tobacco leaves they must be pulled off. Pull back the leaves of me so the bud can bloom, my burgeoning bud, my huge aching bud will bloom, flame, burn into the blue, hot into cool, hot into wet-hot. Oh man, your mouth feels good on my hot stalk, I want to bloom and bloom and . . .

Bong-dong-dong. Dang. Wait, man, my dong clangs too. Blue, cold, alone cold, stripped to the ache. Voices. We are never alone, O beloved. O lost and by the wind grieved, Caswell, come back . . .

Gray light: morning. The sheet off and me with a hard-on up to here. Cigarette smoke. That bong-donging in the hall. Was Sylvester here again, playing with my cock? I dreamed about those roses drooping over there by the window. The nurse didn't take them out last night. I dreamed I was going to bloom. God, I need to do something. My balls ache. Sylvester must have been down on me and I was ready to come. Why didn't he take me and then answer the damned bell? Or is it Mickey's duty-night? But that old auntie doesn't smoke. Sweet old Auntie Mickey and when he takes his teeth out—all right Kincade, enough already.

Poor old Mickey, he never gets enough. Probably gets more than you suspect. More than you ever did in your best week. Just acts pathetic. Was he ever a good actor onstage? Probably not. Just another show stud like you. He claimed when he was young he was swung on by everybody in town. Couldn't get enough of it. Loved it. Now he swings as if he couldn't get enough of it. Knows how the young ones love it. Vicarious loving it.

Anyway it wasn't Tony who was handling me. He's been gone for over a week and never would reciprocate, just squeezed it a little and peeped at it when it got hard. Why does every ginnie think he's doing you a favor to let you suck off his little prick? But Tony was cute, with the map of Old Ireland on his mug. I give up.

Damn the sheet. Bang, my book to the floor. Caswell didn't waken. Waken Caswell, O I wouldst thou couldst . . .

Proust. I was reading Proust last night, I'd read *Swann's Way* and *Within a Budding Grove.* Last week I read *The Captive*—Edie brought me *The Captive* instead of *The Guermantes Way* I asked for.

Edie tries hard, tries to be efficient, shrewd. She's a mess. She wants to be warm and earth-motherly but she's so cold her teeth chatter, poor dear. Thank God she's got money. No more of that fight I had when I first came here. Eccentricity in an expensive double room is a different matter. That cramped little single room they put him in first had a window that opened onto life though. Life poured in from the tenement next door—smells, yells, radios and all. I hoped it would get to Caswell and wind around him and hold him, help me hold him and draw him back. Like the street sounds and the village voices singing and bickering and being alive in *Intermezzo.* Translated *The Enchanted.* No wonder Giraudoux always fails, translated into subwayese. Where else do the street sounds call the heroine back from death?

Look, we haven't come through. What holds us back? Pusillanimity.

Witherspoon for once was not pusillanimous. He came. He sat on that chair, his decent gray stiff hat he doffed from off his decent gray hair, his decently clipped gray hair, his decently expensive four-in-hand knotted carefully. Sitting there with his decently expensive little gift-offering in his manicured fingers—what did he bring? wasn't it an enameled pill box? where did it go?

Witherspoon confessed to me—confessed, pleading to be let into certain sacred precincts, expiating certain sins of slippery omission and stony expulsion, sending Caswell away at Christmastime, just a year ago! The Witherspoon confessed that years ago he sat in a hospital room such as this one while a young man's life ebbed. Tom Caswell's, Caswell's uncle's life. And Tom was younger than Caswell is, a big, strong flirtatious southern boy, senior at Quillquiar's. They had been driving back from a football game, for once just the two of them alone in the car. And then the accident.

Not Witherspoon's fault. No one ever doubted that for an instant. He wasn't fondling the boy or anything like that, he wouldn't have had the nerve even twenty years ago. And he always drove most carefully. But he had to explain to Tom Caswell it wasn't his fault. Only he never got a chance, just as I have not...

It was because of Tom Caswell—uncle and all that—Quillquiar's took Caswell in for his senior year. He knew he was on probation—they had no choice when he failed to meet his obligations. It was practically automatic. Witherspoon was pleading with me to forgive that bit of treachery. And confessing that once he risked all the world to sit doggedly in a lad's hospital room. And reminding me that other men have suffered from aborted expiation and thwarted penance, so the guilt seeped back into the system and colored it poison. What guilt had he? Just for once alone with a youth he lusted after, enjoying his company even if he didn't dare touch him, establishing confidence? Didn't dare touch him though the youth twinkled his eyes and giggled his southern giggle and kept sliding a not-too-casual hand over a rich bulge in the tight chinos—confidence established for other meetings? And the confidence established betrayed by the accident he hadn't somehow kept off them.

And how did Witherspoon know why I sit here week after week? No one knows except Edie and Doctor Brady and Alex and they only know I have to tell Caswell something if he ever wakes up, something that may make all the difference. And Ty knows why, if he knows I am here at all. Alex said yesterday he'd heard Ty had gone to Bermuda. I wish it were Zanzibar.

If I met Ty now, what would I do? He's loathsome in all that vicious deliberate lying. Yet I can't hate him—he's too pathetic. I hate myself for being so easily fooled by a shy eager manner and an outrageous lie. Shy! Sly, ingratiating, scheming egomaniac. Was he only pretending in bed too? So grateful, so fired up, so swept away he swept me away and made me forget Caswell, the deliberate lie, everything bad or good outside our own bodies. Until I heard Caswell on the stairs and before he'd even put his key into the lock I knew how we had been betrayed. Ty's clothes and mine all over the living room—how could I have done that to Caswell even if every word Ty said... But Caswell wasn't supposed to come back until six and was supposed to act as if he didn't know. What a fool I was to believe for an instant he would have been a party to such a charade. I must have wanted another time with Ty an awful lot to have let myself be flummoxed that way. And now I can't imagine my ever wanting Ty at all.

Was it Ty I really wanted even then or was it the new relationship I thought Caswell and I were working into by sharing Ty? According to the artful fabrication I was supposed to have my little diversion with Ty to balance out Caswell's lapse of the day before. Each of us having deserted the other momentarily with Ty and neither mentioning him, equally guilty and circumspect. But of course Ty knew I wouldn't succumb so easily, even with the occasion arranged—Caswell gone alone to a film for the first time—so Ty had to tell me the whole story of how he'd dropped by the day before while I was still at school, thinking I'd already be on vacation but of course I wasn't. And Caswell was the charming little host and after one drink simply took Tyree right in his chair. And then the qualms and tears and the plea that Ty come back the next day and even things out while Caswell sat grimly in a movie. And Ty only too willing to comply now he'd been the unsuspecting partner of Caswell's only lapse from virtue.

How did Ty know I'd believe Caswell had gone down on him in that abrupt way? He'd evidently heard about Caswell's exploits last summer and knew I knew. He made up the whole episode to undermine my resistance, he wasn't there at all the day before. But if he wasn't, how did he know Caswell would be out on Thursday afternoon? Or did Ty make up the whole damned lie after he'd seen Caswell leave? Perhaps Ty even spoke to Caswell on the street and found out Caswell was going shopping for my present and that I was due any minute. But Caswell would have gone back and let Ty in, insisted he come in and wait, and I found Ty in the street outside our place. And Ty probably didn't even know what Caswell looked like. But if Ty saw him come out of that house and had heard so much about him, even had heard him described . . . it doesn't matter. Going over all those possibilities again and again is nonsense. Even if Ty didn't lie to me at all, I betrayed Caswell. Even if he did relapse for a few minutes into the old pattern, I didn't have to jump into bed with Ty O'Neill. But I told myself it was what Caswell wanted . . .

If Ty wasn't there, how did he know Caswell and I hadn't been sharing lovers right along? Lots of fellows who love each other very much still do that. Ty must have been telling me part of the truth. He probably made a pass at Caswell and got a curt refusal and the session with me was more revenge than reunion.

Caswell might have mentioned then he'd be out the next day but I'd probably be in after the merriment at school was over. That must have been the way it was. And Ty knew Caswell might be back any minute and hoped he'd walk in on us! Ty had only to alter the facts a little and I was convinced. And laid.

If that's the way it was, I suppose I should be flattered Ty came up there to see me on Wednesday but the trip back on Thursday was hardly complimentary. It doesn't matter. It only matters that Caswell came in, with his Christmas present for me in his hands, and realized I was in the bedroom carrying on with someone else. In our home, in our private refuge from all that, our enchanted castle. And doing it brazenly as if I didn't care what he felt, symbolically dumping him out. No wonder he fled and won't come back.

Caswell, how pale you are. The terrain of your bed grows more gaunt, the thin peaks of your knees and chest pierce my numb consciousness. Everything I love is strewn broken on that bed and all my wishes and all the doctors can't put it back the way it was. Nothing goes back to the way it was. We can't go home again in this world and there isn't any other. What's over is done, even if I am not done with it.

No morning drum arouses Caswell.

When Caswell dies—cancel that, take it back, run back the reel! Not even the smell of such a possibility is allowed in this room. Caswell will live, the crisis is past, he is mending. Today or tomorrow he will stir. Another day he will open his eyes. He will see me, hear me whispering how we were both betrayed, how much I need him. And he'll smile and get well and we'll live happily ever after.

All right, Kincade. You've had your euphoric fix for the day. Back to earth, Buster. The kid lies there barely breathing, dead to the world. He's lain there for seventeen days now. The chances are practically nil for consciousness, much less recovery. All that apparatus can keep him going only so long. Then—well, Edith will take care of the funeral. She probably has it all arranged for. Only the date remains to be finalized.

I'll be gone. Mark's in Florida. That Christmas card from Lainey reopens possibilities. Frisco, hello? I hope she's not hung up on marijuana or some dyke. And maybe Robby's out there. O Daddy. Fuck me, Daddy, with that great big ugly red thing. Good grief.

The need to be needed. Satirize it, sterilize it—it's still there.

I needed Caswell but did he need me? Was I really what he needed? Did I take advantage of his need to satisfy my own need? I knew I was no psychiatrist but I clasped him to me. I let him—hell, helped him—break off with everyone else: college, family, the few friends he had and all those anonymous men who must have given him something besides their gism. Even operating that crazy way, he might have been better off this minute, 4:39 A.M., December—is it still December? I know I missed Christmas but have I missed new Year's too? Yes, it came and went. I kissed Polly. Well, I was never fond of frantic New Year's carryings-on anyway. It's a January morning and a long time to sunup.

Caswell will have to go back to that psychiatrist he was going to last year, I didn't even bother to find out what his name was. But it seems to me he should have bothered about what Caswell was doing. I suppose Edith somehow convinced herself and the psychiatrist that Fire Island was just the place for a wild twenty-year-old. And Beaton. And me.

She's only his aunt. And her sister was ill in Washington. There was so much to attend to—Edie has to attend to everything a little. If Edie had been more persistent and officious, we wouldn't have had our two months together, I wouldn't even have met Caswell on the beach. Whatever happens, those months were wonderful. And I was learning again to keep myself for one person as I did with Carlo.

Carlo was the only person before the Tyree debacle to touch me. And he only meant to show Hayden what he'd had so long. And I was only eager to show Hayden what a gorgeous tool I had—Hayden and any sixty others who might have been looking. How many got their looksies that afternoon I exhibited my hard-on in the Grand Central men's room? Dangerous, of course, but I couldn't resist hoisting it up above the urinal for the line to see and then standing back giving that whole faceless bevy of faggots a cheap thrill. Call it sharing the wealth, masturbating in public, what you will—it had something to do with feeling tied down, atrophying in one way although never more alive in another. And after the initial shock and regret I felt when Ty told me about Caswell's taking him, I hopped into bed with Ty too damn blithely, more concerned with recapturing that first fine careless rapture with Ty than with recapitulating Caswell's quirks and qualms.

I understood Caswell's alleged weakness by analogy—I wasn't perfect, either. And I was old enough to know things seldom go the way you plan. Love and fidelity are two different boxes, life is change, creative love means shifting arrangements. But the arrangement was all being done by a cynical Don Juan.

Have I ever wanted anyone so relentlessly I would have done what Ty did? I haven't. Not even Caswell? Would I have messed up someone else's life to get him? Would I do it now to get him back? I'd go to Hell for him. Would that be my Hell—lying, wrecking, grabbing? And the bastard didn't even want me—he wanted to have me, take me away from someone I loved more, prove something to himself. Shit, any half-assed rascal can get almost anything. Half of Europe for instance. But the means make the end what it is. What did Hitler and Napoleon end with? What did Ty end with? I wonder if he reads Ayn Rand?

How can I go down into Hades like Orpheus and bring back my beloved? Rhetorical, stupid question. There's no way to die for Cas. And if there were I'd never believe it any more than I can believe that taking Cas in my arms and taking him home, giving him a home, sharing a life full of loving and laughter was wrong for him, even though it has come to this. That October afternoon I knew or at least thought, intuited, he was going to kill himself, but how could I guess that doing what I was told he wanted me to do would cause him to try to kill himself? Cas ran right into the traffic—the cabbie had no choice. Poor Strauss. Another victim. Strauss, Edie, Caswell, but not Mike Kincade—Kincade is no victim, he is the fool. I should have known Tyree was lying, that Caswell would not have done what he said and would never have willingly shared me even if Ty had blown him and I knew Caswell was susceptible to paroxysms of despair and fury and self-destruction. I was not such a fool as it would be comfortable to claim—I simply betrayed Caswell for a few minutes of passionate adulation from someone who spurned me once. I didn't want to be wise or faithful or honest. I betrayed Caswell and myself.

Is it humanly possible to love someone else more than your own ego? Is it ever humanly possible to be self-subduing and strong and wise enough to be responsible for the well-being of another human being? Is that the human tragedy—that we are concerned and want to do what is best for someone else but aren't capable? Capable of knowing what is best for someone else or of doing it, either. Men are not gods.

So we're back to *hubris*, the step over the line into the domain of the gods, the arrogant treading of the sacred purple. I stepped and trod where only the gods may go when I drew Caswell's life from the undertow and took his life into my life.

And now, having done my worst, in this bleak gray hour all I can do is wait. Be here if Caswell becomes conscious for a moment, beg him to stay this side of the Styx. And hardly hope any more.

My tears I will weep for years to come. Tears for my lonely self, for what might have been, for what was and might have gone on and on. Not on and on the same; life does not go on exactly the same but we would have gone on together, getting older, loving each other even more. I'd only begun to love you, Caswell. Stay.

These gray mornings are all alike, these days go on and on more alike than any days I've ever known. Even that numb winter I drifted wasn't this monotonous. Prison must be like this, minus all the expensive padding. I could walk out this minute, so I am my own jailer, my own judge. No one else really knows or cares that I am here. They see me and wonder and forget a moment later. Neither Aunt Edith nor Doctor Brady really believes Caswell can return to consciousness, hear me, believe me, want to live again, throw off the death with delusion that drags him down. But Doctor Brady admits many have lived through worse manglings, there's no apparent reason he must drift like this, further and further beyond our reach. And Brady's a good joe and a good doctor—he sees I may be able to do what he can't do and lets me stay here. He accepts even if he doesn't want to believe. He's so straight, so unimaginative. He would prefer life to be simple but knows it is not.

Doctor Zeeman's mind clicks in new information, whirs and whirls and adjusts all along the line to accommodate the surprising turn of fact, ticks on. And he clacks off to another problem. He must know those hard clacking heels annoy a thousand drowsing weary patients a day and his stinking pipe another thousand or two. Is he callous, perverse, or does he just believe he has earned the right to bully whomever he pleases?

Now the nurses again. Squawking, hawhawing. The bells, the metal trays and cart a-jangle. Are they all perverse, too, callous as ushers gabbing and cackling through a hit musical they've seen a thousand times? Or have they all been instructed to break up the deathlike torpor whenever they can with casual cymbals and merriment? Sylvester is quiet; when he talks to the head nurse I can hear only a murmur between the raucous directions and retorts. Mickey forgets and brags and nickers sometimes.

It's too late now for Sylvester to come back in here. I might by luck catch his eye in the corridor and meet him in the john for a quick squeeze. For a thick dark dong, his gets hard fast. Most of the big black ones I swung on never got really hard. But Harry's did. Eddie's did. And certainly that dancer's at Cal Vernon's did when we jacked each other off and shot all over the place. Phallic fallacy number nine: niggers' jiggers don't get bigger or harder.

Carlo's poem:

Mike's feet are petite
But my peter's petiter.

For my height and all, I guess my feet are rather small—wide and short, like the feet Finnish Tom draws. Ten years ago guys used to say in amazement, "But your feet are so small!" Superstitions go out of style, too. Everyone seems to know now there isn't any way to tell who's got a big one.

Caswell's feet are long and narrow—when he crosses his ankles in bed they look like wings . . .

I hope Cleery's not on duty today—fat, sharp, impatient, her mind like a trained pig's. When she handles Caswell I worry she'll break him apart again. Actually she's pretty deft. Smoother than Kermolian who's a lot quieter and gentler and a little lazy. What a pair.

I wish we had Polly. Maybe I'll marry Polly some day. She's so pert and black and clean and right. A little dykey, too, which isn't so bad under the circumstances since a lot of folks seem to think I come across a little gay at times. How folks do get funny ideas.

On with the pajamas. Aunt Edie's idea of hospital wear—blue silk from Symon's. I suppose when she caught me in my jockeys that time she decided she'd better cover me up. She knew I'd been up to our apartment to get stuff I forgot to ask Alex to bring and she must have figured out I didn't own a pair of pajamas.

I wonder if the dear lady was titillated by the sight of my lovely legs and etceteras. She isn't old, not as old as Alex, in fact. And she may be still quite vulnerable. But I can't imagine her in bed with a man. With a woman? Yes! Good God, lesbian. Well, why didn't she say so? Because she isn't, you ass, or at least hasn't been for a long time. Sublimated. Which is unmated in any fashion as far as I'm concerned. A Park Avenue nun, in a flurry of good intentions, self-indulgence and penance for imaginary sins. And dollars. They're definitely a feature of any fragmentation of Aunt Edith. And maybe she does still tingle a little when a cute number like Polly swishes a cute tail down the corridor and bounces the boobies.

If I had married Phyllis last September . . . To hell with that. I married Caswell in October. For better or worse. This worse pays for that brief best. When I don't pay as I go, I pay later, plus interest compounded of tears.

My bootees. O God, with what tears can I ever pay for these absurd things that, next to Caswell himself, are the most precious things in the world to me—poetry excepted? Will I ever be able to touch them without dissolving in sentimental tears? He knew how cold our apartment floors were and I had only those old ripped sandals I hated and swore at. I didn't realize he had no money at all, he never said a word or even hinted. He must have bought these with scrapings from the money I gave him to buy groceries with. When Alex brought me the box Caswell had dropped on the sofa before he fled and I saw these, my Christmas present—the silly lambswool lining and the little wooden balls on the strings—my God. From that cheap place on Broadway. Full speed ahead, Kincade and dam the tears.

Edie said he had an account in his own name at her bank—untouched since the day he met me. As if that life no longer existed. He didn't say he couldn't get money, he just didn't have any and I didn't want to complicate our tremulous beginning with money arrangements. He didn't need money. He didn't want to leave the house except with me. Did he?

Next time we'll talk about everything. Next time? There has to be another chance or there is nothing. Losing Carlo was bad enough but losing Caswell too? It's a conspiracy to make me suffer, make me pay. I love too much, I enjoy too much—I have to pay.

Mike closed the door softly and went swiftly to the high bed and bent over the face on the pillow—the pale mask that betrayed no life except that out of it sprang the dark rich hair. Mike brushed his warm mouth over the cool lips, the polished cheekbone, the sweep of dark hair, whispering, "Caswell, Caswell, I love you! Come back to me. Please, please don't leave me." He subsided, kneeling on the bare floor, his cheek on Caswell's thin hand at the edge of the bed.

There was bustle in the corridor, doors slamming nearby. Mike rose and was putting on the pongee robe Edie had brought when Miss Cleery pushed the door open and marched in.

The visitors' lounge was deserted, formal but disheveled, the magazines still strewn around from yesterday's abstracted fingering and dropping. Mike crossed to the window and pushed down the top sash. Windows weren't to be opened by just anyone so he was discreetly quiet about it. The cold damp air chilled him in a moment. He shut the window and stood staring out.

When did one finally face the cold raw reality, the absurdity of standing here at five o'clock of a raw January morning, the eighteenth day of dogged useless standing, sitting, reading, lying, waiting? Job gone, everything deserted and abandoned except a living memory, a mortal mistake that couldn't be paid for. Caswell Green ran away. The thing in there on the bed only vaguely resembled Caswell whose intensity was enthralling and exhilarating even when it was jammed into futile ritual.

Not ritual, not design, not complex, not ordeal, not program. What could one call a course of action not schemed out but adopted without a qualm, a rigid routine for which no alternative could exist, an obsessed simplicity that denied chaos, multiplicity, the horrifying way things were? Caswell's summer was stark in its simplicity—stark and bizarre, hateful but undeniable. Just as Mike for the few seconds had not been able to resist the urge to show off his big hard cock for those trembling men, Caswell hadn't been able to forgo sucking off half those who offered themselves to him. Then walking alone on the beach and making his fortresses anew each day.

Later college had proved a mere hiatus and he had gone back to the beach to do what he had to do, even though going back to that nudged him nearer the edge.

Simple welcome routine again—not going out except to shop nearby or to go to the theater or a party as Mike's "other half," taking care of their place, learning to cook, making love, every waking moment loving and being loved. Only the present matters.

No one cares if I live or die but I care if Caswell lives or dies, so I'll stay. If I can just lie there, holding him in my arms, I might draw him back. Would Doctor Brady and Doctor Zeeman let me do that now? Probably not. I don't really care what anybody says if they see me. Let Kermolian and Cleery tell whatever they please. That mad little old woman who wanders in sometimes will understand even less than she does now. She thinks Caswell is her nephew and I am his brother but I'm not one of her nephews—she's sure of that—they're all dark-haired. Maybe when Caswell's body is sounder and all those wrappings and bandages are off I can resurrect him. He's a fully grown young man and even in that dark dream he floats in, in the dark cave he huddles in, his need will respond. I'll have to wait.

But I will play God again and take the consequences. What

else can a man do? I'll read and work on my poems and bide my time. What more can I ask? Who needs money? Fame? According to Freud it's only so much transmogrified shit anyway. But if I had to die so Caswell could live—that would be a poser to stop traffic in my brain.

Fortunately this isn't a neat little melodrama we're caught up in with impulses hurtling neatly to the nexus, clearly labeled good and evil—evil always being selfish, self-preserving, or is it actually self-hating? If I could have caught up to him, shoved him clear even if it meant the cab would hit me, I think I'd have done it. Partly in expiation for my fool mistake, partly because I loved him that much, partly because—one does or one does not. Maybe I'd have drawn back in pure reflex fear. I don't know.

It's the cold raw grayness that makes me think these things, this wrenched-open hour not night or day, this exposed limbo.

Mike stared down the canyon between the wing of the hospital and a row of dingy buildings into the street traffic, more gray, snow-rimmed buildings, the lowering sky and smoke. It was more mazy boring than the meaningless wilderness. He turned back to the room in which he stood.

Someone in white was standing at an adjacent window, four or five feet away. A slim man in white shoes, pants, medical jacket, a blondish young man, thin, his curly hair white-blond, he was looking directly at Mike. He looked down and moved—his cock was lying on the radiator top, his very large pale-skinned cock and his balls! Slowly his far hand grasped the shaft of it and hauled the thick foreskin back off the big pink head. The fingers pressed back hard into the pubic hair and fly of the white pants. The organ swelled and stretched and hardened—it was a very big, very beautifully shaped tool.

Mike gasped and had an impulse to yell, "No. Not here. Not now, you fool!" But he got his breath and looked up at the young man's face. The other smiled and winked at Mike. The wide mouth, the wedge-shaped chin, irregular nose, wide cheekbones, merry gray eyes, wide forehead, the curly light hair—it was all familiar to Mike. The smile, the big square front teeth and the canines slanting in that way—familiar. It was a face Mike had seen many times, the smile a few times maybe. But not that cock. It was up now, rearing up in a delicate curve, longer than Mike's, thicker than Lloyd Stark's, the head huge but beautifully modeled.

"When I used to dream of running into you again, I never thought it would be like this," the young man said quietly. He tucked his equipment back into his pants carefully. "Smoke?" he asked, taking a pack of cigarettes from the breast pocket.

"Thanks. I don't."

"That's right, Sylvester said you didn't. I forgot. Well, I work here, obviously. I'm interning. Sylvester had me the second day. He told me you were out here."

Mike was nonplussed. He ached to get at this young one, get with him. He was sure they had spent some time together but he was equally sure they'd never been to bed. You don't forget a magnificent thing like that. Where? One of the kids who were in and out of the show at the Village Stairs? There was a blond he heard about after he'd gone.

"You're—Angelo, the guard in *Villon* the week before it closed."

"No," the younger man said. "Pinecroft in the Poconos. I was nineteen but probably looked younger."

"Yes." Mike remembered—the gangly blond with the bulgy teasy crotch and the watchful eyes. "I thought you were a kid, like the others."

"I lost a lot of sleep over you that summer," the intern said. "I'd never been in love before. Remember the fat little Czech boy Yanni?"

"Yes, I think so. Dark?"

"Yeah. My buddy. I told him everything. He was in love with you, too. We used to spy on you. At first we were sure you were making out with old Marie. I gave her a plugging myself just to find out. She said you were sneaking off with that frail babe that took care of the nutty old Marmelade or whatever her name was."

"Marigold," Mike said. "Marigold Clattahan. I wasn't making out with Alicia, though."

"Of course you weren't," the intern said. "We kept tabs on that romance. We knew Marie was wrong. We also trailed you into the woods more than once and watched you jack off. I loved it because you always took your clothes off and stood right out in the open. Man, how you loved to handle that big beautiful thing. I tried not to shoot until you shot. I made Yanni stay way back because he breathed so hard you might hear. And that way I had you more to myself. Once we caught you swimming at night in the pool and watched you jack off in the outdoor shower. We were right on the other side of the trellis. The wind was blowing like crazy and the lightning ripped and you pulled at that thing like you were going to tear it off. I shot when you did, right in my pants, and after you left I took a shower and jacked off where you did and had to have Yanni and the other kids jack me off a third time in bed before I could go to sleep. Remember Red?"

"Yes, he was a kid."

"He was seventeen and hotter than a fox. He used to pull out that little rod and whip off a load wherever he was—walking up the hill, in the shower, in the kitchen sink. His bed was a mess. Once he jerked off into a cup of coffee the cook left for a minute. You quit going into the woods. We figured you'd found a babe in that bar around the bend."

"I went to the bar," Mike said.

"I know. I went back to Pinecroft the next summer hoping you'd be there again. God, it was lonesome without you. I even let old Howard have it a couple of times before I decided to see what the Hiway Rest had to offer a hot-pants loner. I met Earl. Remember Earl?"

"Yes, hair the color of yours—a fast lad with a hand job."

"Yes, at first he wouldn't let me touch him but by the middle of the summer I was fucking him once a week. Man, what a tight little ass that was. Know who else I met?"

"The bartender, of course," Mike said.

"Yes, him. A watch-quean. But the one I was fucking once a week was Gus Davies. Don't tell me you'd forgotten him, the motorcycle cop—the big blond."

"With the enormous balls."

"Like goose eggs," the intern said. "He followed me out back one night and we jacked each other off. Old Max, the bartender, came out and watched, of course. After that, Gus and I met down the road a piece."

"I remember the place."

"Of course you would," the intern said. "He told me. You were the first guy he ever went down on."

"Did he talk about his baby brother?" Mike asked.

"Baby brother! Pem was eighteen and his balls were bigger than Gus's and oh, that ass!"

"I take it you met him then," Mike said. "I didn't. I wasn't even sure he existed."

"We went on a so-called fishing trip," the intern said, "for Saturday night and Sunday. The brothers had a neighbor's cabin that had a big fireplace. It rained the whole time. As soon as we got a fire going and a couple of quarts of beer in, Pem stripped and stretched out in a chair by the fire and Gus stripped and started sucking little brother's very big cock. I stripped and fucked the shit out of big brother. Neither one had ever been fucked before but they were both royally fucked that night. We fucked so much Saturday night all we could do on Sunday was jack each other. We'd get sore and stop and drink more beer and somebody'd jack off a load of piss and bubbles. At least that's what they got from me at that point. The cream kept rolling out of those two like they were loaded forever. Seven, eight, nine ejaculations—and there was still a gush of thick semen. They should be in the medical books. Anyhow, look, I've got work to do and you have your lover to look after."

"Sylvester told you about him?"

"Sylvester! You think everybody in the damned hospital isn't talking? This is the eighteenth day. There's book made on whether you ever get to him! I'm betting twenty you do, though it may be a while yet."

"I thought the doctors were skeptical," Mike said.

"What do doctors know? What's happened, what will happen—probably. They don't know any more than anyone else about what is happening or definitely will happen. I'm one of them, remember. I put my money on sex every time. Don't suppose he's in any condition to slip it into yet but when you can, man, get right in there and remind him how good it is. In the meantime, if you want a little reminder yourself—you're the only man I ever loved."

"Thanks. I don't want a reminder."

"Hell, man, you're ripe. First you suck what you saw a little, then I jack off what I've been aching to get my hands on for more than five years now. Then when you're limp and calm and relaxed, in it goes, slow and easy. You're built for it. You'll love it, I'll love it."

"Maybe if you sucked me off a couple of times . . ."

"I don't swing."

"You're built for it," Mike said. "That's a cocksucking mouth if ever I saw one. You're an oral virgin—hey, what's your name, anyway?"

"Paul Schonberg. Doctor Schonberg already. You're a sweet bastard. Open that robe. I'm going to blow you right where you stand."

"You're a fake," Mike said.

"At least let me see what I got to learn to like," Paul Schonberg said. He drew Mike's robe and loose pajamas aside and lifted out his half-stiff cock. "That's it. That's beautiful man-stuff." He wrapped both hands around it and squeezed. "God, I wish I had the nerve to take that right now. Before it gets too hard, right down my throat."

"Easy, Paul. It's been several days and Sylvester was playing with it. And looking at that beautiful tool of yours got me more excited. I'll shoot fast."

"Good." Paul pulled Mike over to the sofa, his back to the corridor, sat on the sofa and took Mike's cock into his mouth, manipulating it only with his lips. At first Paul could take nearly all of it but as it hardened he could take only half of it at each swinging plunge and after a dozen plunges he held while Michael shot and shot, his whole body rocking and his lips clenched between his teeth.

They both became aware again of gongs, marching footsteps, doors banging, metal clanging, the chirr of the elevator, the gray January light.

"You're mad," Mike whispered. "We both are."

"I'd do it again, right now." Paul rose, brushing his mouth on the cloth of his jacket shoulder. "I want all you've got. And I want to give you all I've got. I'll be back." He left.

"And now to rescue Caswell," Mike murmured ruefully to himself.

"What?" a nurse hurrying by asked. "Oh, it's you, Mr. Kincade. How's your friend?"

"Not conscious yet. But I've been away a while. I'd better go see." They went their ways.

Mike's knees were still trembling. It had been a long time since he had done anything so reckless or been so excited. He remembered the big deserted outdoor shower, the wind and the lightning and his wild jacking off with that sweet kid right there on the other side of the trellis, that great gorgeous phallos erupting in his pants. If Mike had known . . .

Paul Schonberg. Standing there showing off what he had to the only man he'd ever loved. The head on that thing, Mike thought. It would hurt. Mike shivered, remembering his feverish compact. Paul would realize it wasn't a fair compact. Everyone said the bigger they were, the less it hurt. Paul would be good at it, loving, gentle. Good God, Kincade, listen to yourself.

Okay, so I'm a virgin. At thirty. Still running away. Or do I want to take Paul and won't admit it? Won't admit the desire, will admit the phallos? Am I going to turn another corner? It wasn't exactly a promise. Shut up. Quiet down. But life is so full of surprises.

Caswell, Caswell, baby, you must live. Life is full of surprises. Wake up, darling. This time be brave. I'll help you be brave. Life is very complicated. Complicated but delightful . . .

JONNY

"Jonathan, Honor," Amos Hanford greeted them jovially from his aisle seat. "Hi, Kim, Kylie. How're you all doing?"

Honor smiled and nodded politely toward Amos and his party but did not stop to chat; she proceeded serenely on into the seats the girl usher had indicated were theirs, in the same row as the Hanfords' but on the other side of the aisle. If her husband chose to play up to the hypocritical old pirate, that was his privilege. They had opened fire in a battle to curb the depredations of the cynical entrenched Old Guard of Eastonport; Honor would respect Amos Hanford as a tricky adversary but she would not pretend she liked him.

Jon knew exactly what his wife's cool behavior meant; he suspected Amos got the message too. Jon was proud of Honor: she had such perfect control, whereas he himself was inclined to be a little too impulsive sometimes. Or to seem so: no one, not even Honor, realized how long and carefully he had controlled certain unworthy impulses. Honor looked very pretty too; without spending much she could look as fashionable as anyone. Kim and Kylie were a handsome young couple; he was proud of his whole family.

Kim had kind of bowed and said "hi" or something to Amos, his polite greeting lost in the theater hubbub, turned and followed his mother into the row of seats, trailed by Kylie. Kim was a fine-looking young college man, inches taller than his daddy, athletic in a lanky, not yet fully developed way, not too handsome of face but a handsome face was not always a great asset. The important thing was that Kylie considered her fiancé something special. For a fraction of an instant Jon speculated about whether Kylie had already discovered just how specially her Kim was fixed in one very interesting way. Even if Kylie hadn't had occasion to find out exactly, she must have a pretty good idea: the girl wasn't blind. Although Kim was nicely modest, he didn't go to any great effort to conceal from Kylie or anyone else the heavy bulge in his pants front. If they'd already gone all the way... well, Kylie was on the Pill of course and they knew they should wait for marriage until Kim had finished at Bowdoin. They were good sensible kids. Jon had never had to worry about Kim's running off on some crazy tangent as, with his genetic inheritance, he might be expected to do.

Several queries, flashes of pride, rebellious surges later but actually only a few seconds in time after Amos's amiable gesture, Jon responded with his dignified "Evening, Amos... Joan, Osborn..." Not kowtowing, not acting as if the Mynotts hobnobbed socially with the Hanfords all the time. Even though Amos was fully aware that Jon and Honor had been the active leaders of the citizens' group who defied Hanford's North Point House corporation and forced them to abandon their piratical scheme to convert the end of Horatio Street into a mall which would be, in effect, the condo's private terrace, Amos apparently bore Jon no ill will. In fact, having been handed a setback engineered by Jon, Amos had finally recognized that Jonathan K. Mynott was a public-minded citizen worthy of respect and, not long after the city council battle, Amos had approached Jon about the postmaster position and practically offered it to him whenever it should become vacant. Honor had of course declared, like some Delphic sybil, that old Amos had made the vague suggestion merely to buy Jon off cheaply and forestall his resistance to any further grabby deals which the arrogant old plutocrat already had in mind to put over on the unwary taxpayers.

As Honor said, it was all very well to remember that the price of democracy was eternal vigilance. No one ever mentioned that the personal cost to an independent man might be the favors he had to forgo, the bribes to relax his vigilance once in a while he had to scorn. Honor wasn't a mouthy woman but she did know how to speak her mind clearly on occasion. She could also, on other occasions, keep her thoughts to herself and never betray her secrets even to her husband.

Naturally Jon had expressed his interest in the position which he had thoroughly prepared himself to be worthy of assuming; he had expressed his gratitude for Amos's interest in his bettering himself but he had carefully made no commitment nor even hinted that he felt himself indebted. Amos might believe he had slyly enlisted Jonathan Mynott in his private forces but he had sprung some big surprises on other high-handed types in his time and he would not hesitate to spring one on Amos Hanford if the spoiled old manipulator attempted to nudge him into anything shady or even into convenient silence. Jon was strict with himself; he certainly did not intend ever to be less strict with anyone else's sneaking over the line of legality or decency.

Jon calmly seated himself beside Kylie and surveyed the summer theater auditorium which was filling up fast. It would be a sell-out performance of course, with all the notoriety the show had received. If people who had driven over from Eastonport saw the Mynotts there and surmised that they had come out of pure curiosity due to the publicity, there wasn't much Jon could do to disillusion them. He and Honor could hardly go around informing everyone they knew that, actually, they had a very special reason for seeing this particular play of the season. He hoped he would be able to deal calmly with the unique occasion but he was extremely relieved that, by pure chance, two other spectators would be sitting in the aisle seats of the row, shielding him from any curious glances old Amos might cast his way to observe Jon's reactions to the far-out play.

Early in July, as soon as the theater announced that Molly Malloy's leading men in *Design for Living* would be Michael Kincade and Ron Devera, Honor had called over and ordered their tickets. Ron Devera meant nothing to them but Michael Kincade meant a great deal. He meant so much more than either of them cared to say that Jon had considered refusing to have Kim along when they encountered Mike again for the first time since their senior year at college.

After some reflection, though, Jon had not said a word for he feared that any move on his part to foil the plan he was certain Honor had in her mind might erupt in an argument on a very delicate subject and that in the heat of such an argument either he or Honor might spill out what they both had been so careful never to mention. He realized that the publicized immorality of the play wouldn't hold up as an excuse for not including Kim and Kylie in the theater jaunt to the larger city. The Noel Coward play might have been considered shocking in its day but that was nearly fifty years back . . . half a century, before he and Honor were born, old hat before he and Honor were twenty, the age Kim and Kylie were. If there was nudity in this production, well, nudity had been accepted on the New York stage and everywhere else as far back as the late sixties, more than ten years earlier.

His refusing to allow Kim to see Mike Kincade on the stage would have been as good as admitting right out to Honor that he had long been aware that Kim's real father was probably Mike and not himself. And that he'd never had the nerve to tell his wife that he had known practically from the day the child was born. Not known of course but strongly suspected, had come to believe. And to accept.

Jon definitely did not hold that Honorette had deliberately betrayed him, that she had trapped him into a hasty marriage when she saw that Mike was completely fascinated by another woman. And never would be a good husband anyway. Honor hadn't been that sure herself what the exact biological fact was; she hadn't been totally sure either until she too had seen Kim growing up, so much taller than Jon or any of the Mynotts or her own menfolks. And so clearly a young duplicate of Mike Kincade in the penis department.

If Honor did have in her mind some weird female desire to take Kim backstage to meet Michael Kincade and there abruptly, dramatically, to reveal to Kim, to both Kim and Mike and, necessarily, to Jon as well . . . Honor could be fierce when she had a bee in her bonnet but she could never be that cruel to her husband or to her son. How Mike might react to such a revolution out of the blue, Jon, who for two years was Jonny, Mike's roommate and most intimate . . . friend? Hell, lover! . . . Who ever could guess how Mike would react to anything?

And there was no real proof if the relationship wasn't immediately apparent to both the older man and the younger, no legal proof beyond the good possibility and that one peculiar physical characteristic they shared. Which Honor would never have the audacity to point out. The surprising six-two of height could have filtered down from some Sullivan grandparent. And so might the other have, although the more probable accounting for it could hardly be overlooked. Even if Honor somehow managed to get Mike alone with herself and Kim. . . . No, it would never happen : Honor was too steady, too good, she was too comfortable in the secret lie she had lived so long.

But if Jon had dragged Honor's secret into the light by refusing to let him even see his father, wasn't it likely Honor would have defended her duplicity, not exactly justified it but defended it, by countering with her kind silence on the subject of her husband's own guilt? Jon had rarely felt he was living a lie after he married Honor but he had been careful not to mention what had gone before.

Honor had always been careful too never to make the slightest allusion. She couldn't have been totally ignorant, although she needn't have ever known much as actual fact. Mike had been a giddy, devil-may-care-but-I-don't type but neither he nor any other man would have mentioned or confessed or bragged about such abnormal exploits to a nice girl, even a girl he was sleeping with. Not now probably ; most certainly not back in those stiff late fifties, the pre-rebellion days before the radicals tried to throw out all decency and reticence and modesty. However, it was likely, about a zillion to zilch, that even the nice, quiet girls like Honorette Sullivan and Wilma Whatever Her Name Was heard some of the gleefully-passed-around rumors about Don Juan Kincade's numerous brief romances with guys as well as the campus queens. Honor had been fully aware that Jonny, who was eager to take her away from Mike even before Lainey snatched Mike away, had been Mike's roommate for two years. And had dated almost no woman at all until Honorette's roommate Wilma sort of made a play for him that fall and he dated her a few times.

The best Honor could think, when Jonny Mynott dated Wilma and even laid her a time or two and then shifted his whole eager attention to herself, was that Jonny had belatedly discovered girls, if not changed his gait and shifted over to normal. Which was exactly what did happen. He'd handed both Mike and Lloyd Stark a big surprise that night at the close of the school year when he'd brought Lloyd to Mike and then turned and walked out of the party and never made a move to see either man again. He'd had Lloyd once, Lloyd had practically offered Jonny his big dick to swing on—he'd never been sucked off by a guy and he'd heard Jonny was the best; also there was that kind of rivalry-fascination with Mike Kincade which Lloyd didn't mention but which Jonny was aware of and which made Jonny's being the first guy to have Lloyd Stark's notoriously huge dick, the King Cock of the campus which a lot of guys had seen up hard but no one, not even wild Mike Kincade had ever dared touch. . . . And Lloyd had let Jonny have it right in the middle of his hot, much-gossiped-about affair with Lainey and the crazy year when Jonny had Mike every time he wanted him, plus half the jocks in the fieldhouse showers and locker rooms. Jonny hardly ever mentioned those other conquests to Mike but he had a feeling he did let it slip to Mike that he'd had Lloyd Stark. He wouldn't have been human if he'd resisted that moment of triumph. Triumph? Silly, childish egotism . . . mysterious detouring through queer-heaven, straight-hell, toward becoming a grown-up man in charge of his own destiny.

Music, sprightly Mozart or Vivaldi, anyway something classical and sparkly, mingled with the assembling audience's murmurs and little social cries. With a shiver of ecstatic anticipation, Jon reminded himself that in a few minutes he was going to see Mike again and, if he hadn't misread the newspaper review of the play, he and about a thousand curious, titillated other theater-goers were not only going to enjoy Mike's performance in a sexy comedy, at one point in the evening they were going to be treated to a good look at every bit of Mike in the nude. And, out of the assembled multitude eager to see the handsome actor in all his naked glory, only he would know exactly what Michael Kincade's fabled big dong looked like fully erect.

Except, possibly of course, Honor and that Jon considered rather doubtful. Her few dates with Mike had probably always ended in the dark. Nice girls like Honorette Sullivan in those days didn't want to see and touch men in that state any more than they had to. A nice girl now, a girl like Kylie...? Well, Elaine Palmer might have carried on as openly over a man's tool as a queer guy but Wilma didn't and Honorette didn't either and wasn't that brazen even with Mike, Jon was sure.

If Honorette had been aware of any considerable physical difference when she and Jonny made out so soon after Elaine snatched Mike away, she was a nice polite girl who didn't betray any awareness. He certainly had not expected Honor to mention anything of the kind; he'd hoped that actually Honorette was one of those many women he had heard about who preferred smaller, less troublesome men. Several of his heavier-hung conquests had admitted they were only so hot to be taken care of by a guy because their girls didn't want to deal with a really huge hunk of man-meat. Honorette had seemed happy enough with Jonny the first time and eager enough to make it with him again as soon as they could. For Jonny it had been not only a kind of reassuring experience he needed, it had been a wonderfully surprising one; he was in love for the first time. And Honorette had happily agreed that it was the first real time for her too. He believed her then; he still believed she hadn't been fooling him. They'd discovered, to their mutual amazement and delight, they were meant for each other.

Jon gazed fondly at his pretty wife who certainly didn't look forty-two any more than he did himself. Honor was intently perusing the program notes, as were Kim and Kylie. He supposed he ought to check out the bios too. Naturally, Jon went right to the notes about "Otto" (Michael Kincade) and was a little surprised to learn that Kincade was better known as a poet than as an actor, although he had appeared in many leading roles in college, on Broadway and Off-Broadway and in Europe over the past two decades. In one of his early appearances he had been one of François Villon's illegitimate sons in a Greenwich Village play in which Ron Devera, only two years older than Kincade, had portrayed the famous poet-thief. In Munich, where Kincade lived for a number of years while his friend Dr. Paul Schonberg did advanced research at a hospital there, Kincade had appeared in several German productions, including some of Rainer Fassbinder's early films.

The program notes weren't a bit shy about making innuendos about homosexuality, which Jon had gathered was at least suggested in the old play. They said Kincade had appeared in one short American film, an early underground all-male but poetic piece which had become a collector's item like *Chant d'amour.* Whatever that was. They did mention that Mike had been married once—once in contrast to Molly Mallory's much publicized many times Jon supposed—to an actress whom Jon had never heard of.

Jon had seen one Fassbinder film. The director himself had played the lead, a blundering working-class fellow who won some money and was exploited by vicious queers. "Fox"-Fassbinder wasn't handsome but in a gym scene he appeared naked, as if determined to show that, although he did not have an attractive face, he did have a very good physique and a notably nice large cock. Jon bet that Mike Kincade got to know that director's big cock well enough. Jon had known him to be active when sufficiently challenged. Like a lot of well-hung studs, Mike was willing to stand still or lie back and enjoy some inferiorly endowed guy sucking his gorgeous big lob for hours but when Mike and Lloyd were finally brought together under the right circumstances—both drunk, Lloyd set to graduate and leave the next day, Justin O'Connor already down on his knees attempting to take all of Mike's long dick down his throat when Jonny brought Lloyd into the room which he and Mike had shared for two whole years, and Jonny stripped the newcomer's big handsome bod naked, Mike beckoned Lloyd over to him. Lloyd went willingly enough right to Mike who handled Lloyd's great big dick which had already begun to harden up as Lloyd stared at Mike's equally big tool, up full force and wet with spit in Justin's drunken, determined hands. In their shower-room jackoff sessions, Jonny was pretty sure neither had ever touched the other, much as they might have wanted to. Mike didn't just touch Lloyd's cock, he went right down on it to the hilt.

In that dorm room Mike had teased Jonny and nearly driven

him mad for one whole year but he hadn't been making it with anyone else, just getting his rocks off with Lloyd in their impersonal shower-room sessions every so often. The next year, in that room Mike was Jonny's any time he wanted him and one wet Sunday it was four times in a twenty-hour period. He'd realized Mike was making it with other fellows as well as the passing parade of girls but he'd never had to see another fellow giving Mike a blow-job and if Mike had ever responded in kind to another guy, he'd never heard of it. It had disgusted Jonny to see Justin slobbering over Mike. He could understand Mike's fascination with Lloyd's great dick but he didn't want to see Mike sucking it. In another few seconds Lloyd would be unable to resist pulling away, getting down, shoving Justin away and trying to suck Mike. Jonny didn't want to see that either.

They had both given him enough but he'd paid any debt; he'd given them each other. He'd turned and pulled out of that crazy scene forever. He'd never regretted his subconscious but nevertheless wise decision.

Lloyd didn't make it through pre-med; he dropped out and became a coach somewhere Jon heard. All those other special jocks turned their backs on the queer stuff just as Jonny did. They enjoyed giving their big dicks a long, leisurely soaping when muscleboy Jonny was staring at them as if planning what he'd do with them; they'd enjoyed the quick blow-jobs and the long, luxurious sucking if there was no danger of their being interrupted. They'd gone on and gotten married and had kids and never mentioned the fun they'd had that way. Maybe some of them still couldn't resist occasional discreet indulgence, the ones whose moral fiber was flabby or the ones whose flesh had gone flabby and needed reassurance that their big peters were still attractive. Mike Kincade had chosen to go on being his irresponsible, irresistible Peter Pan self, not quite grown up, a poet, a vagabond actor. It wasn't a satisfying life for most men; they didn't want it any more than Jon did. In fact Jon wasn't even sure he wanted to see Mike again face to face.

The play opened with a long scene between the star Molly Mallory and a precise but not exactly prissy older man of about Jon's height who was expensively turned out but obviously had not taken very good care of his body. Jon prayed that Mike, at forty-two, would not be a worn-out bum or a gone-to-seed slob. When Mike did come on, he was wearing a hat and trench coat, looked to be in fairly good shape and seemed taller and bigger than Jon remembered his being. And even handsomer, but that might have been mostly makeup. His hair was darker and fuller; about the only sort of gay thing he did was stroke his hair into place when he took his hat off before kissing Molly.

Molly Mallory was a stunning-looking woman with a thinnish figure and a great mane of hair as palely blonde as Mike's had been in those early days but wasn't any more. Half the time she was languidly sexy with heavy-lidded eyes, then she'd suddenly become wide-eyed wise and almost sharp; both ways the actress seemed phony. Mike, Jon was glad to observe, seemed real enough—smart enough in how he said what he had to say but when he moved, a little heavy-footed for graceful, vigorous Mike. Twenty years had made a difference; Mike should have kept up a stricter physical regimen. Jon gloated that, as in college, although they were the same age, he still looked several years the younger of the two.

The other lead, Ron Devera, looked more than two years older than Mike. He was sharper featured, dark with a little beard and mustache, and almost too quick and light in his movements—as if he were trying hard to be cute and young. Ron deliberately showed quite a large crotch-bulge; he wanted all the attention.

The newspaper review had intimated that on the opening night both leading men had stripped. Jon could tell that the "Leo" actor would enjoy making an exhibition of himself and he hoped that what the guy wanted to show wouldn't be disappointing. Of course, compared with what Mike had concealed in his pants, Devera's pride and joy wasn't likely to stand much of a chance.

Down at the nude beach outside San Diego, Jon had been embarrassed at the antics of several blatant exhibitionists who weren't much better fixed than he was and hardly worth a second glance. He couldn't figure what made them tick. He had faced the fact at sixteen or seventeen that he would never have anything special to show or to offer a girl. In high school and his first year of college, if he and the other guys happened to get boners in the showers, no one paid any attention to him except maybe to kid him about how quick he got up hard. Then getting the merest teasing glimpses of his roommate's outsized organ had aroused him; catching, maybe three times, Mike and the star football jock from down the hall jacking off their fantastically huge hard cocks and imagining a thousand times the pair beating off together had driven him to frenzies of masturbation all that first year. Never in all the hundred? two hundred? times the next year that he played with Mike's ever-naked and available, ever-responsive luscious big peter and sucked it off or jacked it off, Jonny never thought of himself although he nearly always shot off his load when Mike gave him his.

In the fieldhouse it had been his hungry stare that turned on the special jocks whose big dicks he wanted . . . and got, some only once or twice like Lloyd, some regularly. Two or three politely reciprocated; others wanted to fuck him up the ass but he drew the line at that variety of reciprocation. That whole year he never got off once alone and he was damn sure Mike never did. Jon wondered if Mike Kincade ever gave himself so freely and enthusiastically, time after time, to anyone else. Was Mike still a sex maniac, would he still enjoy having his cock sucked on and teased until he came, while he studied for an hour before supper, and then go out with a bunch of friends, wind up screwing some hot babe, and when he came back at midnight, ask for and always get another fast and furious session with Jonny right to climax?

Jon allowed himself to indulge in such lurid thoughts; after all, he'd restrained himself for twenty years, it could never happen again, he was permitted.

Nothing much happened in the first act of the play except the woman "Gilda" switched from one lover to the other and back again. At the intermission Kim and Kylie said they'd found it all very amusing and went off to get lemonade. Honor remarked on Mike's darker hair and added weight and expert comedy technique, then excused herself to go have a word with Mrs. Nina Vanderhagen from Easton Rock who had come over with her spoiled young grandson Tony who lived with her, now that his divorced parents were so unsettled. Nina was definitely crême de la crême of Eastonport society, Old Guard and rich, but, although "she owned the half of the town which Amos Hanford didn't own," she sometimes could be persuaded to act for the commonweal against her own and friends' immediate interests. She and Honor had become almost chummy during the Horatio Street battle; she'd wielded her stock in the condo corporation like a club to make old Amos and his contingent change their plans. Jon felt he was balancing the forces neatly when he sauntered over to Amos who stood alone, deserted for the moment by his son and daughter-in-law.

"Might have known Nina would scamper over here once she read that review," Amos chuckled. "For a woman of her age, which is nearer my own than she likes to admit, Nina still has a lively interest in the facts of life, especially the male facts. She embarrassed some of the men, not me of course but some of the younger prudies, at a dinner party she gave last month for the governor, telling us all about the California Chippendale's burlesque shows for women only and the Long Island luncheon clubs where the male dancers strip down to G-strings and wiggle their butts at the women. Nobody could shut Nina up: it was her house, her party, and she insisted on telling us a lot more than anybody wanted to hear about the Dunes in Honolulu with their naked waiters at lunchtime two days a week, back about five years ago when she happened to be out there."

"I think I recall reading something about that fad . . . in one of those magazines at the barbershop. *Playboy* I expect; I can't tell one of them from the other."

"According to Nina the star of the Hawaiian show was a black man who proudly sported a twelve-inch hard-on and he let Nina hold the ruler. It's my educated guess that that jumping-jack's bodonkus gets about half an inch longer every time Nina tells her favorite tale."

Jon couldn't help recalling for an instant the ebony bodonkus of George Petit, the university's champion high-jumper; that fifth limb of his had gone down Jon's throat like a dark snake more than one late afternoon that year.

"Guess Tony Vanderhagen comes by his interest in such things fairly legitimately. When Chief Agostino sent Joe Adrakian in a bathing suit out to North Point beach one night last June to find out if there really were homo orgies going on out there as Agostino had been advised, Joe claimed it was Tony Vanderhagen who sucked him off but he couldn't be too sure since it was so dark out there and there had to be at least six or seven other guys holding him and tickling him and all."

"I never even heard a whisper about any such goings-on on that beach," Jon said. "Usually any local scandal gets passed around pretty fast at the post office. Somehow the women seem to get hold of everything first and pass it on to the men after they've dolled it up to suit their fancy."

"Naturally Joe didn't tell a lot of people he got raped by a bunch of faggots and, as the general opinion was it was college-age summer fellows and one notoriously wild Vanderhagen, the whole mess got the damper put on. Among those who did hear, it was generally doubted if it was Tony who actually committed the dirty deed of depriving our upright policeman of his vital juices since Tony's reputation seems to be more for fancy handwork. I reckon with Tony going off to college next fall and Pete Adrakian out of the way in New York, things around sleepy little Eastonport may be quite a lot quieter in the peculiar sex sector. I wouldn't be surprised to hear that Joe Adrakian had decided to settle somewhere else too. For a real man, not to mention a police officer, Joe seems to get himself raped a little too frequently. With that heavy influx of queers we've been undergoing, we certainly can't afford to encourage them by tolerating known deviates or even part-time deviates in our law enforcement departments or in any other public-paid positions. You must have seen Joe Adrakian around the YMCA gym, Jonathan. You ever notice him acting funny, trying to lead some weirdo on? I heard tell, on pretty good authority, his brother Pete was an outright hustler as well as being a dope-dealer."

"I don't recall ever seeing Joe Adrakian at the Y anytime. He certainly never turned up in any of my exercise-drill classes.

Of course I've heard sniggering comments about Tony Vanderhagen ever since he was about twelve but I never pay much attention to that kind of nastiness. So much of it is likely to be pure jealousy when the young fellow's as rich and conspicuous as a Vanderhagen and anyway kids horse around, go through phases, try out this and that and forget all about it. The spoiled, headstrong brats like Tony, that is; not all kids. I'm sure Kim never did anything I'd be ashamed to hear about."

"Ye-uh, you and Honor have a fine, clean young man there to be proud of. And speaking of sons, here come Ossie and Joan. Wish I were sitting where I could watch Nina's reactions when that big theatrical climax comes along. If there is any at all. I'm always a mite dubious about these theatrical come-ons." Amos chuckled his rich dirty-chuckle and ambled off to join his party.

Jon drew the deep breath he'd been needing. Was it possible that Amos Hanford brought up Tony Vanderhagen just so he could casually get to the Adrakian brothers? Just to let Jon know he knew that Jon had contributed to the fund they got up so Pete, back in Eastonport and out of jail with nothing legitimate to do, could go down to New York and live without dealing or hustling until he could make his contacts and get into acting in porno films? Amos's spies might have got hold of that much information but surely no one could have possibly discovered that, as a gesture of gratitude, Pete had, seemingly kidding, offered to fuck one particular benefactor's tight little ass for him and then, when that generous offer had been definitely rejected, had seriously insisted on at least showing Jon just how big and beautiful his dick was—the already locally famous tool with which he was going to achieve fame and fortune in the Big Apple. And made Jon touch it, at the same time so merry and so nutty in his insistence that Jon didn't feel victimized exactly or undignified. And once he'd gone that far, Jon couldn't resist letting himself go on and do what Pete wanted him to do. Challenged by the sheer bulk of Pete's dark-skinned beauty, Jon gave it all his long-dormant expertise, such an enthusiastic, thorough sucking that the next day Pete begged for one more of those before he left the little burg forever.

That double lapse with Pete, the one with a straight but hot and curious fellow-sailor in the rocks above the San Diego nudist beach and the queer orgy he had inadvertently allowed himself to be led into while he was stationed in San Francisco were his only steps out of line in the twenty years he'd been married. Being naked with other naked servicemen or gym-mates never really bothered Jon: he could inspect and admire and feel no great urge to do anything about even the biggest and most proudly displayed and openly offered cocks but San Francisco in the crazy, rebellious, mixed-up mid-sixties had driven him nuts. It seemed like every hung straight guy in the city was determined to find out for himself if getting head from an expert male was as special as he'd heard. The men who possessed extra-large endowments all flaunted them in ancient, decorated jeans so threadbare and so tight you could see the hair on their balls and tell whether their dicks were circumcised or not. The incredibly endowed proprietor of their favorite health-food store got pissed off at Jon because Jon wouldn't admit he was even curious about other men's meat; he told Jon that he ought to go retire from the real, uninhibited world and live in the hidebound, uptight New England town he himself had fled from—Eastonport. Which Jon decided was exactly what he should do, as soon as his hitch was up. He'd moved Honor and Kim and a vanload of their belongings right across the whole U.S. Another of his impulsive right-angle turns that had certainly been all for the best.

Before the second act of the play began, a young man in glasses came out and reminded the audience that they were all invited to remain after the performance to hear Mr. Michael Kincade read his poetry, including his early sonnet-sequence "Lainey's Room" which was now included in several anthologies and his "Jailhouse Boogie" which was available only in one very different kind of anthology. His statement brought giggles and a little scattered applause from some of the younger people.

Mike was quite a lot livelier in the second act, becoming at times almost as impish as "Leo," when he turned up after being away for two years. In the second scene of the second act, Mike strolled on, wearing extremely sheer white silk pajamas and a thin silk dressing gown which swung open and billowed away every time he moved so that the exact contours of his cock were plainly discernible. It was, intermittently, a most impressive spectacle but Jon was alarmed that that was all they were going to be allowed to see. He'd got the idea that both men flaunted themselves simultaneously and not so coyly. Ten years earlier, around 1970, he'd read that whole casts of plays running in New York shed all their clothes and not too long ago Nina Vanderhagen had had lunch at a place where she had been encouraged to measure a waiter's hard twelve-inch cock with a ruler. Surely, in 1980, even in reactionary New England, they dared go further than teasing in filmy pajama pants.

The rival, the "Leo" turned up; "Gilda" was out, the men bickered over her until they discovered that she had run out on both of them; then they drank a lot very fast and commiserated and ended in each other's arms, sobbing and smooching. Leo stripped off Mike's pajama top as the lights went out. There was applause of course, then quite a lot of whispering during the longish wait for the next scene to begin—some of the whispering, Jon suspected, negative comments about the kissing but more of it disappointment with the supposedly shocking scene of the show. Jon realized that he and Mike had never kissed and wondered if, had Mike been more affectionate and maybe not so sexually obsessed, things might have been different. Evidently some men did find loving other men enough.

Honor whispered across the kids that Nina had begged to be introduced to Mike afterwards. Jon fervently hoped that Honor had not informed Nina Vanderhagen or anyone else that her husband Jon had shared a room with Michael Kincade for two years. If that bit of ancient but suggestive history was ever wafted to Amos Hanford's ears, Amos would immediately be very suspicious. Jon hoped that his off-hand comment about young people taking up and dropping experiments, which was meant at the time only to defuse Amos's gossiping so crudely about Tony Vanderhagen's peculiar activities, might be applied to his own case, should Amos jump to nasty conclusions about Jon's own youthful misadventures. Who could ever be sure what a sly old fox like Hanford would stoop to use as evidence, if he was determined to drum up a quick, damning dismissal? Amos's apparently good-natured compliance with the public interest and his jolly, between-us-men-of-the-world gossip in the intermission only meant he wasn't ready to hand Jon a black eye right away. Or chop off his head, politically speaking.

The new setting was Gilda's elegant penthouse apartment in New York. She'd married the stuffy little art dealer. She entertained some rich but obviously not very sophisticated people who decided pretty quickly to leave when Otto and Leo turned up from a long trip together and acting like two spoiled Katzenjammer Kids. Gilda made her two ex's leave with the others but slyly told them to come back later. The next morning the husband arrived home from his own trip and Mike and Ron Devera popped out of the bedroom, wearing the husband's pajamas which were short in the sleeves and legs and so tight in the crotches that everything the men had was made very evident.

The husband yelled at them to take off his pajamas. Jon hoped they would; they did. The husband yelled for them to put the pajamas back on; they did that too but first they tossed the tops and bottoms around and put them on upside-down and backwards and had a ball shocking poor old hubby and entertaining the applauding audience who all got a lot of good views of two of the most impressive sets of male equipment they could ever hope to see.

Mike's thick pale peter flopped and swung, just as big and beautiful as Jon remembered it. The stud Ron's stuck out a little as if showing himself off excited him; it looked to be every bit as big as Mike's but Jon bet it wasn't really. For an instant Jon let himself imagine being alone with Mike and Ron in their dressing room, being urged by Mike to give him a few deep dips for old times' sake, then shoved down on Ron's big dark one which had reared up when Ron saw Jon taking such good care of Mike. Mike's dick didn't really get hard, despite how healthy and young he had looked on stage: he was sort of played out from all that fast living in Europe and everywhere. But Ron's, which was really huge, became hard as stone until it could no longer withstand Jon's expert onslaught and the man happily surrendered his all.

The play ended quickly after Gilda came in from wherever she had stayed the night and they all tried to be polite but the husband was furious and stomped out. The three lovers laughed and laughed and hugged each other in a kind of mixed three-way as the curtains closed and the lights dimmed. Jon hoped that Mrs. Vanderhagen had got her money's worth. And Honor too. He wondered about Kim and Kylie though. They did applaud as vigorously as anyone and seemed to have enjoyed it all as a lark.

What did take place in Mike's dressing room after the show was hardly what Jon had dreamed up in those few indulgent seconds but was pretty much what he really expected. Ron Devera wasn't there—he had his own dressing room—but half a dozen other people crowded in, including Molly Mallory who dashed about "darling"ing people and being kissed.

Kim and Kylie preferred to wait outside in the corridor so Jon had no chance to see Kim and Mike together. And neither had Honor. Honor introduced Nina Vanderhagen who took on herself to remind Mike, who was looking a little bewildered, who "Mrs. Jonathan Mynott" was. Mike stared at Honor a second, yelled "Omigod!" then turned to stare hard at Jon, grabbed him dramatically and kissed him—on the forehead.

"My little Jonny-cake. Of course. You haven't changed a bit... except maybe the hairline's slipped a little. Well, so has mine and my locks are dyed. What are you doing here, way down East?"

Jon was so choked up over being kissed, finally, the first time ever by Mike, even if only on the forehead, that he couldn't answer coherently. Nina butted in with such overdone praise of Jonathan and Honor that no one could have swallowed it whole. Jon grinned and winked at Mike and shrugged. What he really wanted to do was hold Mike close and kiss him back, kiss him good, run everybody out and... Jon quickly glanced about for Honor. She stood serenely smiling although Jon knew and she knew Mike hadn't remembered who she was, that he had ever dated, dated and slept with Honorette Sullivan whom his roommate had married a few months later. In that instant Jon realized that it didn't matter much to Honor and never had and it didn't matter much to him either that they'd both been aware, from the day the child was born with that dinkus of a two-year-old, that Kim's biological father was Mike and they'd never said a word about it. It was better they had kept that shared knowledge secret. Just as it was probably better they'd both known about but never mentioned Jonny's relations with Mike. It struck Jon that Honor might have imagined that her husband was having occasional such relations with other men. And didn't mind a lot. No tacit deal—she just wouldn't have minded so much she would have allowed Jon's indulging his strange whims to disrupt their perfectly satisfactory life.

Nina was introducing Tony to Mike. Mike shook hands with Tony but hardly seemed to see him; however, Tony had certainly seen Mike and was devouring him with his eyes. Jon could understand Tony's excitement but he didn't care to see the arrogant brat's trying to make out with Mike right there before everyone. "Nice seeing you again, Mike. We live in Eastonport. If you get time while you're here, call and come over and see us. You be careful, Nina: Mike was the campus Don Juan and it still looks as if he's up to his old tricks," Jon said and then had a pang of fear that Nina Vanderhagen, or worse, Mike, might think he was warning Nina to keep Tony away from Mike. But of course no one except himself would think of a thing like that. Except Tony, who'd hate him forever as a suspicious old closet-queer who was bent on spoiling others' fun.

In the corridor Honor murmured that she thought it would be interesting to stay on for the poetry reading. Kim and Kylie were willing but not very enthusiastic. Jon was tempted. He'd never asked to read any of Mike's poetry when they roomed together; he'd glanced over a few of Mike's poems when Honor brought home a volume of them from the library but they'd seemed too personal and too intricately contrived for him to deal with. But when would he ever have the chance to look at Mike again and be amazed how zesty and funny and young he still was? They might not meet again for another twenty years. Or ever. Jon said they might as well stay for it; it probably wouldn't take long and they'd get to see another whole side of their old friend. Kim said "fine" but wondered about that jailhouse poem and bet Kylie she'd learn a few things she hadn't even guessed about before. Kylie reminded her solicitous fiancé that she'd read *Our Lady of the Flowers* when she was fifteen and seen *Chant d'amour* and *Bijou* so she might be better prepared for Michael Kincade's nitty-gritty than he was.

Amos Hanford was waiting patiently at the stage door, enjoying his cigar. Osborn and Joan had met Molly Mallory once in New York and had to do their duty by gushing over her performance, etcetera—not that a woman like Molly Mallory wasn't easy to gush over if you were into all that kind of social folderol and froufrou. At least Ossie and Joan weren't going to put him through the torture of listening to the actor read his poems.

"I've always enjoyed Mike's poetry," Honor said. "We knew him in college you know so we're probably not fair critics. Mike was one of the notable figures on the campus, as a poet and actor, and of course as a romantic figure. He was even more handsome then, so popular. Is it a college fraternity who's sponsoring the reading tonight, Kim?" Honor turned brightly to Kim and Kylie. "You know our son Kim and his fiancée Kylie Cameron, don't you, Mr. Hanford?"

"Sure, sure. Well, you people are welcome to my share of the literary goings-on. These things the youngsters go in for nowadays are too far out for me."

"It's not a fraternity exactly, Mom. It's a lambda group. I saw one of their posters."

"A local gay group. They always use the lambda as their insignia but I can't remember why," Kylie informed the oldsters.

Jon had the impression Kim and Kylie were deliberately pushing a little to tease old Amos Hanford whom they considered a superannuated relic and called privately "the last of the local dinosaurs."

"Gay? not as in 'happy' I presume," Amos drawled, then sang "'Poor little lambdas who've lost their way? Baaa, baaa, baaaa?'"

"I doubt that Kylie's much worried that any of the gay fellows will snatch Kim away from her," Jon said, hoping he sounded a lot more bland and unaware of implications and possible complications than he felt at the moment. "Queen Victoria's been dead for most of a century and nobody believes in witches anymore, even down here Salem-way, do they, Amos?"

"Yeah," Kim said, "no dogs in the manger in our family. Got time to come and have a brew with us, sir?"

Key West, February, 1984